A DUST STORM IN DELHI

Meena Arora Nayak is the author of the bestseller *The Blue Lotus: Myths and Folktales of India*. Her other books include *The Kathasaritsagara of Somadeva*, *Evil in the Mahabharata*, *Endless Rain*, *About Daddy*, *In the Aftermath*, and *The Puffin Book of Legendary Lives*.

A DUST STORM *in* DELHI

MEENA ARORA NAYAK

First published by Tranquebar, an imprint of Westland Publications Private Limited, in 2021

1st Floor, A Block, East Wing, Plot No. 40, SP Infocity, Dr MGR Salai, Perungudi, Kandanchavadi, Chennai 600096

Westland and the Westland logo, Tranquebar and the Tranquebar logo are the trademarks of Westland Publications Private Limited, or its affiliates.

ISBN: 9789390679829

10 9 8 7 6 5 4 3 2 1

This is a work of fiction. Names, characters, organisations, places, events and incidents are either products of the authors' imagination or used fictitiously.

Typeset by R. Ajith Kumar
Printed at Manipal Technologies Limited, Manipal

For my daughter

1

RAGE FILLS ME TO THE BRIM, BUT I WON'T LET IT SPILL. I WANT TO whet the blade of my sword with it so that I can slice off their heads and take back my Sultanate. Lying here in Tabarhind fort, battle-weary and bleeding, my ankles and wrists shackled to the wall of this dark, dank dungeon stinking of rat feces and old death, I replay their treachery. Last night, on the advice of Aetkin, the Sultanate's most senior officer, the keeper of my household, my Amir-i-Hajib, we pitched our tents near the water tank. He had insisted on this location when we strategised for the battle. Both Khwaja Muhazzab, my wazir, and Yakut had felt that the location was too close to the south wall of Altunia's fort. But Aetkin had reminded us that the outer gate of Tabarhind's south wall was low and narrow, completely unsuited to start a charge, because it would take over two ghadis to get all the troops out, and it was also impossible for the war elephants to pass through it. And the North gate, which they would mostly likely use, was more than a parasang away from the water tank, which would put our encampment at a safe distance from Altunia's troops. He had also pointed out that in this month of Ramadan, the sands in the fields of Tabarhind burned—even at night. 'The troops have just returned from the battle in Lahore,' he had reasoned. 'And they've been on the march to Dilli for almost a month, and now they'll march to Tabarhind in this summer heat. Not to mention that the men are fasting. They need at least a good night's sleep so that they can tackle Malik Altunia's forces in the morning.'

How sweetly that snake had spewed poison. Of course, the troops were exhausted. Of course, the sands were burning. Of course, the water tank with its cooling breezes, carrying the fragrance of twenty-guz-tall neem trees that surrounded it, would refresh the troops. Of course, the sun and wind would be behind us when we met Altunia's forces in the morning. It was too perfect. In war, one rarely encounters such perfect conditions. If this were not a pitched battle called by Altunia in his own home ground, I would have seen this perfection as Allah's boundless mercy; but this left me feeling uneasy. But I ignored it. Even Yakut warned me. But I didn't believe him. In fact, I asked him why he suspected foul play. He knew Altunia as well as I did, if not better. I thought Malik Altunia's rebellion was simply a tantrum. He just wanted attention—a small token battle to win back whatever pride he thought he had lost. I was so sure about his motives that I even disregarded my astrologer's readings on the staryab and his calculations in the sands of the takht.

'Akreb, the scorpion, is approaching Al-Mirrekh, the planet of war,' he predicted. 'The scorpion has a sting.' But this was Altunia. Even his sting was innocuous, or at least that's what I believed. Fool that I was.

Last evening, lying in my pavilion in the middle of the encampment, flanked by a quarter of my Dilli garrison, lulled by the breezes from the tank, as I idly watched flying ants and white moths circle around the torches, a thought struck me: their navigation system, which was attuned to the moon, had been thrown awry by the torch fires. They were flying in tighter and tighter circles around these false moons, thinking that their sense of navigation was unerring; when, in reality, they were being led into a death trap.

For a moment I couldn't breathe—the air in my lungs just stilled; and then a fluttering began in my belly, like the wings of one of those white moths. Jumping to my feet, I ran to Adowa and swung onto her bare back. I didn't have the patience to wait for my shahana to prepare her; it had suddenly become imperative for me to ride to the battlefield, if only to make sure that everything was as we had planned for the battle at dawn.

I knew the field lay towards the north of the fortress. A few of us had reconnoitred it earlier, after we set up camp. I had actually seen it even before then, when I had visited Altunia a few months ago, on my way home from Sufi Baba Haji Ratan's dargah, only a few kos from Tabarhind fort. Altunia had welcomed me with his boyish grin, the little crater in his right cheek dipping, like someone was pushing it in with an invisible finger. He had shown me his new acquisition—a glass mirror, he called it—layered molten silver, mounted in ivory, thirteen fingers in circumference. 'It's from Byzantine,' he told me, drawing me into a private room. 'But you have to remove your veil to see its full effect.'

What I saw in the luminous reflection, trapped in the contraption, shocked me: it was my face—but also my father's. I could see acutely his scimitar-arched black eyebrows, his silver-tinged eyes, his blade-sharp Ilbari cheekbones, so typical of his Turkish tribe. Baba's betrayal is still nestled in me, like a thorn that has passed through the skin into the flesh and has ceased to prick—until it's pressed. Then it hurts for hours. To see him in me ... surely this was some unholy trick of the contraption. I know I look a little bit like Baba, but this was something else. I've seen myself many times in shined bronze; in its dull red-gold flatness, I always look more like me than him.

I had thrust the contraption back at Altunia, but he had pushed it into my hand. 'It's a gift for you,' he said. 'Marry me.'

Altunia has proposed marriage to me so many times, I've lost count, and I've turned him down every time. In fact, his proposals that are at times serious, at times facetious, and my refusals have become our own private custom. But this time, before I could refuse, he said, more purposefully than ever before. 'Don't say no yet, Razi. I want you to think about it before you answer.'

Although his new tone of gravity surprised me, I didn't really give the proposal much thought. Back in Dilli, I carefully wrapped the glass and silver thing in thick velvet and put it away in the wooden chest in which Azra, my maid, would keep my winter furs, festival silks, and nacre jewellery boxes, along with childhood mementos I had outgrown but couldn't bear parting with, like my training sword, and items I had never grown into, such as the alabaster doll my mother had purchased from a travelling merchant from Misr when I was two. A few weeks ago, searching in the trunk for my favourite finger protectors, I saw the wrapped mirror again and was reminded that I still owed Altunia a response. That day I sent him a message: 'Sultan-i-Hind Razziat is flattered by Malik Ikhtiyar-ud-din Altunia's proposal of marriage, but she must decline.'

Riding through my slumbering men, I recalled that incident, which was the main reason I had not taken Altunia's declaration of war seriously. I thought he was just miffed at the rejection and merely wanted to show me that it had not emasculated him. That he was still all man.

As I rode out of the camp, Yakut joined me. I accepted his presence without question. I knew that, as always, he had instinctively felt my unease, even from across the encampment, where his pavilion was erected. We rode in quiet alertness, knowing that the Tabarhind guards would be vigilant, and kept a clear distance from the fortress wall that was built in a series of bastions, which, in the dark, appeared like a dense undulating mass.

With mutual, unspoken consent, we rode towards the north and stopped at the edge of the ten-parasang barren patch of land where the battle would occur. It appeared almost ethereal—so quiet—the rocky soil an unending stretch of silver, innocent of the colour red, the night before the battle. All seemed as it should be, so we turned our horses around, but as we drew near the south end of the wall, we heard a sound like a shuffling of boots, and of armour. Pulling up our horses, we quickly dismounted and tethered them to a thicket of bushes. Then we crept closer to see what was going on at this end of the fortress that Aetkin had passed off as simply a wall with a one-man passage gate. The citadel was built on a rocky hillock, and, from down below, all we could see of it was a shadow skyline of crenellated walls and squat towers. Yakut crawled up on his hands and knees, and when he came down, his eyes were wide.

'The south end now has a military gate,' he whispered.

'What?' I couldn't comprehend what he was saying.

'He's built a gate for the troops in the south wall.'

In disbelief, I crept up halfway on the hillock to see for myself. An eight-guz-tall gate of heavy teakwood studded with iron spikes stood in place of the one-man doorway. Its panels hung open wide and pouring out of it were fully armed soldiers in formation. No torches were lit, but I could see the forms of thousands of warriors as they emerged and lined up outside, moonlight glinting on helmets, armours, nailed shields, tips of lances and hilts of swords. A surprise attack! This was no pitched battle at dawn. This was treachery in the pre-dawn.

My immediate thought was torture and death. I was going to torture that reptile Aetkin by breaking every single bone in his body, one by one. And Altunia? His head I would squash like a watermelon under my elephant's paw. Then, I began to plan. Being only five kos away from the attack point, and with the water tank flanking us on the other side, we were basically trapped. Altunia's forces at the south gate would run us down in no time at all, unless we faced them fully prepared. Scrambling down the rocks as fast as I could, I whistled to Adowa and hitched myself onto her back, even as she galloped towards me. Yakut did the same with his horse. We spurred our mounts and sped to camp as though pursued by jinns.

'How much time?' I called out to Yakut.

'One ghadi,' he called back. I, too, had estimated the same time.

'Altunia,' I said. 'Can you believe it?'

'Yes,' he replied, and then added, 'We'll crush him.'

Even as we thundered into our camp, Yakut began yelling orders. I rushed towards my pavilion, telling my shahana to prepare Sundari, my elephant.

'Sundari?' he asked. When I turned to look at him, he shook his head. I remembered Sundari had hurt her paw on the march here and was still poulticed.

'Shall I bring you Batal, the other elephant we have been training?' he asked.

'No. Bring me Adowa,' I told him quietly. I preferred the elephant in war, because it charged passionately, trampling with its paws and goring with its iron-spiked tusks. It also gave me better leverage to target the lance. Sundari and I had faced many enemies together; she understood me. Batal was still learning my language. In this battle wrought with treachery, if I couldn't have Sundari, I would rather have my mare. In any case, she would give me more stealth and mobility and also allow me to fight with my favourite weapon—the sword. Besides, I thought, I would be able to see Altunia's doom on his face when I killed him. He always rode into war on a horse.

When Altunia's arrows began pouring on us, my commanders had just finished ordering the forces into the tighter, half-moon schematic, rather than the flanked layout we had initially strategised. Our elephant-mounted archers had barely been brought into position. Our five thousand cavalrymen were also just falling into formation, but the remaining two thousand infantrymen were ready. My brave soldiers. They fought with all they had. The thought of their fearless spirit makes my chest swell with pride. I drove them hard, and they drove themselves harder. So many of them martyred to the quest of traitors.

Khwaja, my general, had advised me to postpone this battle, at least till after Ramadan, for the sake of my soldiers. Aside from the astrological predictions, it was the wisdom of battle. It had just been a fortnight since we had returned from chasing that rat, Kabir Khan, Lahore's governor, who had declared himself independent of the Sultanate. I should have paid more attention to my father's advice about him. He used to keep a secret dossier on each of his bandagan-i-khaas—his coterie of forty men, whom he claimed to trust, but whose loyalty he tested implicitly at every juncture. Don't trust a chameleon, he would tell me. A jinn resides in him, always changing colour, spitting fire. I had seen Kabir Khan's shifting colours, but I had still given him a chance to prove himself loyal. If the scarred old bastard hadn't helped me in gaining the Sultanate by rallying against Shah Turkan, I would never have rewarded him with the governorship of Lahore.

On Aetkin's advice I had taken the Dilli garrison to deal with Kabir Khan's rebellion. 'The Lahore garrison can't be trusted anymore; it could be tainted with Kabir Khan's sedition,' he had said. But when we reached Lahore, we discovered that most of the soldiers were still loyal to me, and we had expended the Dilli garrison for no reason at all. Could Aetkin have known this? And then, although geared for battle, we hadn't even been able to engage properly, because Kabir Khan had scuttled away with a hundred of his rodents, all the way across the Chenab River, right into the wall of thirty thousand Mongol warriors. So, he had scuttled right back to me and fallen at my feet.

'Remember I saved your father's life,' he wheedled.

Once, Hindu bandits had attacked Baba outside the weaver's bazar in the shahr, and Kabir Khan had deflected the bandit's knife, taking a gash on his cheek so deep, it had not only split his face from ear to chin, but had also sliced through some of his gums and teeth. The scar still emblazoned his face—his badge of loyalty, tainted with corruption and deceit. I should have dragged him behind my horse all the way back to Dilli and thrown whatever remained of him in the dungeon for the rats to feed on; but I let him go. His plea had my father's name on it.

Though we didn't lose many men in Lahore, there were still injuries. The wounded were treated immediately in the field hospitals, but bones need time to heal, and wounds need to be poulticed against infection. The whole garrison needed to recuperate and feel human again before it could transform into warriors. We were also running low on honey, which the chief hakim used lavishly to heal wounds. Other war supplies needed to be replenished, too; we'd been running low on both naphtha and vinegar even before we left for Lahore. Without that Yunani fire, we were only using old-fashioned cannonballs in our projectiles, and without vinegar, we only had water to squelch enemy fire—water that, in the desert terrain of Tabarhind, was a precious commodity. We also needed more wood, wood-cutters, engineers, horses, elephants and weapons. As it turned out, to fight this battle, we needed to prepare for war. 'Prepare for Uhud, fight for Yarmouk,' Baba used to say. I live by those words—a principle that has earned me the title of Lashgarkash: the ideal general. Then, how did I make such a bad decision? I take risks, but they are so calculated that in the gambling dens in Dilli, men double their gold simply by mentioning my name. What happened to me?

'Altunia!' The name sears my lips as it hisses past. By killing Yakut and keeping me alive, the bastard has fully revealed his hand. 'Huge mistake, Altunia!'

I pray to Allah that my wounds don't kill me. I want to live. I want to live so that I can destroy him. And all the others—every single one of them involved in this plot. My body is throbbing with pain, and I'm grateful for that. A warrior trusts pain—as long as it is there, there's battle left in her. I want to count each wound to keep the pain alive, so I resuscitate the memory of how each was received, but I can't seem to recall a single direct engagement with any enemy warrior. For some odd reason, I was the taboo of this battle. Most of the wounds I received were from random strikes, such as a flying arrow that pierced my thigh. The stinging on my arms and shoulders was from when I tried to save one of my brave soldiers from being hacked to death, and the adversary's curved sword pierced through the fabric of my red kazaghand and the chain mail underneath. I always wear red to battle so that even if I bleed, my soldiers do not know it. What an audacious enemy he was, striking at me, even as I sliced off his head. I'm no lightweight swordsman myself. My handling of the sword is legendary. In Hazrat-i-Dilli, people touch their ears when my name is mentioned. There was only one other who was better than I, but even when he defeated me, he conceded defeat.

'Defeat by you is sweeter than victory,' he used to say. Ah, Yakut! Unlike me, he was surrounded in the battlefield—swords, sabers, battleaxes and maces smashing, slashing and hacking at him from all sides. I saw him respond, his arms moving in rhythm—heads, limbs, bodies falling around him like windfall fruit. But more assailants kept coming at him, as though he had become the only ritual of this battle.

Suddenly, warmth gushed from my side, and I realised that in my moment of distraction, a sword had pierced me and cut too deep. Flattening my thighs along Adowa's saddle and pushing my weight into my heels, I grounded myself and, gripping the handle of my battleaxe with both hands, brought it down on the head of the pesky little soldier who was prancing in front of me, erratically swinging his sword in the frenzy of panic. His head split from helmet to throat, the chain mail swinging wildly around the two halves of his face. Then I spurred Adowa to get to Yakut and hew down the swarm surrounding him. But even as she leapt forward, I saw Yakut's head—the pointed helmet, the swishing mail and his face—his dark, moon-eloquent face, clouded with regret—sailing through the air. And then, that soft, deafening thud.

A scream roars out of me. Hot tears burn my eyes. I shake them away. Not yet, I tell them. Not yet. I'll weep for him, but not yet. Right now, my eyes are still gritty from that vision of Altunia's hordes around Yakut—preventing him from coming to my aid, when they threw the net over me—among them my own men, Saif, Mubarak, Muiz. So, this was the reason for Yakut's popularity, the reason his head lies in the battlefield, and I lie here, alive.

Ah Yakut! I lay my head on the cold stone floor; my tears don't listen to me. Not any more.

2

I REMEMBER WHEN I FIRST MET YAKUT. ALTHOUGH, HE'S HAZY IN that memory. What I remember more clearly is my encounter with Guzel, my first, very own mare. Yakut was just the lanky, thin-legged, dark-as-walnut boy with fuzzy black coils on his head and a funny way of talking, who brought Guzel to me.

It was during the festival of Nowroz. Baba had just returned from war after defeating his old enemy, Yulduz, who had captured Lahore and had been preparing to attack Dilli. Yulduz did come to Dilli, but not with his force. Baba dragged him there in chains and paraded him in the streets, his face blackened, barefooted and sitting backwards on a donkey, looking at the animal's arse. Then he had him taken to Badaun in a cage and thrown in the dungeon to rot. That year's Nowroz was euphoric. And Baba bought me a gift that was magnificent—a Marwari mare.

Most of our horses were from Turkistan or Arabia or Ruus, but a new breed was being added to our stables—the Marwari—a very special Al-Hind breed from Marwar. Hindu Saras, my bodyguard, told me that Marwari horses had large hearts and a pious spirit, because the Marwari people showered their horses with the same love they bore their children. And that, because they also included them in their worship, their horses carried the blessings of their hundred gods. Baba himself had fought the battle with Yulduz riding a Marwari—Bahadur. The zenana was filled with Bahadur's stories—stories that the soldiers had brought back—about how, despite being shot in the chest, he had carried the Sultan out of a thicket of enemy fighters, how the Sultan himself had sat in the bloody battlefield and taken his head in his lap to strangle him, and relieve him of his suffering. And how, afterwards, the Sultan-i-Hind had wept like he had lost a son.

On that particular morning, I remember as I came to the riding range, dressed in my new Nowroz salvar and tunic, made of soft blue malham, Baba told the shahana to bring out the present he had got for me. And there she was, being led by Yakut: a big smoky apparition—grey all over, except for the white blaze on her forehead, that ran all the way from between her black eyes to the tip of her nose. I loved her on sight. But then a strange thing happened to me: when I took a step towards her, she snorted and pranced, and suddenly, she seemed enormous. Then, Yakut took something out of the pocket of his tunic and held it near her mouth, and I saw her black lips move over his palm with a flash of teeth—yellowish and huge. My own palms became sweaty. I couldn't understand it. In my eight-year-old mind, I was fearless. Besides, I was used to horses. I had been riding since I was five. Doran amca, our riding teacher, whom we called uncle, had trained me and my brothers, Nasir and Rukn, while we were still in Badaun, where Baba was governor at that time. But, while my brothers graduated to full-grown horses when we came to Dilli, I continued to ride a pony, because unlike their sudden growth spurts, my height crawled up only in hair-breadths. My only experience of a full-grown horse was sitting on it behind a grown up, and the thought of riding this giant all by myself was making my heart pound.

'She's really big,' I said loudly, trying to drown out the drumming in my ears.

'Sixteen hands, Shehzadi. Marwari,' Yakut said.

'How do you know?' I asked him, thinking that if I knew more about her, my heart would feel reassured and return to a normal pace.

'See ears turn in? Marwari sign. Marwari good horse. Big heart. Lucky. See?' He pointed to her legs. 'See white boots? See flame on face? Very lucky,' he said.

I clenched my hands and did what I had been taught; I approached the mare from the left. Then, reaching up, I stroked her along the mark on her nose. When I saw my hand tremble, I pulled it back immediately, because I didn't want anyone, especially Baba, to see. But here was this dark-faced boy with strange hair, staring at me as though he could see inside me. I wanted him to look away.

'You talk funny,' I said to him, imperiously, a tone I had heard Baba use.

'He's a Habshi, Shehzadi,' the shahana spoke. 'He's from a country called Aksum. He takes care of your mare.'

'What's his name?' I asked the shahana.

'Jamal-ud-din Yakut.'

'Yakut…' I said slowly, feeling my lips round on the second syllable of his name.

He suddenly became very still, and I saw him stare at me—his eyes slightly moist. Many years later, he told me that was a bewildering moment for him—the way I had said his name, as though accepting it on my tongue; in that moment he discovered that the heart can race for reasons other than fear. I didn't tell him that back then, I was only trying to disparage him.

'What's my mare's name?' I asked him.

'No name, Shehzadi,' he replied. 'I say faras, which mean horse.'

'Give her a name, my guzel,' Baba added. 'What shall we call your beautiful mare?'

'Guzel,' I said. 'I want to call her Guzel, because she's beautiful, too.'

'Perfect.' Baba smiled. 'You'll be my guzel, and she'll be yours.

Why don't you take her for a ride?' he said, and nodded to Yakut, who ran inside to get the riding block.

I adjusted myself in the saddle, as I'd been taught, sitting straight, holding the reins, thumbs up, hugging the mare with my knees. She began to canter at a steady pace around the horse track, away from where Baba was standing with his entourage, Saras amca and the shahana.

With every step Guzel took, I felt myself bounce, which upset me, because it meant that I wasn't in control of my body, or the mare. Then I began to panic; what if my body shifts and, instead of landing on the mare's back, I land on air? And, even as I thought this, the ground seemed far, far away, and every gallop became a presentiment of a fall.

'Loose fingers, Shehzadi,' Yakut's voice cut through the panic. He was running beside me and Guzel.

His words made me angry. I wanted badly to believe that my anger was solely directed at him, because he dared to talk to me without being asked. He was a slave of the lowest kind, after all, and I was the future Sultan-i-Hind. And he kept talking: 'See ear twitch? She feel you fear. Show her you friend. Trust horse. She big heart. Look between ear and trust. She lead you. Trust horse. She trust you. You not fear. Horse know you fear. She lead you. Trust horse. She trust you. Do not fear.'

'I'm not afraid,' I hissed at him. 'And how dare you talk to me.' His silence after that was so palpable that I forgot to worry about how far away the ground was and became more focused on his not talking. Perhaps he thought I would report him to Baba. The punishment for disrespecting a member of the royal family was a lashing, sometimes even a maiming, and to disrespect the future Sultan—it could possibly even be the dungeon.

I didn't complain about him to Baba when we returned. But it wasn't wholly for his sake, although I did feel a twinge of guilt for having terrorised him. Nasir, my brother, had joined us, and, along with him, his personal Turki Mamluk, Taj-ud-din Sanjar. Baba had acquired Sanjar in Badaun as a personal companion for Nasir. He was about six or seven years older than me and Nasir, and already a legend among the slave girls in the zenana.

'His swordsmanship and his sharp shooting are the best in Hazrat-i-Dilli,' they said in awe. 'Have you seen how tall he is? Have you seen how his frame cuts through the sunlight when he rides?' they whispered to each other, their voices aflutter. Sanjar had completed his military training, but the rumour in the zenana was that he still trained, because he was learning to use the most difficult swords of all—the urumi, that was like a fluid metal whip, the wielding of it a feat in itself. I used to love hearing these stories about him.

'What do you think of Guzel, my guzel?' Baba asked me.

'She has a big heart,' I said, trying to sound grown up.

'She's a big horse. Can you manage her, my child?'

I nodded my head vigorously.

'Don't be afraid, Razi,' Nasir sensed the panic in my eagerness. He was like that—sensitive—like a girl. 'I'll take care of you. Won't I, Abi?' he asked Sanjar, whom he called elder brother.

Sanjar responded, 'I think the shehzadi is brave enough and may not need to be taken care of. But she sure needs her brother.'

I fell in love with Sanjar that day. He was my first crush. The sixteen-year-old with golden-skin and rippling muscles, his eyes very blue under straight black brows; my very own Rustam stepped out from the pages of the *Shahanameh*, whose gilded, illustrated copy I kept carefully wrapped in velvet in my wooden chest.

Yakut once told me that he never forgave Sanjar for the way I looked at him that day.

But I reminded him that it was him I met clandestinely in the stables that night of the sixth day of Nowroz.

3

I HEAR A SOUND—DISTANT—MAYBE FROM OUTSIDE THE CELL. Tuning out all other faculties, I concentrate, but all I can hear is a long-exhaled breath—the perpetual sigh of old stones, like ghosts passing through them. The walls are too thick for any outside sounds to penetrate, I tell myself. Perhaps it's not from the outside at all, but something inside, most likely rats. I try to sit up. But every wound in my body seems to have nested, and my right leg is throbbing like hell's hammer. I wish I could see; it's pitch-dark. I don't even know how much time has passed since I was dragged in here. Is it still day, or is it night?

There it is again, the sound, louder now and definitely outside the cell; like the rattling of the chain lock. I begin to see a light at the far end, a flickering seam underneath the door. Then the heavy wood is dragged open. Clenching my teeth, I pull myself up to sit against the wall, just as a soldier emerges, holding a flambeau. He places the torch in the socket on the cell wall and leaves.

'Sultan-i-Hind, welcome to Tabarhind,' a familiar voice speaks.

Altunia is standing in the doorway at the foot of his own long shadow. The light from the torch falling on the gold embroidery of his wide-sleeved brocade qaba and the golden skull cap in the folds of his dark green turban is illuminating him like an unholy thing of radiance. The short tail of the turban is hanging on his right shoulder, spread artfully on the cascade of his black hair, and his shoes are so shined, twin flames reflect in them. He's dressed impeccably. He's always been particular about his attire, almost fastidious. I used to tease him about it; now I'm sickened by it.

Sliding up the wall, I stand, leaning heavily on my left leg; the chains around my wrists and ankles threaten to pull me down with their weight, but I will not allow him to look down at me.

'Have you come to offer the Sultan-i-Hind marriage, Altunia?' I ask in a voice icy with disdain.

'Maybe,' he says with a facetious smile and, walking towards me, stands right in front of me. 'If I offer, will you accept this time?'

His smile, his immaculate appearance, his flippant manner—I can't bear it. Wrath boils in my gut and I spit it out at him. It splatters on his face, sliming down his cheek. For a moment I see something violent flare in his eyes. Then he quietly takes the tail of his turban and wipes his face.

'You won't believe me,' he says. 'But there's an explanation for all this.'

I laugh derisively. 'Was Tabarhind not enough for you, Malik Altunia? Or did the governorship give you the illusion that you could match the Sultan-i-Hind? Tell me, what's your treachery worth? Another governorship? Badaun? Lahore?'

'You,' he says. His audacity sickens me. I lunge at him. But he sidesteps, and my shackles pull me up short, making my legs buckle. He rushes towards me to break my fall, but fails, and I land on the floor. Loud groans escape my lips.

'You're wounded!' he exclaims.

Is that concern I hear in his voice? And regret? The bastard backstabber! What did he expect would happen after he took me to war?

'Don't worry, Altunia,' I say, clenching my teeth and raising my chin so that I can look at him. 'I won't die. I'll live—to destroy you.'

'How badly are you wounded? Shall I send for my hakim?'

'Go burn in Jahannam.'

'I know you're angry. But will you let me explain?'

'What are you going to explain, Altunia?' Ignoring the pain, I sit up. 'Are you going to explain why you stabbed sixteen years of friendship in the back? Are you going to explain why, instead of thanking me for Tabarhind, you took me away from my Sultanate? Are you going to explain who you sold out to and for how much? What, you bastard? What are you going to explain?'

'Please, Razi. It's not what you think.'

'No? And Ya… Y…?' I can't even say his name. My voice collapses, as though his name is a distant shore and my voice, a mere wave.

'I had to save you. The only way was to kill him.'

I shake my head at the incongruity of his words. 'Stop it,' I say with clenched teeth. 'He called you a friend.'

'I loved him like a brother,' he says.

My fingers itch to wrap around his throat. If I had a sword, his head would be at my feet this instant. 'Get out,' I spit at him.

He stands, looking at me for a moment, then turns away, saying, 'I'll return later. When you've calmed down.'

I lie there, watching his back, and then his shadow, retreating along the wall and across the door of the cell. When a soldier comes and shuts the door, I let my body sink into the floor. I know I'm dying. I'm bleeding out from the sword wound in my side. And I know an arrowhead is lodged in my thigh. What I need to do, if I want to live, is stem the bleeding in my side, remove the arrowhead from my thigh and cauterise the wound so that it doesn't fester. Thankfully, Altunia has left the torch, whether by accident or design. I need the light to do what needs to be done. Sitting up as quickly as I can manage, I slip off my kazaghand, pulling one arm out of the sleeve as far as the shackles allow, and reach for the shoulder seam of my tunic to tear out the fabric. It is sticky with blood; my fingers ache and the chains on my wrists are heavy, but, finally, I am able to rip away the sleeves. And then, using my teeth, I tear strips and tie them, as tightly as I can, around my belly to stem the bleeding from the wound on my side.

The arrowhead is a bit more challenging. At least it isn't animal bone, I think, or I would be dead with the poison; nor does it seem to be forked-headed, which would be impossible to remove. It's most likely a steel point, which is usually fitted to a reed shaft. I know the shaft that I had broken was reed. Steel-point arrows are the easiest to pull out, and if I can get my teeth around it, I can possibly extract it. But I also know that as soon as the arrowhead surrenders the flesh, blood will gush out. And this is a thigh wound—one can bleed to death within a ghadi from the blood loss of a thigh wound. What I really need is a tourniquet. I could make one from another strip of the tunic, but I have nothing to use as a windlass to tighten it enough to cut off or, at least, slow down the flow of blood.

'Think,' I tell myself, but the scheme I come up with requires extreme dexterity: tie the strip of cloth around the thigh, quickly pull out the arrowhead with my teeth and use that itself as a windlass. I would have to staunch the flow of blood with one hand, while I inserted the arrowhead into the knot with the other. It can be done; but the risk is high. I could faint from the pain when I extract the arrowhead or, if it takes me too long to insert it in the knot, I could lose consciousness from blood loss. Finally, I decide not to risk it and just let the arrowhead remain where it is until I can tend to it with a better chance of success. Of course, it could get infected, but I don't want to think about that—at least, not yet. What I want to think about is escape. The unfought battle, and now Altunia's visit has convinced me of one thing, he doesn't want me dead. Whatever motive he has, he wants me alive. To be sure, I could just let him take care of me and then try to escape when I am recovered, but even that thought is repugnant to me. Besides,

I can't wait that long. I need to leave Tabarhind, gather whatever remains of my soldiers, regroup the nobles who still support me, and return to challenge Altunia.

The fact that Altunia came to see me without his bodyguard further bolsters my escape plan, because it probably means that the next time, too, he will come alone. When he comes again, I will wait for the right moment and then jump him, so that I can wind my wrist chains around his neck and strangle him. The only hitch I see in this plan is that Altunia is a big man and very powerful, and I am enfeebled. I wonder if I can overpower him.

'You can't match his muscle power, but you can beat him with strategy and technique,' I hear Yakut's voice in my head. This is what he advised me, after Altunia defeated me in our first fencing match. I won the re-match, and I intend to succeed at this escape, as well, using strategy against his strength.

Mulling this plan in my mind, I lie down. The effort of bandaging the wound in my side has exhausted me, and my leg is throbbing so badly, it's sucking dry the little energy I have. Telling myself to breathe, I will the pain to spread through my body so that it hums in every nerve and simply becomes a part of each breath.

It was Yakut who taught me this technique. Once, when we were young, a nail pierced my heel. He and I were visiting the construction site of the minar in the citadel. No one was allowed in the minar at that time, but I had persuaded Yakut to take me there. While climbing to its second storey, I stepped on a nail. It makes me smile to remember how he reacted when he saw it sticking out of my heel. A string of foreign words spewed out of his mouth as though he was cursing the nail; or perhaps, he was cursing me.

'Just pull it out,' I told him, bravely, even though my throat was choked with pain.

'It'll bleed. A lot,' he warned. 'And if the wound goes bad … I must cauterise it.'

The thought of branding the spot that was already radiating pain was terrifying, but I wanted him to see me as a fearless soldier, just like himself. 'Do it,' I said.

He built a small fire and then told me to lie down. Handing me a piece of wood to put between my teeth, he said, 'When the pain hits, just bite on this. Then, breathe. Feel the pain—really feel it with each breath, and let it spread through your body. Keep your focus on the pain. Soon, it'll become part of your breathing, and you won't feel it any more.'

'How do you know that?' I asked.

'Lashings,' he said, simply.

I didn't get to try out his technique then, because when he touched the burning twig to my heel, I fainted, and when I came to, it was already bandaged, painful but bearable. But the next time I got hurt in the training ring, I breathed the pain, as he had told me to. It worked—a technique to survive wounds, of the body and, perhaps, also of the heart.

'Breathe,' I now tell myself. 'Just breathe.'

4

EVERY INTAKE OF BREATH IS REDOLENT OF FLOWERS. THIS IS HOW I remember Nowroz. Amaryllis and rose, purple jarul, red gulmohar and white champa spill in abundance everywhere, as though someone in the sky has emptied a huge basket of them all over Dilli. They bloom in the palace gardens in the citadel, border fountains, stepwells and tanks, and spread through neat beds along pathways that connect one locality to the other in the shahr. They also sneak into every nook and corner of the zenana, arranged in vases all along the corridors and in the rooms, strewn in bath waters, sometimes even showing up in delicacies served for dinner. And drunk on their scent, mynas chirp from sunrise to sunset, their excitement presented in an ensemble with the nostalgic kook of the koel and the guttural gutur-goo of the pigeons. The season of Nowroz arrives with such exuberance in Dilli, it can't contain itself.

When Baba became Sultan, he brought the season to the Qila of Lal Kot. He had gardens planted from end to end, laid out like velvety, colourful rows of ornamental calligraphy, punctuated by black marble fountains in front of the three palaces—the Qasr-e-Safed, the White Palace that used to be Rai Pithora's imperial palace and had become Baba's Daulat Khana; the newly built Kushk-e-Ferozi, the Blue Palace, that houses the zenana; and Kushk-e-Sabz, the Green Palace, where, during Baba's time, the Sultan's adult sons and royal guests stayed, and also those nobles who, fleeing the Mongols, came to Dilli for refuge.

For the six days of Nowroz, multi-coloured banners hung on the twenty-guz-high walls of Qila Lal Kot, making the citadel look like a rainbow land, visible to travellers from as far away as the Aravalli Hills. Moat bridges were lowered outside Chaumukha Gate that has eight guardsmen and four right-angled internal gates, through which one path leads to the Masjid-i-Jami and minar, two to markets in the shahr, and one to Qasr-e-Safed. For the festival, instead of holding court inside the White Palace, Baba had a pavilion specially constructed every year in the maidan outside Bhind Gate to share the season's advent with the populace of Dilli and to welcome visitors, who came from as far away as Misr. What a sight Baba's pavilion used to be—all white—flying pennants of the Sultan's colours, black on the right for royalty and red on the left for justice, their tails so long they competed with the kites that the Hindus flew from their rooftops to celebrate their Vasantautsava. Over the entrance of the pavilion was inscribed Shams' motto in decorative Kufic, 'All Praise Belongs Only to Allah.' Inside the pavilion Shams-ud-Din himself sat on a jewelled throne flanked by lion heads. Over his head was a black parasol studded with pearls, and on both sides, his jaandars stood at attention, holding swords and lances. With the Sultanate's triangular sharbush on his head, a golden belt around his waist over a silk qaba embroidered in pure gold thread, displaying the title of 'Sultan' and his names, and the Darbash—the royal baton—in his hand, he looked as magnificent as Afrasiab, the legendary king of Turin.

No one, except Anneh and I, knew that underneath his imperial sharbush, strings of pearls, and gilded tiraz qaba, Baba was a simple man, preferring cotton tunics to silk. People only saw the grandeur, which created such an ethereal aura around him that women were known to faint in his presence. He used to tell me and my brothers that such pomp was necessary to exalt the Sultan, because Sultan-i-Hind is the representative of the Khalifa in Baghdad. He is Yamin Amir al-Mu'minin—the right-hand man of the Commander of the Faithful.

When I was young, I used to escape from the zenana and go and sit beside Baba. He had a small wooden throne made especially for me, which, one Nowroz, was so copiously studded with mother-of-pearl, that for those six days of the festival, Baba called me his Inci—his pearl. I would sit on my throne, hour after hour, watching Baba welcome each guest, royal or common, making a mental record of every word he spoke—a lexicon I intended to use when I became sultan.

The first five days of Nowroz were reserved for royal visitors and travelling merchants. But on the sixth day, when the day and night are of equal length—the day that the legendary Jamshid defeated the evil demons and had them raise his gem-studded throne to the heavens, so that the sun's rays shone in each gem to illuminate the truth—Baba freed one thousand doves, and an equivalent number of prisoners who had been incarcerated for petty crimes. Then, in the afternoon, he visited his Sultana and his concubines in the zenana, bestowing presents on them.

On that particular Nowroz, many of the gifts were from the plunder of Yulduz's rich coffers—yards of the finest cottons, silks, satin and gold brocade, gold necklaces studded with rubies and emeralds, aigrettes studded with pearls, gold pins with flower motifs of jade and lapis lazuli, glazed ceramics and glassware vessels from Maghreb, and fragrances that captured the essence of flowers that bloomed in the spring seasons of distant lands.

Kushk-e-Ferozi was a beehive of activity on any given day, but on festival days, it became a whirl of concubines, children, slave girls and eunuchs. Back then, the four-storied palace housed the Sultan's private quarters and seven households, one of which was my mother's, who was the Sultana. The others belonged to Baba's concubines. My mother and I had ten rooms to ourselves—one half of the top floor of the palace. The other ten, on the west side, were my father's rooms.

Nasir and Rukn's mothers shared the third floor. Although Rukn's mother was the chief lady of Baba's harem, Nasir was Baba's eldest son; therefore, both concubines had similar apartments—each with ten rooms. All the other women of the zenana and their children—daughters, and sons who were twelve years and younger—lived on the second floor, along with the women who were purchased to be given away to the nobles. There were also schoolrooms on each of the upper three floors, where all the zenana's children received lessons in Persian, the Six Pens, mathematics and the Sharia. Nasir, Rukn and I normally received lessons in my study room on the fourth floor. The ground floor housed the slaves, the serving women, their children and the zenana's eunuchs. It also had the pantries and kitchens. My father was a generous man, and no household lacked lavishness or slaves. Altogether, aside from twenty royal children and their mothers, fifty eunuchs—six each for the Sultan's chief queen and chief concubine, and the rest for the other ladies—and my own personal bodyguard, Hindu Saras, about three hundred people resided in Kushk-e-Ferozi. All day, the staircase on the east end of the palace kept up a continuous pitter-patter of feet, as slaves, serving girls and eunuchs ran up and down on this errand or that. The other, west staircase, was used almost exclusively by my father and the royal ladies. Anneh's visitors also came via the Sultan's staircase, but they needed her permission to come up and had to be accompanied by one of her eunuchs, unless it was the ladies of the zenana, who needed no escort.

On festival days, my mother presided over the palace like the queen she was. But she was a sickly woman with a weak heart, and when she felt unwell, she remained mostly confined to her quarters, conveying her orders through her trusted personal servant, Ilbari Khatun, a Turki woman from Baba's tribe. Tall and sparse like a babool tree, there was no softness in Ilbari, but she loved Anneh with every bit of her thorny being, and she carried out her sovereign's orders like a military general.

That Nowroz, Ilbari tried to keep the top floor as quiet as possible because Anneh was indisposed, but the excitement in the floors below from Baba's gifts couldn't be suppressed. In every corridor of the palace, wooden horses, dogs, monkeys and birds wheeled and careened, pulled on strings by my windstorm-like younger brothers, who were being chased by a horde of squealing slave children. My sisters, Shazia and Aisha, had half the household in a tizzy, shouting orders from their room as they prepared a wedding for their new dolls. Serving women went in and out of rooms, and up and down the east staircase, carrying trays full of sherbet and sweetmeats, while slave girls rushed about, helping the ladies try on a new farajjiya, a new salvar-tunic, a necklace or tiara, holding up polished bronze plates for them to see the effect. And, in the background of this rapturous pandemonium, the silvery smooth strains of rabab and sarangi arose from the entertainment room in Baba's quarters, as musicians prepared for the evening of song and dance that the Sultana would host. Baba was not quite a music enthusiast. He said it was against Islam. But he knew that the men of his kingdom and the women of his zenana enjoyed it, and so he allowed it. I had heard that he was more opposed to it in Badaun. In Dilli, the influence of Sufi Khwaja Qutb Saheb's sama ceremonies of dancing and singing had made him more tolerant.

Amidst it all was Husni Begum, Rukn's mother and Baba's chief concubine, climbing up the westside stairs to see Anneh on one pretext or other and then, quarrelling with her, standing at the door of her room, uncaring of the fact that Anneh was sick. They quarrelled all the time. Mostly, Husni spewed venom and my mother wept. Husni hated the fact that my mother had been a shehzadi, Sultan Ai-Beg's own daughter, and was Baba's legal wife, while she was just a lady of the harem, a mere slave girl, albeit an expensive one, from Turkistan. Rumour was that my father had purchased her from a slave trader in Ghazni for twenty-five thousand dinars, although she herself used to boast that he had paid no less than fifty thousand. My father named her Khudawande-i-Jahan Shah Turkan—the most excellent in the world. She was his favourite concubine, a great beauty of milk-white skin and midnight-black hair, and a figure that resembled a spittoon, even after she birthed Rukn. I had heard women in the zenana talk in hushed tones about how, after her son's birth, she had forced the midwife to tighten her birthing belt to cinch her belly so much that her womb had squeezed to the size of a pea and could never again hold another infant. But she accomplished what she wanted; a waistline so narrow that a gold, belt could be circled around it twice. She never observed purdah, loved gold and was forever devising ways to disparage the other zenana ladies and bring misery to my mother. I hated her when I was a little girl, and, as I grew older, I learned to recognise her as my greatest enemy. Sometimes I think that if Rukn hadn't been her son, he and I would have been close. He was a little bit like me—passionate; but he was misdirected, mostly by his mother's indulgence.

On that Nowroz, I had no interest at all in the zenana's tizzying chaos or entangled squabbles. I was devastated. The realisation of the fear that I had felt that morning when I met Guzel, had left me traumatised. I couldn't bear that I had been betrayed by my own body. All day, I kept seeing myself as though from outside of my self—the pounding of my heart and the tremor in my limbs, a visible thing, a thing I needed to annihilate. But, in order to do that, I needed to confront the object of my fear. I had to go and see Guzel, but on my own, in private. I was certain that if I spent some time with her, without anyone watching me, I could defeat my fear and never be afraid again. But when could I go? Perhaps at night. But how? Even if I was able to get out of the zenana without my nurse, Azra and Hindu Saras finding out, how would I get out of the palace and then exit Bhind Gate? Kushk-e-Ferozi was located in the north end of the citadel, and the royal stable was on the south end, past Bhind gate, on the other side of the wall that divided the compound. In addition, the palace's immense wooden door secured with iron bolts was heavily guarded day and night. And on this day, when it would be the venue for the evening's entertainment, the guard at the palace was doubled. Even if I was able to get out of the palace, how would I cross the area in front of it and the gardens, to exit the gate in the division wall and get to the south end, without being seen? The whole citadel was lit up with flaming torches.

But I had to do it. I couldn't live another minute, knowing that fear crouched in me, waiting to pounce right out of me for the world to see.

Ultimately, it was easier than I had anticipated. My plan was to wait till it was dark and Hindu Saras handed me over to Azra, then, somehow evade Azra's eagle eyes and mingle with the servants leaving the fourth floor via the service stairs and then exit the palace with the women who came from the shahr to provide different services. I was a little bit shorter than a short woman, but I hoped that, dressed a certain way, no one would recognise me.

My initial plan was to use the cover of the women who came to assist with the cooking of the Nowroz feast. But then I heard from Azra that they would leave right after they cleaned up, at sundown. So, I abandoned that plan, because I knew, that at sunset, the palace would still be active with slave girls and guests. And, outside, men would still be watching wrestling matches and flying kites. Then, by chance, I heard Ilbari tell Azra that that night some women from the shahr would be coming to massage my mother before she went to sleep. She had been complaining of pain in her back, and the hakim had prescribed a deep, marjoram oil massage that night. Normally this would happen before the first sleep, but because Anneh would be hosting the music performance during the time of the first sleep, the masseurs would come after the Isha prayer and massage her before the second sleep. I knew these women would leave the palace late at night, when all the men would have left to visit their ladies, and the torches would be extinguished.

That evening, as always, after the Maghrib prayer, Azra helped me change into a cotton salvar and tunic, and, making sure I was settled in bed, dimmed the lights and left my room. I knew that, unlike other nights, she would not return to check on me, because she was going to watch the dancing girls and musicians from behind the screen meant for the serving women.

After she left, I lay in bed, keeping myself awake. I had hours to wait. For a while, I listened to the wailing of the sarangi and the tinkle of ankle-bells, and when I tired of that, I began to play a game with myself—as I often did—of giving my fears gargantuan proportions in my mind: I imagined my heart beating in such agitation that it popped right out of my chest—a bloody thing lying beside me on the bed, my chest a gaping hole. I imagined the sweat collecting in my palms, forming rivulets, pouring onto the bed clothes, dripping on the floor, my room a lake of sweat. I saw my limbs tremble so much that my veins snapped off and my body flooded with lawless blood. These imaginary scenes were my way of making a mockery of my fear by rendering it ridiculous.

Finally, the music stopped and I heard people leaving. Soon after, when the call for the Isha prayer came, I got up. Taking the shawl that I had borrowed from one of the slave girls earlier and hidden in the wooden chest, I slipped out of my room and went down the corridor to Anneh's chambers. Inside, I could hear the gentle voices of the masseurs and my mother's groans of pain. After some time, I saw five women emerge, one of them carrying a lamp. They all wore ghaghras, the long skirts that Gujjar women wear, but the embroidered odhnis that covered their upper body were similar to the shawl I had on. Pulling it down to cover most of my body, I followed the women down the service stairs, first, at a distance, and then when they got to the palace gate, as closely as possible. My heart was thumping, but as I had hoped, the guards hardly even looked at me, and I stepped out of the gate along with the women.

At Bhind Gate, which is the entrance to the palace compound, the guards once again let me pass along with the women. But from here on, I was on my own. While the women headed to Chaumukha Gate to leave the citadel, I had to sprint from one shadow to the other to make my way to the stables. It was dark, as I had expected, but I had to be careful, because there was still an occasional flash from the lamps that the men returning after the Isha prayer were carrying.

The stable seemed unguarded at first, but when I drew close, I saw the soldier near the entrance. This was the tricky part. I had known the stable would be guarded and had racked my brain to come up with a believable excuse for my presence. Finally, utterly frustrated, I had left this to chance—an option I rarely ever choose. And so, there I was, having made it to the stable, but unable to go in. Standing in its shadow, I wondered what to say to the armed guard that would convince him to allow me to enter. Just then, luck favoured me: someone passing by the stable called out a greeting to the man on guard, and he stepped away to chat. I was able to slip in.

Inside, it smelled pungent—of fresh hay, fodder and horse dung. I didn't mind the smell at all; it was strangely comforting. There was one dim torch in a sconce in the middle of the corridor that ran from one end of the stable to the other. This corridor led to ten sections, each with seven-eight horses, and some with slumbering grooming slaves. Tiptoeing from one section to the next, I peered in, trying to identify the horses in the near darkness. There seemed to be so many of them; although I knew that there were no more than a hundred in this stable that was exclusively for the royal family.

I found Guzel towards the end of the stable. She was in a stall with four other horses. To my surprise, it was lit; a lamp with a low wick was hanging from a nail. And, even more surprising was that standing beside Guzel was Yakut. He was a mere silhouette, but I knew it was him. He was speaking to her softly in a strange language. And Guzel, her smoky hugeness blurred, seemed to blend into his hand that was caressing her side. I stood just inside the stall, watching the two. I hadn't counted on Yakut being here, but this struck me as a stroke of good luck. With his help, Guzel and I could become acquainted very quickly. For some reason, the fact that he would see me in my fear didn't bother me; perhaps because he had already witnessed it, or perhaps because I felt safe with him—this boy from a foreign land who intuitively seemed to know what I was feeling.

He must have felt my presence, because he stopped talking to Guzel and said softly in Farsi, 'Who is it?'

I stepped into the light of the lamp. Even now when I remember his face at that time, I am amused. His jaw literally dropped, and his eyes opened wide. In that feeble light, all I could really see of him was a set of very white and even teeth, and bright white eyes. Neither of us spoke for many heartbeats. Then the gaping hole closed, and he started to say something. I heard a splutter, and then nothing. Walking up to him, I said softly, 'Yakut,' pronouncing the syllables carefully. 'Will you teach me how to make friends with Guzel?'

He didn't say a word. I could smell horse on him and something else, like coconut. Many years later, after he had become a full-grown man, towering over me—his frame so tall, his tailor in the shahr had to have a special tape measure made just to fit him for his tunic and qabas—I found out that he oiled his hair with the extract of coconut to keep his curls from becoming stringy and rough. He also used a loofah on his skin to exfoliate it. These little bits of feminine vanity in him were so incongruous, I pocketed them like pebbles and threw them at him whenever I wanted to heckle him. But at that time in the stable, I was hardly thinking about him or why he smelled of coconut. At that time, he was simply a means by which I was going to become a master rider.

Without a word, he took my hand and placed a bit of jaggery in it and raised it towards Guzel's mouth. I didn't even think about reprimanding him for touching me; I was too busy concentrating on Guzel's reaction. The whites of her eyes flashed as she bent her head to smell my palm. My hand trembled, and, as though he had felt the tremble in his own blood, Yakut put his hand gently under mine and held it in place. Guzel's nostrils twitched and then I felt a wetness tickle against my palm, as her tongue grabbed the jaggery in one big swipe.

Yakut's teeth gleamed at me, like tiny doves lined up on a ledge. Then he took my hand and placed it on Guzel's neck, guiding it down in a soft caress. Her warm, sleek skin twitched under my palm, and I heard her snort, in a way that made me think of how I must sound when Azra rubbed sandalwood oil in my hair and I wished she would continue forever.

'Guzel like Shehzadi,' Yakut spoke for the first time. I put my nose against Guzel's neck and breathed her in.

After that, for five more nights, I would go to the stable as soon as the household slipped into the oblivion of the second sleep. Every night, Yakut met me there, placing a lump of jaggery in my palm and teaching me how to become friends with my horse, with soft words and a firm hand. My fear of her size vanished in that first night, and, in the following five nights, I became attuned to the movements of her limbs and face. Yakut taught me more about horses in those six nights than I learned in years of training. He also taught me everything he himself had learned about Guzel—from blowing small puffs in her nostrils to help her recognise my scent, to relaxing her by tickling her sweet spot, which Yakut showed me was just above her nose.

'Who taught you about horses?' I asked him.

'Babek,' he said. 'First slave master.'

'In Aksum?' I remembered the name of the place the shahana had mentioned. 'Where is that?'

'Not Aksum. Aksum home,' he said. 'I no slave Aksum.'

'Tell me about yourself,' I said.

He leaned his head against Guzel's side and closed his eyes.

I waited, but he didn't tell me. Not that night.

5

MY LITTLE TRYST WITH YAKUT SOON ENDED. I ENDED IT. IT WAS MUCH harder to leave the palace after that first night. I couldn't escape Azra and Hindu Saras' watchfulness for long. Also, every night of my rendezvous, a thought nagged at me: if Yakut was ever caught with me, he would most likely lose his life. The more I knew him, the more that thought pained me. In any case, I didn't need him anymore. I was ready to face the world on Guzel.

Now I saw Yakut only in the daytime, when I came for my daily ride, accompanied by Hindu Saras. Soon, I also joined Nasir, Sanjar and Rukn on the track. Yakut wasn't allowed to ride with us, but he always stood on the side of the tracks, watching me intently. What I remember most from those days is the pride on Baba's face. What I realised later was that that pride tethered me to Yakut—it was a victory we had achieved together. The smile on his face as he watched me was the smile I felt on my own face.

Soon after that, Yakut started military training and went away to live in the barracks in the lashkar that was located on the other side of the shahr. Four years later I, too, started military training. Anneh didn't approve of it. 'Humph,' she would grumble, her pale, narrow face, pitted with faint scars of childhood pox, tight with displeasure. 'Daughters are not sons. Why doesn't the Sultan understand this? It is my bad fortune that I did not produce a son, but why does my daughter have to suffer for that?'

'It's not suffering,' Baba would reply. 'Allah himself has written zafer in her fate.' This was another name he had for me—Zafer—victory, because soon after I was born, Baba had triumphed over the hill tribes, who were considered too willful to be controlled. And to reward him, Sultan Ai-beg had manumitted him.

I tried to convince Anneh that this is what I wanted to do; but she just couldn't conceive of a girl who wanted to live the life of a man. Anneh never understood that it wasn't a man's life that I desired but a life that was of my own making. She thought she had failed as a mother, because her daughter didn't turn out like the other girls in the zenana, and I wanted her to realise that that was her utmost success. I wasn't interested in oohing and aahing over jewellery and dolls or finding perfect pebbles for a game of stones. I wanted to play war. When I was little, my favourite toy was a wooden sword that Baba had got me from one of his campaigns against a Chandela king. It had probably belonged to the prince. It had a sun-gold hilt studded with dozens of star-shaped amethysts—an insurgency in the skies. I used to challenge Nasir and Rukn with it in mock battles and defeat them. Zafer. Always zafer. Anything less was not my style.

The one person, who, to my surprise, did understand my desire to learn weaponry, was Rukn's mother. But I discovered soon enough that that wasn't surprising at all. Because when I was just a zenana-bound princess, even though I was Baba's eldest child, I was merely a contender for Baba's affection; once I began training to be a warrior, I became a contender for Baba's throne.

A few days after I started training, Azra came to tell me that Husni Begum had summoned me to her room.

I was getting ready to step into the lotus bath that Baba had installed in Anneh's wing. Azra had just had it filled with warm water from the boilers on the ground floor. After being in the field from sunrise to mid-day, constantly drawing the bow and shooting arrows at targets, my muscles screamed for a deep soak. I loved archery, but it was proving to be the bane of my life. The ability to shoot from a moving horse or an elephant, while lying, sitting, standing, or even leaping made this the most versatile of weapons, but learning to lock the fingers and clench the arrow was a challenge I had not expected. My palm and fingers were full of blisters as big and white as pearls. Second year trainees were allowed to use ghustuwana, the archer's protective rings for the thumb and forefinger, but a neophyte, like me, was expected to first learn the raw feel of arrow and string. Most other first-year trainees laughed off the blisters and just let them harden. For me, they weren't so easy to ignore. They were so prolific that I couldn't hold an arrow in place without wincing. I found myself concentrating more on disguising my pain than on target practice. This bath was my reward to myself. Unlike the boys in training, who could only visit the public bath once a week, I had the privilege to soak in my own private bath every day, and I shamelessly took advantage of it.

'What does she want?' I asked Azra with a groan.

Azra made a spitting sound with her tongue and teeth and then pursed her lips. She was fond of chewing paan and always had bits of areca nut in her mouth that she spat out at moments of disgust.

'Fine. I'll go to her after I've bathed,' I said, stepping into the water, fragrant with roses and swarming with lotuses.

'You know Beauty doesn't like to be kept waiting,' Azra said. Shah Turkan's name, Husni, meant beauty, but only Baba and Anneh called her by her name. For everyone else she was Shah Turkan; however, in private, they all called her 'Husni' in a way that sounded like a disparagement of beauty.

Just the thought of the abhorrent impending visit ruined my bath. Every time a floating lotus drifted towards me, I swatted it away, my mood darkening even more. I hated that she had so much control over my emotions. After my bath, I quickly dressed in my tunic and salvar with the help of a slave girl, who also loosely braided my wet hair. When I descended the stairs to the third floor and arrived at Husni's apartment, a slave girl directed me to the low chaise lounge that was placed in the centre of the room.

I rarely ever came to these rooms, but every time I did, I saw a new display of opulence. This time it was the chaise. There were no carpenters in Dilli, at that time, who had the skill to make this delicate piece of furniture. Husni's was probably imported. It was upholstered in golden velvet, a fabric which was also extremely hard to get. Women in the zenana would have killed for it. It was made in Misr and exported to Baghdad, and Baba only received it occasionally from visitors coming from the Khalifa. I can't say I was surprised to see the gold chaise in the room. I knew from Azra that every time Husni won in chaupar against my father, she asked for something none of the other concubines owned. Her matches with my father and her skill at the game were a perpetual topic of discussion in the zenana. As I sat down gingerly on the edge of the chaise, I saw across from me, on the thick carpet, a chaupar board laid out with carved wooden pawns and gilded cowrie shells and I wondered how many of her victories were simply my father's indulgence.

I waited for Husni for a long time. This was not new. She always made me wait every time she summoned me. So I sat and waited, asking myself why I didn't just get up and leave. Finally she deigned to come out of her inner apartment and looked at me, surprised, as though I was there unexpectedly. 'Oh, Razziat,' she exclaimed. 'Welcome.' She never called me Razi or Shehzadi, like the other ladies. It was always my full name—Razziat. 'I was taking a nap. I must be such a mess,' she said, smoothing her hair with a hand.

I looked at the two heavy braids on either side of her face that didn't have a hair out of place, but didn't say a word.

As she walked towards me, I couldn't help but notice her—her tunic of yellow silk that was like a shimmery second skin, her impossibly thin waist that was caught in a gold and ruby belt, the malika necklace on her chest that was shaped to the exact contours of her breasts and the quince seed beauty spot on the apple of her cheek that was the exact onyx of the kohl in her eyes; both a perfect foil for her milk-pure complexion.

Settling herself gracefully on the floor cushion across from me, she looked my way. 'I hear you've started training with the shehzadas.'

A sick feeling began to build in my stomach. Baba was so enamoured of her that I knew just one word from her would be enough to persuade him to withdraw me from training.

'I asked your Baba about it,' she continued. 'He thinks you'll make a great warrior. But I also hear that your mother, my dear elder sister, doesn't approve.' She paused, looked at me intently, and then continued, 'I just wanted to tell you that I fully support what your Baba says. I think you'll make a great warrior.'

At that moment, a mere finger's push would have toppled me over, I was so surprised. But then, almost immediately, suspicion and questions rose in my mind—What does she want? What devious plot is she spinning? What could her motive be?—I looked at her to see if her face would give away her true intentions, but she just sat there looking innocent, eyes artfully enlarged with kohl. I realised she was waiting for me to say something.

'Thank you, teyze,' I said, dutifully.

Her benevolent smile was of a queen's. She gestured to me to come and join her on the floor, and when I did—sitting a little away so that no part of me touched her—she said quietly, almost genuinely, 'I think we women would make better warriors than men. You know why?'

I shook my head.

'Because we use our …' She tapped her forehead with a henna-tipped finger.

I nodded. I couldn't believe that we were speaking the same tongue, that her thoughts were my thoughts, that she understood what drove me. I didn't know what to make of this knowledge.

She took my hand and caressed it gently. 'Sometimes I wish I had a daughter like you. Brave. Beautiful.' Then she suddenly stopped. 'Oh, you poor girl.' She turned my hand over and looked at the callouses on my fingers. 'Your lovely hand. Look what you've done.'

'It's nothing,' I said, quickly pulling my hand out of hers.

'Does it hurt?'

'A little,' I said and then wondered why I had just told her that.

'I'll give you something for it,' she said. 'It's a salve that heals cuts and callouses and also keeps the skin soft.'

'I'm fine. I don't need anything. The shahana says the callouses only hurt for a few days and then harden.'

'Such a brave girl,' she said, reaching out to caress my hair. Her ring got caught in my wet hair. 'Oh no. So sorry, dear child,' she said. 'This ring. It always catches. Hold still.' She shifted a little so that she was behind me and had better access to my head. I sat quietly, disconcerted, feeling little tugs in my hair as she tried to untangle the ring. This close, I could smell her perfume—a complex smell—like musk mixed with jasmine mixed with the crispness of jewels—nothing as common as roses, which most of the women in the zenana wore. She struggled with my hair for a bit and then called her girl: 'Come and help me untangle the shehzadi's hair from this cursed ring. I can't seem to get it out.'

The girl appeared immediately, and, kneeling behind me, freed my hair in no time.

When the slave girl went back inside, Shah Turkan returned to the cushion again, facing me. 'Where were we?' she said, settling herself. 'Oh yes. Callouses. Let me give you the salve; it's made of a plant called gwarpath—aloe vera. It grows wild all over Dilli and people here use it all the time to heal cuts and wounds. I've had the hakim make some for me, as well. Not for callouses, of course, but for my heels; they don't like Dilli's winters. See?' She slipped off a silk slipper and showed me the heel of her foot. I was shocked to see peeling skin. In that moment where she so guilelessly displayed her imperfection, I felt a strange affinity with her. Was she, too, misjudged?

'They're so much better now,' she continued, passing a quick hand over her heel. 'You should have seen my feet two weeks ago. The salve is really very effective—for all skin ailments, even callouses. Did you know that your Baba keeps a couple of vials of it in his bags when he goes on campaigns?'

I shook my head. I felt like thanking her for sharing this private detail about my father, but then I berated myself for it. How could I be feeling grateful to her? What was happening to me?

'It's really a warrior's salve,' she said with a smile. 'Let me get it for you.'

She got up and went inside and then returned shortly. In her hand was a small flat-bottomed, greyish glass vial closed with a stopper that was held in place with a metal clip.

'Here it is,' she said, holding it out to me. 'Just a drop once or twice a day, and you'll see how your callouses disappear.'

I stood up and took the vial from her.

'Go now, my Razziat,' she said. 'I just wanted to give you my best wishes.'

Holding the vial tightly in my hand and feeling a bit out of balance, I quickly returned to my room.

'What's that?' Azra pounced on me as soon as I came in.

'Something made from gwarpath. She gave it to me for callouses.'

Azra snatched the vial from my hand. 'Don't you touch it,' she cried. 'It's probably poison or some such thing. She's no well-wisher.'

'She really was being nice today.'

Azra made the spitting sound again and turned towards the door.

'What're you going to do with it?' I asked her.

'Bury it.'

A week after my visit to Shah Turkan's room, I became violently ill, vomiting and retching, till I thought my very innards would spill out of my mouth. Anneh called the hakim, who gave me a powder that I had to take with water twice a day. 'The shehzadi has eaten rotten food,' he said.

'But no one else in the palace is sick,' Azra reasoned with him.

I couldn't quite keep down the water and powder either, but after two days, I felt better, and on the third day I went back to training. A few days later, during target practice, I began to feel a headache on the right side of my head, just above the ear, and within an hour, it spread to the other side, in a single streak of pain, like a snake slithering under my scalp. The pain lasted for about a day and then it was completely gone, as though it had never been there. A few days after that, my tongue began to feel heavy, like a stone was tied to it, drowning it in my mouth. When that was gone, the bones in my right arm began to hurt, from knuckles to the wrist and then elbow to shoulder. The tongue ailment had prevented me from speaking, but it had not hampered my training; the pain in the arm, however, made it impossible for me to lift any weapon. I hadn't said anything to Azra after the first bout of sickness, but now I was forced to go to her. She immediately called the hakim again, who came and prescribed another powder. 'Sometimes these muscle pains accompany ailments of the stomach,' he assured Azra and Anneh. 'The shehzadi should recover soon.'

But I didn't recover. I got worse. The pain began to spread all over my body, like a new layer of skin. I had no appetite and no energy. I stopped going to train, stopped riding, stopped sleeping. All I did was lie listlessly in bed, every fibre of my body aching. One day, massaging my head, Azra suddenly screamed. She had noticed a black patch on my scalp. She said, many years ago she had seen something similar on an aunt whose husband's second wife wanted to kill her. This time, instead of calling the hakim, Azra summoned a woman from the shahr.

She was dressed in a black ghaghra and had hair in a hundred braids that looked like serpents hanging from her head. She sat on my bed and examined me, probing me everywhere, and poking me in places, asking if it hurt. Where she poked, I didn't hurt, and yet I hurt all over. She peered and sniffed at the patch on my scalp. Then she lifted my lids and looked under them, as though she and the cause of my sickness were playing hide and seek and the cause was hiding under my lids.

'The shehzadi is under a bandish,' she finally declared to my mother and Azra. 'Someone has tied her to a power.'

Anneh began weeping loudly and Azra was so angry, she forgot to spit. 'Can you break it?' she asked.

'To break it we have to find the bind. Did anyone take the shehzadi's hair or nail?'

Azra looked at Anneh, and then they both looked at me. I shook my head. What an odd question, I thought. Why would I give my hair or nails to anyone?

'Did anyone give the shehzadi anything unusual? An amulet a taweez, anything?'

I shook my head again.

'The vial of aloe vera!' Azra suddenly remembered and told the woman about the vial she had buried behind the zenana. They both rushed down, and when they returned, Azra was holding the vial, which was covered in soil. Following the woman's instructions, she emptied the vial's contents into a wooden bowl. The liquid trickled out sluggishly, and along with it came a squiggly little lock of hair.

The woman with the hundred braids burst out laughing. Then she picked up the bowl and handed it to Azra. 'Burn it,' she said. 'Make sure it burns to ashes.'

'What if she had used the salve?' Azra asked, fearfully.

'She would have died. But even if she hadn't used it, she would have eventually died. The juice of the plant is mixed with a timed spell. If it had been buried long enough, it would have been very difficult to save the shehzadi.'

My mother's weeping became louder. Then she wiped her tears and resolutely walked out of the room—on a mission. I heard her yelling and screaming at Shah Turkan from the top of the stairs. But, other than this, Anneh could do nothing. She couldn't even complain to Baba; he believed in the stars that the astrologer read, but he had no belief in the work of the jinn. Besides, there was no proof; it was only a vial of aloe vera, which, in fact, was one of the cures for callouses. As for me, after this incident I swore off all salves and instead willed away the pain of my callouses, accepting them with the same resolve as I did the hilts of my lance and sword.

6

FIVE LASHES FOR BEING LATE, TEN LASHES FOR MISSING A LESSON, AND fifteen for leaving the tabaqa without permission. Both Nasir and Rukn bore the marks of this punishments on their backs—Rukn more than Nasir. He was always late for training in the morning. It wasn't that he lingered in bed—that was more Nasir's guilty pleasure. Rukn just squandered away his time. Right in the middle of the morning Sharia lesson, with which we started our training every day, he would suddenly remember his falcons and slip out of the lashkar to ride all the way to the citadel and visit the roof of the Green Palace, where he kept their cages. The military cantonment is on the other side of the shahr, and he would miss, at least, two coaching sessions getting back, if he came back at all. Or, in the middle of a weapon's exercise, he would develop a sudden urge to go to the elephant stables and watch them getting their afternoon wash. Rukn often started his day with pain and sometimes ended it with pain, as well. And, in his last year of training, his days of punishment numbered more than the days he was in training. From flying falcons, he and his friends had discovered how high they themselves could fly on wine and women.

I, on the other hand, was the most diligent trainee. Generally, all trainees in the military camp are supposed to be treated equally, no matter who they are or which tabaqa they belong to. However, each unit has a superintendent—a shahana, who runs his unit his way, setting his own rules about infraction and punishment, with no interference even from the Sultan. Nasir and Rukn were in the tabaqa for children of manumitted slaves and Turki nobles. I was in a unit with just girls. Our shahana was a eunuch—Baktut. He believed that mental punishment was more effective than physical. That's why the number of lashes a trainee received in his unit were fewer than what was meted out in the rest of the tabiq, but his tongue was the sharpest of them all. My experience of the latter was more than my fair share, and my experience of the former was non-existent. It wasn't that I was spared physical punishment because I was a shehzadi; Nasir and Rukn, despite being shehzadas, were treated just like the other trainees, and they both had welted backs to prove it. And it also wasn't that I was the only female trainee. There were two other girls in my tabaqa; both were daughters of free amirs; although one of the girls left a month after I started training. The other girl was the daughter of Baba's Sar-i-Silahdar, the overseer of the armoury. The girl's name was Shadab. I still remember her. She was a year older than I. We weren't really friends; more like adversarial peers. She seemed to compete only against me; whereas, my competition was with all the boys with whom we used to compete every six months in the specific skills of archery, lancing, sword-fighting and horse-riding. The boys also competed against each other in hand-to-hand—a training the girls did not receive.

Shadab was an excellent lancer. She had the perfect body for it—tall and wiry—her deceivingly thin arms packed with strength that helped her throw the lance at record distances, beating even the boys' throws. For me, this weapon was the hardest to master. Although, I look a bit like Baba with my fair skin, high Ilbari cheekbones and very dark eyes that give the illusion of being black, my physique is quite different from his. He was a big, handsome man. I am small-boned, like Anneh. The lance requires immense strength in the arms, along with height to provide the leverage a warrior needs to throw it. I would never have the latter, but I was working on the former, and it was proving to be quite a challenge.

When Shadab started training, she was lean and flat-chested, like a boy; but, by the end of our first year, she had filled out, her breasts and hips clearly contouring under her clothes, her curves conspicuous, no matter the thickness of her tunic.

Once, after a lancing competition, which she won, we were walking out of the field, when we heard two boys talking and laughing. One of them said, 'She doesn't need a lance to kill; her bouncing balls are enough.'

It was clear to whom they were referring. I looked at Shadab. She looked away, her face red. Then she suddenly swung around and lunged at them, her arms locking around one boy's neck in a choke hold, making him gag and gurgle. When the other boy recovered from the surprise of Shadab's attack, he tried to pry her arms off his friend, and when he couldn't, he began pounding her head with his fists. I threw myself at him, grabbing him around his waist and pulling with all my strength, biting him wherever I could.

One of the assistant trainers saw us and rushed over to pull us apart. 'Who started this?' he yelled.

We all just stood there, panting, the boy whom Shadab had had in a head lock was coughing and spitting blood that was pouring down his nose.

'Speak up,' the trainer demanded. 'Or all of you will receive the maximum punishment.'

The boys and Shadab were whipped fifteen lashes each. The only difference was that the boys were bare-backed and Shadab was allowed to keep her tunic on, which wasn't a concession at all, because if the whip cuts through skin, it drives shreds of fabric into the cut, making the healing process much longer. In fact, people have been known to die from infection caused by the contamination of clothing.

I, on the other hand, was simply let off with an incongruous warning from Baktut. 'Wrestling is only allowed under supervision and only in hand-to-hand training,' he said to me. 'You have not been cleared to receive this training, Shehzadi. If you break the rules again, you will be dismissed from the tabaqa.'

'That's it?' I said. 'No lashing?'

He shook his head and dismissed me.

I was in disbelief and thoroughly embarrassed, I was also livid at the unfairness, for which I thought Baba was responsible. I would have gone to him right there and then and confronted him, but he was on campaign. I also felt that I needed to apologise to Shadab, but I didn't know what I would say. In any case, she stopped speaking to me all together. Every time I looked at her, she turned her face away, and my unmarked back felt the acute lack of pain. Shadab left training in the middle of the second year. I heard she was to be married to the son of an amir in Garhwal.

My resentment at being treated differently grew every day, and I could hardly wait for Baba to return, but then Azra told me that Husni had been telling everyone how I was being exempted in every way; whereas, her son, Rukn, was bravely bearing not just the rigours of training but also the discipline of punishment. I also heard that she intended to tell the Sultan to stop my training, because my delicate body was so unsuited for military training that the shahana was afraid to punish me. Now I began to dread Baba's return.

Then, one day, during an equestrian exercise, I lost control of my horse. He kept bucking, trying to throw me off. It was a new horse—one I had never ridden before. I thought perhaps I was doing something wrong, but I couldn't figure out what. Since Guzel, I had ridden plenty of new horses. Yakut had taught me how to quickly build a relationship with my mount, and, from Baktut I had learned well the dozen different ways of riding a horse in battle—to sync the weapon I was using with what I did in the saddle and the stirrups. Both these methods had helped me pass equestrian training with excellent scores. So, this lack of control in a mere exercise was galling. I could see the scowl on Baktut's face becoming more and more ominous as he watched me struggle with the mount. In frustration, I did something I had learned never to do. I used the whip. The horse suddenly arched his back and threw me off. I landed on the ground.

'Don't punish the horse, Shehzadi,' Baktut shot out at me immediately. 'Control it. Otherwise, your own horse will become your enemy.' I already knew this, and when he began reiterating again, what a controlled horse would do in battle, I intoned the words I had learned by heart.: 'A well-controlled horse will ignore the clamour of battle. It will not hear the strike of metal or the beat of drums. It will not be startled by enemy weapons flying around him. It will only hear his rider's commands. It will only respond to his rider's cues.' I also knew very well that the whip is a means of communication with the horse, not a tool of punishment. I was angry at myself for letting my frustration get the better of me.

Quickly coming to my feet, I came and stood beside the horse. He was now standing calmly, except for a faint twitching in his side. But as I made to get back into the saddle, Baktut stopped me. 'Your horse is bucking every time your legs touch his sides, Shehzadi. Don't you think he's trying to tell you something? Did you look under the saddle before you put it on him?'

I shook my head.

'What were you doing when I was giving saddle training two months ago?'

'I ... I missed that,' I replied, trying to control the rising anger in me. He knew very well that I had been absent on those days. It was another privilege I had, which now I fully intended to forgo. Every month I was allowed to take two days off for my monthly.

Baktut looked at me pointedly, then drew in a breath, his nostrils dilating in disdain. 'Take off the saddle and look under it carefully.'

When I lifted the saddle from the horse's back, I wanted to beat myself. A babool thorn was sticking out of his flank. The saddle and my pressing legs had driven it so deep, that it was almost three-quarters in, and blood was oozing out of the wound. With shaking fingers, I pulled out the thorn; a stream of blood gushed out with it. Baktut called a stable boy to take the horse for treatment and ordered another mount for me. But for me the rest of the day was a blur. Baktut repeated the lesson about saddles and also the proper use of the whip. I heard it all, but I learned nothing that day. All I could think about was the sharp, white thorn digging into the horse's flesh, and how I had continued to err, without pausing for a moment to figure out the problem. How could I have been so heedless, so lacking in control? And the worst part was that I was hardly penalised for my deplorable negligence. If any other trainee had hurt the horse as I had, Baktut's whip would have taught him a lesson for life. All I received was a reprimand that was tame even for a two-year old.

Then there was an incident with the sword that wrecked me. The sword was my favourite weapon. I excelled in it, because, as compared to the boys, whose much bigger shoulder muscles tired out easily, I could train in it all day. A trainee's schooling in swordplay is so rigorous and punishing that only a few qualify for its competition. It starts with weeks and weeks of just striking repeatedly on blocks of clay—twenty-five strikes, then fifty, then a hundred, and more and more, up to a thousand—first with one hand, and then with the other. Then the clay blocks are replaced with blocks of leather, and, after weeks of slashing that, blocks of black ironwood. Striking, striking, striking. Relentlessly. Only when the swinging of the sword became a reflex, are the trainees taught the difference between blows—light, hard or severe—to pierce just the top layer of skin, to cut through flesh, or to slice though the bone. To replicate bone, the lashkar imports pungali wood from the southern region of the Kakatiya where it grows in the forests of Orugallu. This wood comes closest to bone in hardness, which is harder than any wood, because it is one quarter water. Only the most accomplished trainees are given the privilege to practise on pungali.

In my competition cycle, only I and two other boys—Saif and Badar—had earned this privilege. The conclusion of this training was an in-house competition for which arm's length of pungali wood blocks, the thickness of a man's upper arm, were cut, covered with leather to replicate skin and nailed vertically to boards above and below. At the competition, Saif, Badar and I were made to stand in front of the block panel, side by side, about two feet apart—Saif, then Badar, and then I—each us before the block we would strike.

It was a simple test: Baktut called out the strike for each of us—skin, flesh, or bone—and we had to pull out the sword from the baldric hanging on our side and make the strike—all in less than three counts.

Saif was the first to go. 'Flesh,' Baktut barked the order, and Saif's sword struck the wood, cutting through the leather and half-way through the wood. A passable strike, but a bit too deep.

Badar was next. His test was 'bone.' When he struck the block in front of him, it swung in two pieces in a perfect severing.

Then it was my turn, and, considering the first two tests, I was sure my test would be 'skin,' so I mentally lightened the strike that I would make. But when the order came; it was 'flesh.' I instantly readjusted my mind to exert the controlled force that would slice through leather and just the first few layers of wood—a perfect flesh wound.

However, when my sword struck the block, it not only sliced through the leather but also through the whole block of wood; and to make matters worse, it continued to swing in an arc so wide, its tip drew a line through Badar's sleeve, piercing the top layer of his skin. For a fraction of a moment, I didn't know what had happened. Then I saw the blood flowing down Badar's arm. I was stunned. Everyone was stunned. Baktut started barking orders. Badar was taken out of the room. Saif was also ordered to leave. I just stood in my spot, staring at the puddle of blood on the floor, devastated. If I had had to cut 'bone', Badar would have lost an arm.

'Maybe the tegh is not for you, Shehzadi,' I heard Baktut say quietly.

I looked at my sword, the three fingers of my hand still holding a perfect stance on the hilt. Sheathing it, I walked out of the room and got on my horse. I rode back to the citadel, uncaring that I was unaccompanied by a bodyguard, and going through the gates, headed straight to Anangtal, the water tank behind the palaces. This is where I came, when I needed to be by myself. Just the single-minded, sheer terror of descending the six levels of zigzag steps built against the walls in the tank, and then sitting at the bottom, one step above the water's rim, surrounded by the disquiet of toothed walls—the malaise very quickly becomes its own therapy.

Hindu Saras found me there some hours later.

'Someone replaced pungali with deodar,' he said.

'What?' I couldn't comprehend what he was saying.

'The block you cut. It was deodar. The softest wood.'

'How? Who?'

'You know who.'

'How did she know which block would be assigned to me and which test?'

'*He* knew.'

'Who? Baktut?'

'No, his assistant, Salah-ad-din. He makes the test order for the trainees. He was in her pay.'

'Where's he now?' I asked him.

'Dungeon.'

I nodded. 'Do you think he'll confess her name?'

Instead of replying, Hindu Saras ran a hand down his chin; he does that when he doesn't want to give an answer. But, as it turned out, there was no point in hoping Salah-ad-din would confess. The following morning, his body was found in the dungeon—very finely cut into three pieces—at the neck and at the thighs—a precise sword slicing through skin, sinew and bone.

No one ever mentioned that incident again. No one blamed me, not even Badar. He went back to training, once his stitches healed. He and I actually became good friends and spent time together during competitions. But how could I forgive myself? How could I forgive my tegh—a weapon I trusted like my own reflex? It was true that the competition wood had been replaced, but if the tegh was so in-tune with my reflexes, I should have felt the lightness of wood, even as I struck and controlled the swing. I felt betrayed by the very weapon I considered a part of me.

At the conclusion of three years of training, we were awarded a tegh of our choice from the various types of swords that the Sultanate manufactured. But to select a perfect sword a soldier needs to know herself—her strengths, her weaknesses, her decisiveness, self-confidence, or lack thereof, her personal relationship with right and wrong, and the agreements she has with herself regarding injury to the enemy. These swords are not just different in size, they are also different in the wounds they deliver. After trying out the heavier Paralak and Tarawatah, and the sharper Khurasan Bakhari, I settled on the shorter, lighter Nibah tegh made from an alloy of soft iron, silver and copper. It was perfectly suited to both my physique and my disposition. It was also capable of delivering a cut that could kill.

'Always keep this sword by your side,' we were told when we received it. 'Because you are now Mamluk soldiers, and a soldier, even with all other weapons but the sword, is no soldier. A tegh is all a soldier needs.'

I savoured the comfort of always having my Nibah by my side, but Baktut's words still haunted me: 'Maybe the tegh is not for you.' I lived with my tegh day and night, but I didn't wholly trust it. I knew I had to re-learn this trust. And for that I needed another trainer—a horse whisperer, who I had heard had also learned how to decipher the whispers of swords. I had heard that he had completed his training and had won the grand prize in the final competition for which he had been awarded the coveted Saif-i-Hind—the sword of Hindostan—a double-edged blade forged in the karkhanas of Dilli from melted iron eggs that were imported from the Deccan, its edges shined to such a sheen that they appeared as white as salt, its hilt studded with ivory and silver and etched with the words: 'Awarded to the best of the best by Sultan Shams-ud-din, Iltutmish.' I also knew that recently he had been appointed as a junior shahana, the assistant superintendent of the royal stable, and given a Turki horse of his own.

7

I WON YAKUT AT THE ANNUAL COMPETITION. EVERY YEAR GRADUATING trainees compete in an event that is held in the lashkar's maidan. It's quite a show. The trainees prepare for it for days, assembling in formation, standing shoulder to shoulder against the long end of the hippodrome, and then parading in a circle in full battle gear, equipped with all their weapons and shields; five hundred or more, all thundering across the maidan, a force ready to be deployed in battle. Almost all the nobles, who are in Dilli, attend it, and the Sultan is invited as the chief guest. It's also open for public viewing, and the whole city turns out to cheer the champions.

I competed in two championships: swordsmanship and archery. The latter was especially satisfying; all my targets had had Shah Turkan's face. After her machinations had made me suspect all healing salves, I had learned to just bear the blisters, letting them harden into rock solid protrusions. From then on, the rigid sheeshum wood bow, with which all trainees are initiated, became my ally. And, once I graduated from the sheeshum bow to the more methodical Hindvi composite bow, with its hard core, mountain goat horn belly and sinew covered back, I mastered archery in record time. My small, agile frame, put me at an advantage for shooting targets both fixed and moving, whether from a racing horse or from a stationary position.

For first place in any competition, the prize was of the Sultan's choice. My father had personally selected a set number of items as awards: a Katarah blade with the Sultan's motto carved in the cross bar of the hilt, a robe of honour made of yellow silk, the colour of nobility, and a ring studded with cornelian, one of the Sultan's own colours. He used to alternate between these, but occasionally, he would surprise the winner with something unexpected, and sometimes he even allowed the Mamluk to name his prize. When I won the archery contest, Baba handed me a wooden box that had a carving of the huma bird, whose very shadow denotes royalty. It was an insignia on Baba's throne and also on his royal umbrella. Inside the box were six ghustuwana, the leather rings that protect archers' fingers.

'For my Arash,' Baba whispered softly to me, calling me the legendary archer from Persia, who sacrificed himself for his country.

And after I won the best of swordsmanship, Baba slipped a baldric belt, embroidered elaborately with gold thread, over my right shoulder and across my body, straightening it at the waist, where I would slip in my sword.

But I took it off and handed it back to him. 'Forgive me, Baba, but may I name my own reward for this victory?'

He tilted his head and, looking at me curiously, said, 'Yes. Name your reward.'

'Jamal-ud-din Yakut.'

'Explain yourself,' Baba commanded.

'Nasir and Rukn both have a Mamluk as their private companion. I, too, want a Mamluk companion,' I said.

'You have Hindu Saras. Are you replacing him?'

Hindu Saras, my bodyguard and companion, is a Hindu from Bundelkhand—not mountainous and rugged like most jaandars who were selected to their position for their intimidating looks; he is rotund and soft-cheeked with sparse tufts of hair on his jowls. And he is a eunuch. But his appearance is quite misleading. He has a grip that is more tenacious and lethal than death; if he catches a hold of anything—a limb, a neck—he can wrench it right off.

People used to say that he still suffered bad memories of being castrated when he was seven. He is of royal blood—a grandson of the Chandela king, Vijayapala, whom my grandfather had defeated. He was taken as part of the raid in Bundelkhand, and Khalji, who was Sultan Ai-Beg's lieutenant at that time, had him castrated. For years Hindu Saras served as Khalji's boy, and after he died, Ali Mardan's and then Iwaz's—his asexuality passing from one amir's pleasure to the next. The way my father acquired him is legend. Apparently, Baba saw him in the street on one official visit to Iwaz's court. A bull had gone wild in a marketplace, and Hindu Saras, who was probably no more than fifteen at that time, had stepped into the street and grabbed one of the bull's horns, not letting go till the horn had been wrenched right out of the bull's head. Baba paid Iwaz one hundred gold dinars and brought Hindu Saras to Dilli and installed him as my bodyguard. No one knew what his real name was, and he never revealed it. So, he just became Hindu Saras—Hindu, because of his religion, and Saras, because it means eunuch. All my life, I've called him Saras amca, Eunuch uncle. He was fiercely loyal to Baba, and he has loved me intensely from the moment he saw me. For me, he has always been as malleable as gold, but he is impossible to talk to; his response to most of what I say is to rub a silent hand down his chin.

'I love Saras amca, and I would never replace him with anyone,' I said to Baba. 'But I need someone who can help me continue my training in fencing and riding. I want to be the best swordsman in the sultanate. I want to be the best rider. Yakut is an expert at both. You yourself awarded him the Saif-i-Hind, and I've heard you say that he's your best Mamluk. And I want the best. Don't you think your daughter deserves the best?'

Baba agreed to give me Yakut on one condition: whenever I rode with him, I would always be accompanied by Hindu Saras. 'Come to my private chamber in Qasr-e-Safed one half ghadi after the Asr prayer,' he said to me before he left the maidan.

I was so excited at the prospect of having Yakut in my life again that I arrived at the Qasr during the Asr prayer, even though I knew Baba would be in supplication. The guards at his door bowed to me and told me to wait. Just as the prayer ended, I saw Yakut walk down the corridor towards Baba's room. In my mind, I still remembered him as a thirteen-year old boy, slender and self-assured. At seventeen, he still appeared self-assured, but he had also become lean and very tall—sharp, like a lance. Seeing me standing outside Baba's door, he stopped. A wide smile spread across his face, his eyes very warm and crinkling at the corners. I felt a little dizzy. I think I smiled back. He was never one to hold back his feelings; I was the one who wore masks.

When the summons came from inside, it was only for Yakut to enter. 'The Sultan will summon you in one half ghadi, Shehzadi. He has asked you to wait outside,' the guard said to me with his head bowed in apology.

I often wondered what Baba said to Yakut that day. Whenever I asked Yakut, his eyes would get this flat look, as though all he could see was his immediate surroundings—no reflection of the past, no anticipation for the future.

8

THE DAY AFTER YAKUT BECAME MINE, I SENT HINDU SARAS TO INFORM him that he would be accompanying me to the minar that evening. The minar is a victory tower that my grandfather, Sultan Ai-beg, started building soon after Sultan Ghor made him governor of Dilli and he defeated Rai Pithora Prithviraj, Dilli's Chahamana ruler. But he was only able to build one storey of the minar, along with the Masjid-i-Jami adjacent to it, before he died in an accident, playing chaugan. When Baba moved to Dilli from Badaun and became Sultan, he resumed work on the minar and also added his own designs to the masjid. Once, before the work began, Baba took me and Nasir to see it. I was about seven and Nisu was six and a half. This is one of my favourite memories, because this was the first time I actually saw my beloved Dilli—what it was, and the dream of what it could become.

I remember that day; it was very early in the morning, before the Fajr prayer. I was riding with Baba on his horse. Nisu was following on his own pony, and a dozen jaandars were in the rear. We rode along the inner wall that Baba had recently built in the citadel to section off the palace compound from the minar and the masjid, and, as soon as we trotted through its northern gate, I saw it: the thirty-two-guz high, one-storey minar, like a massive stump of a sandstone tree, inscribed with giant carvings of Quranic verses in Naskh calligraphy undulating along its alternating angular and circular flutings. Baba proudly showed us the names of my grandfather and Sultan Ghor carved in sandstone.

'Can we go to the top, Baba?' Nasir asked.

'After salah,' he promised, shepherding us towards the masjid.

Handing over our horses to the attendants, we entered the masjid's courtyard of pillars. 'This used to be Rai Pithora's family temple,' Baba told us. 'But the quwwat—the strength of Islam—has turned it from a Hindu temple into a masjid.' The way he said it, it sounded like miraculous alchemy. It was only later, when I began to learn about the complexities of the Sultanate's administration and the different faiths of its people, I discovered that the differing sandstone pillars of the Jami Masjid, some carved with bells and chains, others with lotuses and flowering vessels, and still others displaying near-naked women with slashed off noses and breasts, had actually been wrested from Hindu and Jain temples—twenty-seven of them. The temples themselves had been ransacked and their structures pulverised, not so much to show the infidels the might of Islam, but more to erase the memory of Hindu rulers from their hearts. I also discovered these very infidels were the masons who installed their temples' corbelled domes and iconographic pillars in the masjid, converting their house of idols into a sanctuary of the faithful. Their signatures were everywhere: on doorways and archways, as though they were broken-hearted lovers engraving their names in the memory of their lost beloveds.

When I took over the Sultanate's affairs, I began to realise that people are just people; they don't care if they are ruled by a Hindu or a Mussalman. As long as they have a livelihood, a roof over their family's head, food for their children, and freedom to believe, they're happy. The temples that Sultan Ghor's soldiers tore down in Dilli to build the Jami Masjid were soon forgotten by the Hindus as simply lost places. They still had their faith and their gods, and they found them—under trees, in stones—and a flower garland or a dab of vermilion is all they needed to recreate their places of worship. I don't think Baba ever really understood this. Perhaps, his faith was too opaque to allow him to see the glimmers in others. Or perhaps, his own faith had all the light he would ever need. That day, as we stood before the arched stone screen—free-standing yet anchored to the plinth, built to veil the serene hush of the qibla gah beyond it, I saw what faith looked like in my father's face.

By the time we emerged from the masjid after prayers, the sun had risen, its rays silken on the buff of sandstone slabs of the minar. Entering through the narrow door, we climbed the dark spiral stairs and emerged on the sunlit balcony. And there before us, in the luminous early morning light, was Lal Kot: twenty guz-high double walls of rubble stones, as thick as three arms' length, housing everything from granaries to soldiers' quarters to dungeons, with enough space between them to allow for two horsemen to ride through, shoulder to shoulder. They formed a crooked, oblong boundary line of the citadel, punctuated by twelve circular bastions and five out of the ten gates that the citadel would ultimately have. Beyond the walls was the wilderness that would become the shahr—the city of Dilli. At this time, it was no more than the vast green spread of Sanjay Van forest, sprinkled with tiny clusterings of houses and shops, like the early inflorescence on fruiting trees. As the years passed and Dilli spread, Sanjay Van contracted, and by the time I became Sultan, all that remained of it was a small hunting forest for royal entertainment.

To the west of the minar was the eight guardsmen, four-faced Chaumukha gate. To the right of it was the Mandavi Gate that led to a rudimentary cloth market. Further east was Badaun Gate that led to the small grain market, and beyond it were the buildings of the military lashkar that were under construction, as were the roads that were being forged through forest and wilderness. On the northwest side was Ghazni Gate—the gate through which Sultan Ghor's forces had stormed the citadel. To ensure that no enemy would ever again breach it, my father had it reinforced with four interior gates that were guarded day and night by four marksmen, who stood in the domed platform of its bastions, with bows perpetually drawn.

Inside the citadel, my father had built two internal semi-circular walls—the one on the west of the palaces and the water tank sectioned off the stables and the riding grounds, and the one on the east side partitioned the palace compound from the masjid and minar. And guarded like a sultan's treasure within the walled circle, were the royal stable, gardens and palaces—the brand new Kushk-e-Firozi and Kushk-e-Sabz, shining like newly minted blue and green gems, and Qasr-e-Safed, freshly painted and gleaming like a white lotus.

Nailing it all to the ground of Dilli was the iron pillar that stands in the centre of the courtyard of the Jami Masjid, directly in front of the stone screen. It's been here since before my grandfather converted the temple into a masjid. Neither he nor my father removed it. Perhaps, they both hoped to disprove the story that the locals tell about it,or, perhaps, they wanted to prove it, or perhaps for them, too, it signified an axis, albeit a loose one. They say that when King Anangpal Tomar brought it here from Vidisha and installed it, an astrologer told him that the pillar had been pushed in so deep that it sat on the head of the world serpent, Shesh Naag, who, the Hindus believe, holds up the Earth. That's why as long as the pillar remained installed, the Tomars would rule this land. But Anangpal, not believing the astrologer, had the pillar pulled out, only to discover its bottom slick with blood, presumably from having hit the serpent's head. Worried that he had brought calamity upon himself, he ordered his men to reinstate it. The pillar went back in its hole, but it never again fit firmly. It has always remained a bit loose; like a loose nail—Dilli killi—and that's how Dilli got its name.

Standing in that balcony of the first storey of the minar, my legs shaking from being far above ground, my knuckles white from gripping the railing, I saw Dilli being born; I was witness to it. Even now when I remember that sight, I feel a thrill pass through my body. I also remember Baba's face at that moment, ruddy from the climb and something else— perhaps pride.

Another memory that always bubbles up, whenever I think about that first visit to the minar, is when we were about to descend the stairs and I looked down the spiral. I was so scared, I giggled and threw my arms around Baba's middle.

'Are you scared already, Razi?' he asked. 'What'll you do when I add more stories to this minar and the stairs go all the way up?'

'How up?'

He pointed to the sky and laughed. 'It's a victory tower. The Victory of Islam and the Victory of the Sultanate. Dilli will become a great city. I promised your grandfather.'

From that day, the minar became my own personal victory tower, and the Dilli I saw from its height became my dream. I had wanted to visit the minar ever since, but it was under construction for many years and was closed off to visitors, by order of the building superintendent, signed by the Sultan. I had ridden by its fenced enclosure numerous times on my way to the masjid and had often thought of invoking royal privilege from the lanced guards who protected the site. However, I resisted the impulse, because I knew my visit would go on record and I would have to justify myself to Baba, and I had no real explanation. So, all I did was watch it from afar, from the fourth-floor veranda of Kushk-e-Ferozi, seeing its stories slowly rise, slab by slab, each storey emerging from the midst of the one below—a promise unfolding.

That day, perhaps elated by my victories, or in a burst of bravado inspired by Yakut, I was ready to risk Baba's ire. To ride on the same path again, circling the citadel to arrive at the minar, with Yakut by my side—it felt just right—like it was meant to be.

That evening, when I stepped out of the gates of the Blue Palace, I saw Yakut standing to one side, his horse beside him; it was a brown slender-bodied Turkoman with a long neck, sloping shoulders, muscular legs and earnest eyes. The way the animal leaned his muzzle slightly towards him, even though Yakut wasn't touching him, I could feel the bond between them, as though the air they breathed, only they shared.

As soon as Yakut saw me, he straightened his back and bowed his head slightly. I nodded at him with deliberate nonchalance and swung myself onto Nudrat, a sedate white Arabian that Saras amca was holding for me. Next, he too mounted, but Yakut just stood there.

I waited a moment and then said imperiously, 'We will ride to the minar, Jamal-ud-din Yakut. Did you not get the message?'

I wasn't quite sure how to behave with him: treat him like a lowly slave or talk to him like an equal? Command him to do what I wanted, or ask his opinion? Expect him to treat me like a shehzadi or like a friend? None of these questions would have mattered with any other slave, but this was Yakut—a boy I had trusted with my fears six years ago, although he hardly seemed to be the same boy whom I had got to know in those six nights. This Yakut made me nervous and a little shy. So, I hid behind the familiarity of the royal mantle. He looked at me for a moment and then bowed his head again, but in that moment, I saw the concern on his face, and it took me back six years. His face still had the same transparency. Perhaps, he was indeed the boy I used to know; just older.

'My apologies, but it's not safe to go to the minar, Shehzadi,' he said. 'It is still being constructed.'

'That's why we're going at this hour. The sun is descending, and the workers have left for the day. We won't be in anyone's way.'

He suddenly smiled, and my belly fluttered.

'You haven't changed, Shehzadi,' he said.

I was quite surprised at the familiarity he assumed, but it didn't irk me; instead, I began to feel comfortable. How easily he had set the tone of our communication.

'What do you mean?' I asked.

'You're still breaking rules.'

'Rules are for other people,' I said haughtily. 'I am Shehzadi Razziat.'

He nodded and turned to his horse. The quick flash of white I saw on his face filled me with the warmth of memories. Drawing in a breath, I raised my chin and turned Nudrat towards the path leading to the north wall.

He rode a little ahead of me, and Hindu Saras followed a few feet behind. We didn't talk at all; watching his straight, long back and noticing how the last rays of the sun sparkled like diamond shavings in the tight curls on his head, I suddenly wished I had words that were not just redolent with childhood memories.

Going through the masjid entrance of Chaumukha Gate, we dismounted and handed our horses over to stable boys. From there, we headed to the minar enclosure where Saras amca spoke to the guards on duty, and they stepped aside to let us enter.

Up close, the minar was a thing of awe. Three stories of it were already complete, and the fourth was being constructed. Walking towards it, I kept looking at it, tilting my head back more and more to see along the alternate angular and circular flutings of the stories, all the way up to the vaulting of each balcony that looked like a massive sandy-red honeycomb. I couldn't look away. 'Watch out. Be careful,' Yakut kept warning me, and I would glance down momentarily. On the ground were stacks of sandstone and quartzite slabs and large trays of slaked limestone mortar mixed with rice water and chir pine sap.

When we climbed the stairs, Hindu Saras took the lead to light the way with a lamp. It was chilly inside and moist, smelling of crisp, fresh limestone. We emerged on the landing of the third floor; its centre was just a scaffolding of wooden poles and knotted ropes, with suspended plumb bobs to ensure that the vertical line remained true.

Picking my way through hammers and chisels that lay strewn about, I went to stand against the balustrade. Up there on the third storey, although breathless and shaky from its height, I couldn't help but gaze at Dilli. I could hardly recognise it. Ten years ago, it existed only in Rai Pithora's citadel and in its immediate surroundings. Now, Dilli shahr extended thousands of guz, precisely sectioned into seven bazars and carefully planned housing localities, each within a framework of flowered pathways. From up there, Dilli seemed like a giant spider's web— buildings and parks and maidans all caught in the gossamer of its flowery radial threads.

I was so enchanted by Dilli's transformation that I almost forgot Yakut's presence. When I finally turned to look at him, I caught him staring. He had been looking at me all this time. Putting my arms around my belly, self-consciously, I sat down, scooting back into the angle of the fluting in the minar's balcony.

'Sit,' I said to him, and he lowered himself across from me, folding his long legs under him. I kept willing myself to say something, but I didn't know what to say. He, on the other hand, was looking at me as though he had already asked a question and was expecting an answer. 'What should we talk about?' I asked him.

His gaze was direct and his face too honest. 'Why did the Sultan select me for your service?'

'Are you questioning the Sultan's decision?'

'No, Shehzadi. I would never do that. I'm just thinking that there are many other accomplished Mamluks in the Sultanate.'

'I asked for you,' I replied.

Delight was clear on his face, and then, suddenly, there it was, that ready smile of his. How easily smiles come to him, I thought. He hadn't changed at all. I remembered how his smile at everything I did right with Guzel in those six nights bolstered my whole childhood.

'I am grateful to the Shehzadi,' he said.

I gave him a brief nod. 'You will help me practice with riding and fencing.'

'I'm honoured, Shehzadi, but may I ask, why me?'

I wanted to tell him that he was the only one who had seen my fear, called me out on it and then showed me how to overcome it. And yet, I hadn't felt diminished by his help. But it was too soon for such revelations.

'Do you not think yourself capable?' I deflected his question.

He sat up straighter and replied, 'I received the Saif-i-Hind from the Sultan. He also honoured me by making me a junior shahana and rewarding me with a mare. I was the best horseman in the tabiq. I am capable.'

'What have you named your mare?'

I was surprised at how uncomfortable that simple question made him. He looked away, and I saw the knot in his throat bob up and down. I waited for a while, and when he didn't answer, I asked him again. His hesitation in telling me his mare's name had made me curious.

'Desita,' he finally said, with a quick glance at me. I think colour rose to his face; his skin flushed and glowed.

'What does it mean?'

'In my language, it means happiness,' he said softly. 'Contentment.'

'That's beautiful,' I said and wondered if he knew that my name, too, meant contentment. It wasn't till many years later that I discovered that he had, indeed, named his mare after me. If I had found out then, I don't know how I would have reacted. For me, our relationship was only six nights old. For him, it was six years.

After that, we just sat in silence and watched the last of the sun. It gave the balcony an intimacy, creating secret spaces between the angles of the fluting. In the month of Rabi' al-Awwal, the days are so short that when the sun descends, it disappears almost instantly. When it did, and the balcony dimmed, Saras amca appeared like a shadow to let me know that it was time to return. I got up and moved towards the stairs, where Saras amca waited, holding the lamp to guide the way. Standing on the first step, I froze. The stairs were so deep and the darkness so dense, it seemed like I was looking down a bottomless hole. Suddenly, Yakut was standing right behind me; I could feel the warmth radiating from him. He took the lamp from Hindu Saras and held it up in a way that the stairs were revealed almost all the way to the bottom. Taking a deep breath and, without looking down, I descended slowly, placing each foot squarely. He remained behind me, holding the lamp all the way to the end.

9

YAKUT'S PRESENCE IN MY LIFE CHANGED ME THE WAY A GRAFTED plant changes. I began to grow differently, as though my very rootstock had changed. From a desperate little girl who sought happiness in her father's approval, I began to discover my own happiness. From someone who used to combat fears with ridiculous masochistic imaginings, I began to accept them as a coherent part of me. And all the while Yakut sheltered the tiny shoots of my courage until they burgeoned. With him, I learned to laugh my joys into the wide sky and have them shower down on me, and through him I learned to tunnel my sorrows to see the light at the end of them.

He seemed to want for nothing. How was he so replete in himself? I still wonder. He didn't ever seem to need anything; every moment of his life was just another assimilation. It was like he was a river that simply flows, and whatever occurs in its course—rapids, currents, sun's rays, dimpling rain, ablutions, even drownings—all just become a part of it. I, meanwhile, was a bundle of needs, full of aspirations—each, a striving unto death. His yielding boggled my mind.

I used to get so upset at him for not wanting more, for not reaching for more. Mamluk culture is all about ambition. Baba manumitted him and then gave him the office of the royal cup-bearer, and that's where he remained, while most of his peer Mamluks were awarded iqta land grants and governorships. It's true that the Sultan's cup-bearer is a position of the highest trust, but it's a mid-level position, and it doesn't demand any real management, except of the wine cellars. Yakut was one of the Sultanate's most accomplished Mamluks and should have been managing a governorship, or, at the least, using his knowledge of animals, overseeing the stables and the acquisition of war horses and elephants. Once I questioned him about why he didn't ask Baba for more.

I had been waiting for him on the steps of Anangtal, a place where I often met him in our leisure, to just savour his companionship. The water tank is a popular haunt for lovers, friends and gossiping women in the late months of spring, so I avoided it in that season; but for the rest of the year, it is quite deserted. Yakut and I normally met there in the late evenings, after Baba retired for the day.

That day he didn't show up till the moon was high in the sky, and when he did come, it was only to tell me that he had to return to work. A dead lizard had been discovered in one of the vats of wine in the cellar, and he was conducting an emergency investigation to find out whether it was by accident or by someone's nefarious design.

'Is Baba all right?'

'Oh yes. His wine is different. This one was fermenting for the next banquet.'

'Someone wants to poison Baba's guests. Why?'

'That's what I'm investigating. Maybe it's nothing.'

'What kind of lizard?'

'I don't know yet. I'll find out.'

'Why are you chasing lizards, Yakut? You should be governing an iqta, or managing the stables as an amir. You're Baba's most experienced horseman.'

'The Sultan trusts me.'

'I know that. That's why he should award you a governorship of his most important region.'

'Dilli's my home. Why do you want me to go away?'

I smacked his arm, infuriated. 'You know that's not what I mean. Stop being obtuse.'

'I'm not,' he said, smiling and rubbing his arm. 'But why can't you believe that I am satisfied being the Sultan's cup-bearer.'

I didn't believe him. So, one day I asked Baba why he had stopped promoting Yakut.

'He's a Habshi,' Baba replied. 'I can't make him a governor. The people will never accept him, and if I place him in a position above other Turki nobles, it'll create dissension in the ranks. Yakut knows this. He understands.'

My heart hurt for Yakut. He hid it well, but, surely, he must have felt the pinch of injustice. Perhaps, this prejudice was also the reason why he didn't have any friends. In all the years I knew him, he just had one friend. A fellow soldier from his tabaqa—Altunia.

I knew Yakut trained in a tabaqa of Mamluks of questionable background; many of them either dhimmies, belonging to faiths other than Islam, who paid a religious tax, or captured slaves from foreign lands. There were also a couple of orphans, whom Baba had adopted in his family of Mamluks. That's how Yakut and Altunia met and became friends. Altunia is an orphan. He was left at Khwaja Qutb-ud-din Saheb's dargah-i-khas as an infant, and when he was six or seven, the Sufi pir gave him to Baba. Yakut and he practically grew up together.

I met Altunia a few months after Yakut and I became friends. I remember that day well. Yakut and I were scheduled for sword training and I was waiting for him in the maidan behind Qasr-e-Safed, when a guard came to tell me that he had arrived. 'Send him here,' I said, wondering why he needed permission.

'Shehzadi, he has another Mamluk with him. He's asking for permission to bring him,' the guard said.

I was instantly curious to know whom Yakut had brought. He'd never mentioned a friend, or anybody else for that matter. 'Tell him I will be pleased to meet his guest.'

When I saw Altunia for the first time, I had a moment of panic. His tall frame, the muscles bulging under his crisp qaba, the sparkle in his brown eyes, and that detestable flirt of a dimple in his right cheek, just at the hairline of his beard—it all took me by surprise. And to make matters worse, he came and knelt before me and kissed the ground at my feet, as though he was pledging allegiance to a sultan. I was terrified he would see the sudden wobble in my legs.

Yakut saved me. His low, familiar voice, as he introduced Altunia, was like a safety net: 'Shehzadi, this is my friend Ikhtiyar-ud-din Altunia. He's an excellent chaugan player. The other day you expressed the desire to play chaugan. I brought him so that you can meet him. He will be a worthy opponent.'

'Excellent,' I said, raising my chin and stiffening my back to appear as imperial as I could. 'Ikhtiyar-ud-din Altunia, I am happy to make your acquaintance. We will discuss the game of chaugan later. Right now, I must begin my sword practice with Yakut. You can stay and watch, if you like.'

Fencing with Yakut, I tried to show off the most difficult manoeuvres, all the while berating myself for it; especially because I couldn't seem to sustain even simple parrying. I was too conscious of Altunia watching me.

'Remember the trick is in the wrist,' Yakut reminded me as I made another awkward thrust with my sword. 'But you must balance the body so that all you execute is the wrist; nothing must throw off the body. Watch,' he said and began to show me. That day, I resented Yakut's skill. Instead of appreciating the smoothness and artistry of his strokes, as he painted a landscape with each thrust and parry, I scowled at every perfect move he made.

'He's just a showman, Shehzadi. Come try your skills on me,' Altunia said from behind us, and Yakut and I both turned to look at him. He was standing there grinning, the dip in his cheek an impertinent crater. Then he unsheathed his sword and came towards me. Suddenly he was on the floor and Hindu Saras' hands was around his neck.

'No. No, Saras amca,' Yakut called urgently. 'Stop, please. He's my friend. He didn't mean any harm.' But when Hindu Saras' fingers continued to squeeze Altunia's neck, and he began to gasp for breath, Yakut turned appealing eyes to me. In my mind, I exulted to see Altunia helpless on the floor, but I waved at Saras amca to let him go. Altunia jumped up, coughing and massaging his neck. Then he bowed to me and, placing his sword at my feet, said very softy, 'I am your servant.' I couldn't tell if his vocal cords were hurting or if he was mocking me.

Stepping back, I gestured to him to pick up his sword and took a stance. It was a short match, with both Hindu Saras and Yakut watching Altunia—Saras amca like a hawk and Yakut like an angry mother bird. Altunia and I advanced and retreated, we lunged and faded as we parried, but then he began to cut and thrust with such force that soon he had me off balance. I lost the match, and he went down on one knee and placed his sword at my feet once again.

'Congratulations,' I said to him as evenly as I could, even though I was out of breath and smarting from the defeat. Then I invited him for a rematch in seven days. I never minded losing to Yakut, but losing to Altunia—it shredded me.

For a week, I trained fervently with Yakut, driving myself to the limit. He didn't question me; he seemed to understand why I had to win.

'Altunia is very good, but you're a skilful fighter,' he told me. 'You were just too focused on his weapon and his hands. That's why you missed it when he changed his stance. Remember, your focus needs to be more on the opponent's core—the middle of his body. That'll tell you what move he's going to make.' Then he told me about Altunia's weakness—he relied too much on his muscle power. 'Overpower his muscle with your skill,' he advised me.

I won the rematch. Sometimes, when I used to compete against Yakut in a friendly match, he would let me win. He never made it obvious, and it was always a difficult win, but I could tell when he purposefully missed a strike. And sometimes the victory was all mine. In either case, it was always sweet victory. But this victory against Altunia? I was so happy I wanted to plant a flag on the citadel's rampart.

Altunia accepted defeat graciously enough, but I could tell from the way his eyes lost their glint that he hated losing as much as I did. That victory of mine also put an end to any flutters of the heart I felt for him. After that match, we became very good friends. He, Yakut and I—and Hindu Saras, our silent partner—we were a team.

Behind my eyes, a collage of memories—Altunia, Yakut and I fencing, shooting targets, playing chaugun; Altunia grinning from ear to ear, gloating about his first victory over me; Yakut conceding yet another defeat; his smile indulgent, his eyes full of something I knew in my heart but never acknowledged. Sunset behind the almost-finished minar; the camaraderie of sandstone and the horizon. The three of us sitting on the last step of Anangtal, just above the cool, clear water; Hindu Saras two steps above us, and the stairs zigzagging behind us, all the way to the sky. Sharing lives, dreams and hopes; Yakut talking about his days as a slave in Baghdad, in Al-Mansura. Of Aksum, his home, he never spoke. Altunia sonorously quoting Qutb Saheb in a string of random Sufi directives; his legacy from having spent the first five years of his life with him in the dargah: 'Shun hypocrisy'; 'Keep the secrets of friends'; 'Take the sorrows of the world on your shoulders'. And I, normally the most reticent of the three, so loquacious about my dreams of being Baba's heir to the throne of the Sultanate. I can still hear my own impassioned declarations of change that I would bring, spouting from within the folds of memory: no more oppression by the Chihalgani, Baba's handpicked council of Turki noblemen; no autonomy of iqta landowners; centralised power; one law for all subjects of the Sultanate; Hindus made dhimmies—protected people through Jizya; no more intolerance of religion; less ties with Baghdad, more focus on Al-Hind; better roads, more hospitals, more parks, more gardens, more madrasas, more scholars and poets, more craftsmen; Dilli the centre of the world, not just Dar-ul-Islam. Sitting in that water tank with my two best friends, I dreamed up a new Dilli. Yakut and Altunia smiling fond smiles, dreaming those dreams with me. And then to celebrate the dreams, Altunia pulling out his pouch of hashish—another habit he had acquired at the Sufi saint's dargah. Yakut hated that stuff, but I would let Altunia talk me into it every time. I remember the first time he placed a pinch of dried leaves on my tongue. Nothing happened for a while, and then suddenly the water in the reservoir became so clear, I could see the shimmery iridescence of the tiny fish in it. The sky above became a blue I had never seen, and the stairs around us began to spin into a jagged spiral. The next thing I knew, the sun was down, and it was already time to go back to the palace. I can't remember those few hours in between. All I can remember is Altunia laughing and laughing.

10

THE SOUND OF MY CELL'S DOOR BEING PULLED OPEN BRINGS ME BACK to the present. I try to drag myself up to sit; instead, I almost collapse on my face. I must have fallen asleep, because I feel disoriented and my body has forgotten the synthesis with pain. I am so angry at myself for not remaining vigilant. And now I've also lost the element of surprise I wanted to use to jump Altunia.

I see a soldier enter the cell and replace the old, burnt out torch with a fresh one and leave. When Altunia comes in, I use the wall as leverage to raise myself up. Then I sit and watch him walk towards me. He's wearing different clothes, and I realise that this is another day—perhaps two days have passed, or even three? Panic begins to curdle in my stomach.

Altunia comes and stands close to me, looking down at me. 'What happened to your clothes?' he asks. Then he reaches out a hand as if to touch the bandage on my belly. I recoil.

'You should really let me send you my hakim to examine you. It looks like you're pretty badly wounded, Razi.'

'Go to hell.'

'You were not supposed to get hurt.'

'You called me to battle, you bastard. What did you think would happen?'

'They had instructions not to hurt you. I want to marry you,' he says.

The seriousness of his tone surprises me so much, I begin to laugh. Has he really done all this just to get me to marry him? The fool. Does he actually think that after taking away my Sultanate and killing Yakut, I'll agree to be his wife?

'I'm serious, Razi. That's the only way.'

'I'd rather die than marry you. And what do you mean, "the only way"?'

He's quiet for a moment. I look up at him, and I'm taken aback by an expression I have never seen on his face before. Even in the dim light, I can see an intensity, a righteous zeal. Then he begins speaking: 'The Ulema—the religious leaders and the Turki nobles—they're all against you. You threatened their power. They were already bucking from taking orders from a woman. Then you go and remove your veil. And then, to make matters worse, you make a public display of lusting after a Habshi. What were you thinking, Razi?'

I stare at him in shock. What happened to him? This is not the Altunia I know. He's talking like the most conservative of them. He's never talked like that, or even had a thought like that. This Altunia is not the friend I've known for sixteen years—a friend who not only understood my imperatives but also supported them. And for him to talk about Yakut in this manner—a man he called his brother ... I want to smack this Altunia in the face.

He must have seen the intent in my eyes, because he raises his hand, as if to stall me. 'I'm telling you what motivated them. Think what tarikh—history—would say about them serving a woman and a Habshi? They couldn't conceive of it. I warned you about this when you became Sultan. You did it, Razi. You killed him. And they would have killed you too, if I hadn't pulled you out of the battle.'

'And what will tarikh say about you, Altunia? What will you be known as? Backstabber? Traitor? So, what did they offer you in exchange for killing a friend you loved like a brother and capturing the Sultan of Hind: the woman who made you, the woman you profess to love? I gave you Baran and then Tabarhind. That wasn't enough for you? How much, you bastard? What did they promise you? Another iqta? Badaun? Lahore?'

'I told you already. You won't believe it, but I did it for you.'

'Don't you dare, Altunia! Don't you dare say that!'

'Just think, Razi. How could they—those proud Turki men bound by traditions, and those scholars of Islam—how could they tolerate your free thinking? But, if you say yes to me, you'll be liberated from their constraints. You'll be free to do anything you want. Go without a veil, change laws in Tabarhind, meet people, sit with men and discuss philosophy and religion all day. I won't stop you. And no one will dare say a word. You will be Malik Altunia's wife—Malika Razziat.'

'Malika?' Contempt drips from my voice. 'You have it all wrong, Altunia. I am Sultan. Sultan Razziat-Ud-Dunya Wa Ud-Din. Go tell your friends, Sultan-i-Hind Razziat still lives and her sword is thirsting for their blood.'

'Don't you get it, Razi? They're too powerful. They'll destroy you. But I can save you. Let me save you.'

'Save me?' I say derisively. 'You bastard. I'm here in this dungeon because of you. Can you give me back my sultanate? Can you bring Yakut back?'

'I told him to stay away from you. But that fool loved you too much. I warned him that he would be his own ruin. And yours.'

'Let me see if I have this right,' I chew out the words. 'I'm a woman who has dared to become Sultan by public consensus. I have revealed my face in public so that my people can see me for who I am; I contaminated my Turki nobility by having a Habshi for a friend and a mentor. But I will be absolved of all this if I marry you?'

'Yes,' he says.

'I'd rather suffer the tortures of dozakh. Now get out, you bastard.'

'You're not thinking, Razi. This is really your only way out.'

'Get out!'

'Please, Razi. Why won't you listen to me?'

Rage is drumming in my ears, urging me to lunge at him and strangle him with my chains. I can feel the impetus building in every cell in my body.

Suddenly he turns around and walks out.

Seething, I hit the floor with my fists; the iron bracelets jar against the bones in my wrists, and I shout in frustration and agony.

11

I DON'T REGRET MY DECISION TO GO WITHOUT A VEIL. IT IS TRUE that I did it on an impulse, but it was the kind of impulse that is the outcome of a build-up, like rain. For raindrops, falling to the earth isn't a choice or a decision, or even a dilemma; it is the only course of action. Some people may call it a command from Allah.

I had been ruling Dilli for a little over a year. It was ath-thalatha—the third day of the week, the day of public court. On this day I listened to cases filed by subjects of the Sultanate. This was also the court of Mazalim in which plaintiffs could have complaints of injustice heard. This day of the week was established by Baba, as were the protocols of the Mazalim court. He had installed two complainants' bells that anyone could ring at any time—night or day—to have his or her petition heard directly by the Sultan. These were large iron bells strung around the necks of the giant marble lions that sat at the entrance of the Qasr-e-Safed, a remainder from the days of Rai Pithora—an ostensible continuity of strength and power that used to represent the Chahamana might, and now represented the Sultanate. Baba was a master strategist; he strung together the power of Rai Pithora with the justice of his bell to let the people of Dilli know that the Sultanate surpassed the Chahamana in governance.

I had been accompanying Baba to this court since I was fourteen. While he sat on his gold-leafed throne with a jewelled huma bird perched on its back, its wings spread to harken goodness and Allah's justice, I sat on a jewelled seat on his left, watching his every expression, or lack thereof, as he listened impartially to the arguments presented by the plaintiffs and defendants. Observing Baba pronounce verdicts, I began to understand how and why he decided upon them. Afterwards, I would visit him in his retiring room and discuss the cases with him, and he would explain to me his reasoning, often punctuating his words with phrases of wisdom from the Quran as well as Qutb Saheb, who was Baba's spiritual mentor. Later, when I sat in the seat of judgement, I would often repeat these lines to myself; they gave me strength and the courage to judge:

> Be ever steadfast in upholding equity, bearing witness to the truth for the sake of Allah, even though it be against your own selves or your parents and kinsfolk. Whether the person concerned be rich or poor, Allah's claim takes precedence over all.

And Qutb Saheb's words:

> O judge, be humble; you may think you are all powerful, holding the fate of people in your hands, but in Allah's eyes, you are the one on trial.

Once when I told Baba I was afraid of making a mistake and giving the wrong judgement, he said to me, 'Truth and equity are two foundations of justice, Razi. Recognise the truth and be equitable in your judgment.' He also taught me that a Sultanate can survive for centuries with non-believers, but it cannot survive a moment with injustice. My father with his noble dignity and a silver light in his black eyes was so awesome, that people couldn't raise their eyes beyond his feet. Yet he sat on the throne with deference for the position and gratitude to the people who accepted his justice without question.

I may look like my father, but I doubt that I sit on the throne like him. However, I do know that I deserve the throne. My people put me there..

That day started like any other day of public court. I arrived at the Qasr-e-Safed on my elephant with my entourage of twelve bodyguards, preceded by kettle drums that ceremoniously announced the arrival of the Sultan. The courtroom was full—the maliks and amirs of Dilli standing to the left of the throne, among them my own appointees, and the remaining from Baba's cadre of the Chihalgani, whom he fostered, nurtured and appointed to the most crucial posts in his Sultanate. He shared a bond of trust with them: they had all started young, as military slaves, most of them having been purchased when Baba was Governor of Badaun or right after he became Sultan. After training, they became pages in his court and stayed in the citadel, which brought them very close to the Sultan and to each other; so much so that Baba gifted them wives and concubines, and, very often, even their children intermarried. Most of them were so allegiant to Baba, that their support extended to Baba's heirs.

It is with their help that I had become Sultan. However, in my year on the throne, I had slowly been cutting the strings that tied me to them. Some of them had become too old to manage positions of responsibility and others remained rigid in their old ways. I had my own ideas of ruling; they were still loyal to Baba's methods. A few adjusted to my changes; others didn't and were replaced with my own men. Yakut was one of them.

He was not in court that day. As Amir-i-Akhur, the Master of horses, he often travelled to horse markets in and outside of Dilli.

Standing on the right side of the throne were members of the Ulema—scholars of religion. Although they had no say in the verdicts, they insisted on being present, to ensure that no decisions violated the tenets of Islam. Baba had kept more faith with the Ulema than I did. Often in his assemblies, he used to call upon them to interpret a complex situation as per the Quran. I, while upholding the protocols of Islam, trusted my judges to discern the facts.

The rest of the court room that day was packed with citizens. The accused and accusers, along with persecutors, stood at the very front, among them the young Hindu prostitute who had rung the bell of injustice. She was wearing red, the colour of a petitioner that Baba had mandated, and she was in chains.

I, too, was dressed in red—the colour also of justice. Over my red salvar and tunic, I wore a red silk qaba embroidered with gold flowers and fronds. And over that I wore a red burqa, a full body veil that covered me from head to foot, leaving just a netted window for the eyes.

All heads remained bowed as I walked to the throne. Settling into it, with my legs folded under me, I gave the order to my Amir-i-Dad to begin the proceedings. There were two cases before me: the first case was of Malik Bakhtiyar-ud-din, who was the Shahana-i-Mandi, —the superintendent of markets. He had repeatedly come to work drunk and disrupted the markets. The second case was of the Hindu prostitute, who had been sold for thirty silver tankas but refused to cohabit with her new master. This last case had been tried in the community court—the Panchayat, as all Hindu cases were, and the prostitute had received thirty lashes for disobeying her master, but even after the punishment, she had stayed with him only one week, and then run away. She had been caught and tried again; this time receiving fifty more lashes and another injunction to serve her master. However, yesterday evening, she had managed to come to the citadel and had rung the bell, appealing for justice.

I had been dreading Malik Bakhtiyar-ud-din's case ever since I had read the file. He was a friend of my father's, and I knew him well. When I was little, he used to teach me finger games. Thanks to him, I held Nisu and Rukn dumbstruck for years with the trick of dismembering my thumb. He was a good man, but he had a particular fondness for wine. Islam forbids alcohol, but the Hindus say their gods not only allow it but also encourage it. Even Baba, who was less tolerant towards Hindus, allowed its use, but only during celebrations. I knew, though, that some of our Muslim brethren imbibed on a regular basis. I had no objection to what they did in their own homes, but they had to abide by the law that prohibited drinking or display of drunkenness in public places and places of business. There had been many complaints from some fruit and vegetable vendors about Bakhtiyar-ud-din coming to inspect the market inebriated. The qazi had wanted to prosecute him after the first offence, but I had told him to send him a stern warning. However, even after the warning, he had appeared in the market one day, so drunk that he had knocked over a sack of tomatoes. It was this vegetable-seller who had filed the case of loss of income, and the qazi had moved it to the Muhtasib Court—the court of censor. A farman had been issued in Bakhtiyar-ud-din's name with the charge of drunkenness in a place of business. It was now the day to prosecute him.

The prosecutor presented many witnesses—merchants and sellers, who had interacted with the shahana and had seen his inebriation. Then the tomato-seller was called. He was a dwarfish old man, wearing a white tunic and salvar, freshly washed and so starched, that the fabric crackled when he moved. He clenched his hands under his chin and earnestly described the incident: 'It happened when Malik sahib's men were weighing the turnips. Then Malik sahib lost his balance and fell, and my whole sack of tomatoes was crushed under him. In the commotion, my other vegetables scattered everywhere. I tried to gather as many as I could, O Great Wali, but those little urchins; thieves, all of them. They descended like a horde of monkeys and stole everything.'

'My good man, can you tell us what caused Malik Bakhtiyar-ud-din to lose his balance?' the qazi asked him.

'He was drunk.'

'How do you know this? Do you have any proof?'

The man looked at the qazi fearfully. 'O Wali, how can I prove that Malik sahib was drunk that day? I can only tell you that he was swaying on his feet, and when he was talking to me, such a strong smell of spirits came from his mouth that I had to cover my nose with my turban cloth. Like this.' He took the tail of his turban that was hanging on his shoulder and covered his mouth and nose with it to demonstrate.

The qazi called other witnesses who had seen the malik in the market that day, and they all swore to his state of inebriation. When the prosecution rested, I turned to the accused and asked him, 'What do you have to say, Malik Bakhtiyar-ud-din?'

'I...I don't remember, Sultan,' he replied in a trembling voice. 'Maybe the man is right. I only remember my wife's anger. When I came home, she was angry because my clothes were stained red.'

There was snickering in the court. The wazir raised a hand for silence, and I gave the verdict. Guilty. His punishment: To be kept in a dugout for ten days with just a jug of water. A common punishment for drunkenness in a public place. Maybe he would survive the sentence; but considering his age and addiction, more than likely, he wouldn't.

After Bakhtiyar-ud-din was led away, the second case was announced, the Mazalim case of the prostitute. The merchant was presented first, because he was the accused. He was a man in his forties, and there was nothing particularly distinctive about him. He was of average height and had a little bit of a belly that protruded from under his brownish qaba that was embroidered along the sleeves, indicating that he had a certain amount of wealth. He was swarthy with a sparse greying beard, and he had narrow eyes lined with kohl. Under his brown turban, his hair was greyish and probably also thinning; meagre strands of it lay on his shoulders. Every other merchant in the Sultanate looked like him. He certainly wasn't handsome, but he wasn't particularly ugly either; he was just unremarkable. I wondered what issues the girl had had with him to want to escape not once, but twice. Then she was presented to me. She was waif-like, with wide, doll eyes in a thin face and deep depressions in the clavicle; cleaned and well-fed, she would be quite pretty. I could see why the merchant was taken by her.

It seemed a simple enough case. The woman was sold legally for thirty silver tankas. The merchant had a bill of sale and three witnesses. Legally, he owned her. It was as simple as that. But ringing the bell of injustice is serious business; if anyone rings it without reason, the punishment is death. And if there is reason, but the Sultan decides against the complainant, the verdict is normally the severest punishment enjoined by law. In her instance, it would been cutting off her feet.

'Why did you run away from your owner?' the qazi asked her.

She muttered something, but her head was hanging so low over her breast that it was difficult to hear her. At the order of the Amir-i-Dad she lifted her head and looked his way. Then her gaze shifted to me. I drew in a sharp breath. The look in her eyes was something else—wild and aflame. There was a fire inside her. The qazi had to tell her several times to lower her gaze. No one was allowed to look directly at the Sultan. But she kept staring at me. When the qazi asked her the question again, her eyes seemed to search for mine behind the net. If I hadn't been wearing the veil, our gazes would have met squarely. But in that instance, when her eyes couldn't find mine, I saw her defeat. I knew what she had seen: my eyes captured behind the fine mesh. I myself had sought my own eyes behind the net many times in the bronze mirror.

'Tell the Sultan why you have been running away from your owner,' the qazi said to her one more time.

This time, she raised her chin and said quite clearly, 'What does she know of real life? She herself is hiding behind a veil.'

There was an audible gasp in the court, and then everything suspended on that intake of breath, as though poised on the verge of it, waiting to exhale, waiting for me to pronounce the sentence, which could only be death—not at her crime, but at her audacity to sneer at the Sultan. I could feel everyone's eyes in the court looking at me, urging me to pronounce the order of execution.

I stepped down from the throne and left the court room, gesturing for my jaandars to remain where they were. Behind me, the silence erupted in exclamations. Going into my retiring room, I asked my serving ladies to help me remove my veil. They thought I had come to rest. Instead, I returned to court.

The quiet that fell in the court this time was not just the brink of noise. It was aphasic; rendered so by disbelief. I saw men who never deigned to look at me, stare at me, horror in their moving, speechless throats. I saw beards of the Ulema shaking, but no sounds came out of their mouths.

Walking to my throne and kneeling in it, I said quietly to the prostitute, 'What do you have to say? Tell me. I am listening and I will attempt to understand.'

'He … he …' She started to speak and then clamped her lips tightly. When their tremble had diminished to just a quiver at the corners of her mouth, she tried again. 'He likes to wear a bagh nakh—a tiger claw—on his hand when he paws me.' Then she pulled down her shirt to show me where the tiger's claw had raked her breast, the torn skin oozing blood and pus. 'He likes to do it when I am screaming and writhing in pain. I'd rather die than go back to his house.'

'What do you have to say for yourself?' I asked the merchant.

'I paid thirty tankas for her,' he declared.

'Give him thirty tankas,' I ordered the Amir-i-Dad. 'And castrate him. And make sure that the woman is taken care of. After she has healed, give her employment in Kushk-e-Ferozi.'

As orders were recorded and the merchant and prostitute were led out, an old man at the back of the court shook his fist at me and shouted. 'A Musalmaan to lose his manhood because of a Hindu prostitute? A shameless woman's justice. If your father were alive…'

The solders immediately arrested him and led him away. I would pronounce his sentence of execution another day.

12

‘HOW COULD YOU DO IT?’ SHAZIA’S VOICE WAS HUSHED IN DISBELIEF. ‘Weren’t you afraid?’

She had come to see me right after I returned from court. Word had spread fast, as I knew it would. I could almost see the vines of rumour getting longer, their tendrils more prolific, winding through the corridors of the palaces, attaching themselves to women’s tongues, sprouting on men’s bearded lips, nestling in shocked nooks and crannies of all conversations in the zenana and the Kushk-e-Sabz. I didn’t care so much what form they took in the Blue and Green palaces; what I wondered about was the shape they would take in the coteries of the White Palace, where the Shamsi bandagan, my father’s nobles, still huddled, and had the power to topple sultans. But even more than them, I was bracing for the reaction of the Ulema.

The Ulema—jurists of Islam, guardians of the Sharia Law, policemen of moral conduct, and adjudicators of right and wrong behaviour. Even my father, despite his supreme power, never challenged them. Whereas, my entire rulership posed a challenge to them. Baba had a conflicted relationship with the Ulema, a relationship that, I think, echoed his own crisis of faith. He saw himself as the protector of Islam, and he faithfully practised it, but he was also deeply spiritual. That’s why, I think he connected more to the teachings of Sufi pirs, because their practice of dhikr made him feel closer to his God. When we were little, he used to tell us a story about his first encounter with a Sufi darvesh, whom he met as a young slave. One time his master gave him some money to buy grapes, but he lost that money. Scared to return home without the grapes, he sat in the marketplace crying. A Sufi darvesh saw him and asked him what was wrong. When Baba told him, the man took him to the fruitseller and bought him the grapes.

'How can I repay you?' Baba asked him.

The Sufi told him to count the grapes in the bunch.

'Thirty-eight,' Baba replied.

'Then say Allah's name thirty-eight times today.'

'But I always supplicate myself five times a day,' Baba said.

'Why only remember God five times, when you can do it all day?' the Sufi replied with a smile.

That advice became Baba's own personal goal. Before he parted from the Sufi that day, he asked him again, how he could return the money that he had spent on the grapes. 'I'm only a poor slave,' Baba said.

'But when you grow up, you will become a rich and powerful man. Pay me then.'

'How will I find you?'

'You don't need to find me. I will be present in every Sufi ascetic you meet. Pay me by taking care of ascetics like me.'

That encounter was one of the reasons why Baba made Dilli a safe haven for Sufi fakirs. His coffers were always open for their care. However, the Sharia-minded jurists resented this and were constantly on the look out to discredit the Sufis.

I remember a case that I once observed in Baba's court: it was a charge of prostitution against a Sufi, Faqr-ud-din. He was a disciple of Qutb Saheb, and he was famous for the effectiveness of the amulets he gave to people. Wherever he went, hordes used to collect around him. And that was the grudge the Ulema, especially, the Shaik-Al-

Islam, Najm-al-Sughra had against him. He was just too popular, and they were jealous. Faqr-ud-din had a very special ability. He could levitate. In the ecstasy of dhikr, his body would become weightless and rise up. People had actually seen him perched on the parapet of the dargah. The Shaik used that to build his charge. He said Faqr-ud-din had learnt the skill of flying, which, in any case, was against Islam, to visit prostitutes. When the case was tried in court, Najm-al-Sughra presented many arguments and witnesses, but Faqr-ud-din didn't refute any of them, even though he knew his punishment could be death. His only response was: 'If Allah has appointed this hour for my martyrdom; so be it.' The Shaik won the case and the Sufi was beheaded. His head was hung from the same parapet to which the flight of his faith used to elevate him. I remember Qutb Saheb himself came to plead for his disciple's pardon, but Baba could do nothing against the jurists.

When I became Sultan, Najm-al-Sughra was still Shaikh-Al-Islam; and his stance was still as indelible as the austere prayer mark on his forehead. Just like Baba, I had no authority to remove him; he was appointed by members of the Ulema. That morning when I removed my veil, Sughra had been present in court. His face is still etched in my mind—his henna-emblazoned beard shaking in outrage, the vitriol of condemnation in his eyes.

When Shazi asked me if I had been afraid to remove my veil, it dawned on me that I actually hadn't been afraid. Despite seeing the reaction of the jurists and knowing that they would be beside themselves with anger, I hadn't demurred. 'No, Shazi, I wasn't afraid,' I said to my sister. 'Because I knew it was the right thing to do—the right thing for the Sultan. The people of the Sultanate need to see their Sultan, to see in her eyes the light of justice and equality. If they can't see this for themselves, how will they trust me? Did you hear what the woman said to me? What prompted me to do it?'

'Everyone's talking about what she did and said and the judgement you gave in her favour; that too, against a Musalmaan. I'm so proud of you,' she said, hugging me. I could feel the tremble of memory in her body. Shazia is four years younger than I. She's the daughter of Bismillah Khatun, one of Baba's concubines. Many years ago, Shazia was married to a qazi's son, who was training to be a religious scholar, but within the first year of marriage, she left him and returned to her mother. She even gave up her right to the mehr her husband had promised her when they were wed. He had been raping her every night and whipping her every day, claiming it all as his husbandly right. I saw the ugly welts—those that were visible on her arms and back, and also those that she hid in her tears. When she first returned from her husband's house, the women in the zenana were shockingly unsympathetic, and, some of them, like Husni, were downright vicious. They belittled the abuse she had suffered by telling her that her sin of leaving her husband was much greater than his for causing her pain, which, in any case, was a woman's burden to bear, and that she would burn in Jahannum for leaving him.

Shazia swore never to marry again, which, of course, set all the ladies, including her mother, on a mission to change her mind. I always felt protective of Shazi, but ever since she returned, I tried to be the wall behind which she could hide, if she wanted to, or use as a support to stand.

I put my arms around Shazi and held her tightly for a moment. 'I'm not sure that others will think as you do,' I said to her ruefully and silently thanked cosmic forces that governed life and death that Shah Turkan was no longer alive, or this would've swelled into a tornado.

'Thank Allah that Shah Turkan is . . .' Shazia began.

'I know, I was thinking the same thing,' I said, and we both looked at each other and shared a grateful smile.

'So, are you going to keep it off?' she asked. 'You know, remain unveiled forever?'

This question had been nudging at me since I left the court, but I had been pushing it away.

'I don't know yet,' I said. 'I haven't decided. First, I need to figure out how to deal with the Ulema. I'm worried about what they'll say and what they'll do.'

'Don't back down, Razi. Promise me, you won't back down now that you've taken up the fight. Someone needs to fight this fight and show them.'

I wanted to make that promise to Shazia instantly, but I knew that first I needed to douse their virulence before it destroyed me. 'I need to think,' I said, sitting down cross-legged, on my bed. 'I have to do something different, something that they're not expecting. A surprise strategy to deflect their assault.'

'Like in a battlefield?'

'Yes, but not in an actual battlefield; maybe in the public arena of Dilli. I could use the common people as my weapon.'

'What do you mean?

'I've taken this action for the people. And remember, it was the people of Dilli who supported me in my claim to be Baba's heir.'

'How can anyone forget that victory?'

'Maybe if I can make them see that my unveiling is part of my mission to ensure their wellbeing, they'll stand behind me again.'

'I don't know, Razi. You know that the Musalmaan fear the Ulema. They're so afraid of violating Holy Law.'

'What if I show them that what I'm doing is not against Holy Law; it's just different. A different interpretation to unite religion and governance. Actually, come to think of it, it's not that different from what Baba did. The only difference will be how I implement it. He believed in keeping a distance between the ruled and the ruler; I'll remove that distance. I think the Sultan owes it to her people to be visible to them. What if I go out and meet people? I'll let them look me in the eye and tell me their concerns. I'll let them see in my face how much I care about their lives. I'll make them realise that a woman Sultan is no different from a male Sultan; it's only the veil that creates the difference. Once they see that, they'll support me, and the Ulema won't be able to do anything.'

'So, are you saying that you'll meet the people without a veil?'

'Yes,' I said. 'Yes. No veil. I'll never wear the veil again.'

Shazia sat down across from me on my bed with her legs crossed under her, as well, and beamed at me. 'What'll you say to them?'

'The truth. For a woman, wearing the veil is mustahabb—recommended; it's not fard—obligatory. And for a sultan, the wellbeing of her people is the utmost fard. Besides, isn't modesty commanded for both women and men? If they are so bothered by my unveiled face; let them lower their eyes. And it isn't as though I'm going to uncover myself any further.'

Shazia blinked at me a number of times. I could tell that ideas were hatching in her mind.

'What if you…' she began and then shook her head. 'No, it may just make matters worse.'

'What were you going to say? Tell me.'

She got off the bed and, taking me by the hand, walked me to the adjoining room, where I dressed. A bronze plate stood on one side. She lifted it up before me and said, 'Look at your tunic.'

I looked, but I had no idea what she wanted me to see. She put the bronze plate down and came and stood directly in front of me. 'See this,' she said, moving her hands in the air over her breasts. 'This is what a woman's tunic does. It moulds to her curves. Faiz used to say that no man can remain modest if he looks at a woman's breasts. Even if he lowers his eyes, the images remain in his head. And that's what moves him to passion. I know this, because … because he … my husband wasn't a modest man.' She quickly lowered her eyes, but I had already seen the moisture in them. Rubbing it out with her fingertips, she gave a self-deprecating little laugh and said, 'Do you see what I mean?'

I looked down at my breasts. Admittedly they were much smaller than Shazia's but the clear rise of them was indisputable.

'So, what are you suggesting?'

'What if you wore a looser tunic—like a male's? It'll be less distracting.'

'You mean wear a man's clothes?'

'They're really not very different from what we women wear. Just think about it.'

I did. I also remembered the time when I was sixteen and had wanted to tie my breasts to stop being a woman. How silly I was. Thanks to Yakut, I realised soon enough that I didn't want to stop being a woman; I wanted to be equal to a man.

'I can see how that might work,' I said to Shazia. 'In fact, I think you may have just found the perfect way to help me carry out my plan. That's why you're my favourite sister,' I said, hugging her. 'You're brilliant.'

'I don't know, though, Razi. It's just a suggestion but ... Promise me that you'll think about it first, before you do anything. I'm worried that it may anger them more.'

'I promise, I'll think about it.'

'Baba would have been so proud of you,' she said softly.

'I'm not so sure about that, Shazi,' I said, feeling my own eyes become moist from an old sorrow.

I did think about it. Then I sent for Azra's daughter-in-law Jamila. She had trained under Azra and had taken over her duties some years prior to my becoming Sultan. Overnight, Jamila had new clothes made for me—a man's tunic in my favourite colour—turquoise blue, a gold brocade qaba, and a turquoise blue turban. The following morning, I was scheduled to tour the grain market, and I intended to use it as the first test of my reincarnation.

I lay awake that whole night. Over and over, I kept replaying that moment when I walked into the court, unveiled. The magnitude of what I had done took on a whole different shade at night. What had felt like the right thing to do, now trickled through my veins like frozen clots of sin. And when I tried to shut out that image, the old man's pronouncement: 'Shameless woman!' 'Shameless woman!' built to a crescendo of damnation. When the clamour in my head became too much to bear, I did what I used to do when I was child. I imagined worse scenarios. I imagined myself standing in the market square with thousands of people in a circle around me, hurling rocks at me, blood pouring down my naked face. Then I imagined my severed head hanging from the tip of a sword, thrust out from a hole in the wall of the Chor Minar—the tower from which the heads of thieves are displayed. Mine was the greatest theft of all; I had stolen the modesty of men. But the scenarios I used to imagine when I was young were all too far-fetched to be real. None of the scenarios I created in my mind that night were improbable.

The first thing I did in the morning was send an order to Yakut to accompany me to the grain market. I knew he had returned to Dilli the night before. Then I called Jamila to help me dress. When she helped me into the first item of clothing—the blue tunic—I had a moment of panic; it hung so loosely around my body, I felt like I wasn't wearing anything. Jamila must have seen my anxiety, because she waved a velvet qaba before my face and began laughing when I sighed with relief. Adjusting the folds of the qaba over my front, she tied a loose cummerbund at the waist. Then she sat me on a stool and braided my hair into two braids and then tied the turban on my head.

When I looked at myself in the polished bronze and saw a short slim man, I was pleasantly surprised. But when I looked at my face, I was horrified. How strange my face looked that morning. Stark. Raw. For fifteen years, concealed behind the veil, I hadn't bothered to curtail the narrative of emotions on my face. Now, I was afraid I wouldn't know how to control their revelations. Before I began wearing the veil, I used to wear masks to hold my face captive. But after I began wearing it, I had learned to liberate myself. And here I was, free of the veil but seeking my mask again. For a moment I almost asked Jamila to bring me the veil, but then I quickly turned away from the bronze and, without allowing myself another moment to think, adjusted the baldric on my shoulder, slipped my sword into it, and headed for the door. Hindu Saras met me outside the room. He nodded at me without any change of expression, as though he saw nothing out of the ordinary. That bolstered my courage, and raising my chin, I descended the stairs. We rode together to the Qasr-i-Safed, where my bodyguards were waiting, along with my elephant, Gul, whom I normally used for city tours. And standing to the side was Yakut. When he looked at me, I saw a slight widening of his eyes, but other than that, he didn't display any reaction. That made me realise how anxious I had been to know what he thought. His cryptic response made me feel more on edge.

Sitting in the howdah on Gul's back, as soon as I exited Chaumukha Gate and headed towards the shahr, my heart started hammering. Facing people in the citadel was one thing, but facing the people outside ... In all my adult life, I had never been to the shahr without my veil. Word spread fast. Everywhere I went in the grain market, men and women came out in throngs and stood ogling at me, aghast. I saw many old men, staring at me in, what seemed to me, pained incredulity, as though they were witnessing a sinful sight that they would have to carry to their graves. Had I missed seeing the fault line? Were people only perceiving the unconventionality of my face and not the fact that I had made myself completely accessible? Had my unfiltered royal countenance created more distance between me and my people? But then, I noticed, there were also others—both men and women, whose eyes filled with curiosity and also hope. Riding on my elephant that day, unveiled and in male clothing, I couldn't tell exactly what to make of the public reaction: were they thinking that I was defying the Ulema, and they wanted no part of my defiance? Or were they seeing my defiance as their own empowerment? I wasn't even sure how Yakut felt. Seeing him riding ahead of my entourage, all I could see was the straight, rigid line of his shoulders and the stiff alertness of his arm, as his hand gripped the hilt of his sword.

As soon as I returned to the Daulat Khana, I summoned Yakut. His reticence had been bothering me all day, more than I wanted to admit. I had never seen him like that. He was not one to hold back his thoughts, and I wondered what about my unveiling had caused such restraint. He had, in fact, seen me often without a veil; although, it was always in private, after dark, in the moonlight sometimes, and sometimes in the light of the rising sun. I was aware that this unveiling, in the full light of day, and for all to see was something else, and I was anxious to know what he thought.

As soon as he was announced, I ordered my jaandars to leave us, and, when he entered, I deliberately sat facing the door. I didn't want to give him a chance to hide his thoughts.

He stopped just inside the door, and I clearly saw the intake of breath, the flare of his nostrils. Then he lowered his eyes and bowed and stood in silence. I wanted him to say something, but he just stood, gazing at a spot near my feet. I was bursting with questions, but I didn't know how to begin. His silence was vexing. Finally, I said: 'Did you find us some good horses?'

'A few. The Sultan will be invited for an inspection, as soon as the animals are rested and fed.'

I nodded.

More silence followed. He kept looking somewhere near my feet, his hands hanging by his sides; while I watched his lowered face, the fingers of my right hand worrying Baba's lotus ring that I wore on the middle finger of my left hand. Suddenly, he looked up at me. There was something so raw in his eyes, I felt my cheeks blaze. Oh, how I longed for my veil in that moment.

'What did you think about the tour today?' The question popped out of my mouth. This was what I had desperately wanted to ask him, but that moment rendered it irrelevant.

'You are Sultan,' he said, still looking at me. 'If you see yourself as a man, then so will your people.'

I couldn't believe what he was saying. 'If they will question my judgements because I am a woman, I must show them that I am no less than a man. And if I have to wear male clothing and uncover my face, then so be it. That doesn't make me a man; it makes me a woman who is willing to do whatever it takes.'

He didn't respond to that; just bowed his head. But his disapproval was palpable. His back was so stiff, it was like he was holding a beam of castigation on his shoulders.

I stood up. Anger was building in me, and it was too vehement to bear sitting down. I wanted to scream at him: 'You're the one who taught me to be this woman.' Instead, I straightened my own shoulders and waved him away, imperiously. I had nothing more to say to him.

I was remembering that time, on my sixteenth birthday, when I had sobbed in his arms after I found out that I couldn't be Sultan, because I was a woman. He had let me cry then and had told me that the strength of a person is not in conventions but in convictions.

13

ON MY SIXTEENTH BIRTHDAY, I RECEIVED TWO GIFTS FROM MY parents—the Saif-i-Hind sword from my father for completing my military training, and a veil from my mother for becoming a woman.

Early that morning, Baba came to my room himself to bring me my present. I stood before him, trembling with excitement as he lifted the tegh from the silk cushion that one of the eunuchs was holding and placed it in my hands. 'Go ahead, Guzel. Take a look,' he urged, his eyes twinkling at me. 'Take it out of its sheath.'

Firmly gripping the silver and ivory filigreed hilt, I slowly drew out the blade from its red velvet sheath. It sparkled—long, slim, slightly curved like a lion's claw, textured like watery silk. Its beauty took my breath away. Baba placed his hand on mine on the hilt and brought the blade up so that I could read the Kufic letters emblazoned on the metal in gold: *Shehzadi Razziat-al-Din.*

'Do you know what it means?' Baba asked, and when I shook my head, he said, 'It means, *Princess Razziat of the Faith*. Congratulations for your sixteenth birthday.' Then he kissed me on the forehead. 'Till yesterday, you were Shehzadi Razziat, but from today you are also the upholder of the morality and honour of the Sultanate and the Faith.'

Tears pouring down my cheeks, I sheathed the sword and clutched it over my heart with both my hands. 'I promise, Baba, that I will always respect the Saif-i-Hind. And I will uphold the morality and honour of the Sultanate all my life.'

'I know, Razi. I know,' Baba said. There was a sheen of moisture under his eyes too. He kissed me again on the forehead and then tweaked my cheek, as he used to do when I was a little girl. 'Don't forget to also enjoy life. You have worked very hard these past three years.'

After Baba left, I dressed in the new salvar and tunic that Azra had had tailored for me. Once she had finished braiding my hair, I told her to hold up the bronze. Then I slipped the baldric over my neck and carefully slipped the sword in place. It hung perfectly—on my left side, just at my hip. A smooth grip of the hilt with my right hand, a quick flourish and I would be ready to strike with my Saif-i-Hind that had my name on it.

'Will you take a tegh to see your mother?' Azra asked, admonishingly.

'It's my present from Baba.'

'It'll still be here, waiting for you, when you return. You mother may have a present for you, as well.'

Ignoring Azra, I sheathed the sword and let it hang by my side. I would not be parted from it even for a moment.

Anneh was sitting on her bed when I entered. She gestured to me to come and sit beside her, and I did, carefully holding the sword to my side, and then setting it by me. 'It's the Saif-i-Hind,' I told her proudly. 'Baba gave it to me.'

She smiled and then stretched out a hand to Ilbari. Her maid draped a folded green and gold garment on her arm. Anneh shook out its folds and then slipped it over my head. I could feel its silken length fall from my head and pool on my thighs. Anneh arranged the fabric around my face, till my eyes were directly behind a cut-out that was covered with a fine mesh. 'You have now become a woman, Razi,' she said. 'May Allah grant you a long life of virtue and honour.'

I had been expecting this. All of the ladies in the zenana wore veils in public. I knew that it demonstrated status and nobility. That's why the common women in the shahr did not wear it. The only noble woman I knew who went out in public without a burqa was Shah Turkan. Even Shazia had started wearing one recently. I had asked her how she felt with it.

'Strange,' she replied. 'It's really quite a bother. It keeps getting in the way. But I do feel strangely protected and free.'

'Free? What do you mean?' I asked in disbelief.

'I can't explain it,' she said. 'It's like inside it's my own private space. My Anneh says that each woman feels differently about her veil.'

I wondered then how I would feel, and now that I was wearing it, I couldn't decide. I jiggled my shoulders to feel the fabric's touch. Then I felt along the lower edge where it pooled on my lap. I could feel its spread around me, but it left the sword uncovered. Pulling at its border, I tried to bring it over the length of the sword; it just wasn't wide enough. I realised that when I stood up, the fabric would fall around my feet, but the point of the sword would protrude awkwardly from the side. I would have to keep my hand on the hilt all the time to keep the sword straight against my leg. That would be so annoying. But, of course, I wouldn't wear the sword inside the burqa, or how would I pull it out? So, it would always be on the outside, separated from me. I hated the thought. And that's when I began to feel slightly suffocated. My breath hit the fabric in front of my lips and my eyelashes felt like they were getting snagged in the mesh over my eyes. Reaching up, I tried to hold it away from my face. 'You'll get used to it,' I heard my mother say. 'I wanted to give you this when you turned fourteen, but you were in training at that time. Ilbari told me to wait till you completed it. And now you have. From now on, you must always wear it when you go out, especially when you meet men. No man should see your face.'

'Why not?' I said, my voice sounding muffled and strange to my own ears.

'Because your face is very precious, silly girl.'

'But how will I talk to Nisu and Rukn and Baba with my veil on? Besides,' I said, 'they've already seen my precious face.' I knew I was being cheeky, but I wasn't altogether thrilled at the idea of having to wear this thing whenever I went out. How would I practise sword fighting? How would I ride?

'You don't have to cover yourself in front of your father or brothers; only other men,' Anneh replied.

'What about Yakut? Can he see me without it? And Saras amca? What about him?'

'It's okay if you are unveiled before your Saras amca. But not that boy, Yakut,' she said, lifting up the burqa's end and peeling it off me. 'Yakut is not related to you. In any case, you must not see that slave so often.' She began folding the fabric. 'You're not a girl any more. You've become a woman. And if you have to see him for any reason, then you must veil yourself.'

'But he's my best friend.'

'I know he's your friend,' she said, squeezing my hand. 'But now you must create some distance between him and you. The veil will make it easier.'

'Anneh, please. I don't want to wear this when I go to see Yakut. How I will practise with this thing on?' I pleaded with her. 'I'll wear it everywhere else. I promise.'

She took my chin between her two fingers and thumb and shook it. 'Let me tell you a little secret,' she said with a smile. 'When you wear a veil, you'll see that every man will treat you with extra respect and honour, because that is what a veil does. It makes men treat women differently—with the respect that they deserve.'

I wasn't sure if I liked the idea of Yakut treating me differently and distantly, but the thought of him giving me a special sort of respect was enticing. I wondered how he would show this respect.

And suddenly, I could hardly wait to appear before him in my burqa, just to see how he would react.

When my mother stopped speaking, I thought our talk was over and made to get up, but Ilbari came close to her and whispered something in her ear. Anneh smiled and nodded. 'Go ahead and tell her,' she said.

'Shehzadi,' Ilbari began, sitting down on the carpet at my feet. 'You are growing very quickly. You'll notice that men who used to see you as a child or a friend will look at you differently.'

'How will they look at me?' I knew what Ilbari was talking about, I had seen it happen with Shadab, during training. But I was curious to know what else she and Anneh had to say about it.

'They'll see you as a woman; not as a little girl any more. Some men will get distracted by the changes that are happening in your body and will react in a way you may not like. A veil will protect you from their eyes.'

'Exactly,' my mother added. Then she took my hands in her own and looked at me gravely. 'A veil is for your protection. Also, we are women, and for us the veil creates a moral boundary. It reminds us that we are women. Think of the veil as your morality.'

'But don't men have to be moral. Why don't they wear a burqa?'

'Aha!' my mother said, as though she had been waiting for just this question. 'Of course men have to be moral, but Allah has made us women special. The veil gives us an inner strength, much more than men have. Allah has made us women very special and has given us this special gift to make us strong.'

I had never thought about that. I liked the idea of inner strength. It sounded like I had muscles growing inwards. I tried to visualise it and the image made me smile.

'That means if you know something is wrong, you'll have the strength to say so and to act against it,' my mother kept talking. 'Only strong people have this fortitude, and women are made especially strong.'

I nodded and hugged her, feeling better about having to wear the burqa already. 'Thank you, Anneh,' I said.

'Do you have any questions?' she asked.

I shook my head, and then, out of curiosity, asked, 'Can I take it off when I become Sultan? How will I sit in the Sultan's throne with my veil? A Sultan can't hide her face.'

I saw Anneh and Ilbari exchange a look. A dread began to coagulate in my stomach. My mother put her arm around me and gave me a sideways hug. 'Baba loves you very much,' she said gently. 'You are his favourite child. But the heir to the Sultanate must be a male. It's a man's job. Don't be upset if Baba chooses Nasir.'

Once, when I was very young, Anneh had become terribly sick, and the hakim had thought she would die. Sitting by her bedside, Baba had taken me in his arms and cried. The sobs racking his body had passed through mine, and I had clung to him, terrified that he was going to shatter. That's how I felt when I heard Anneh's words—like I was going to shatter. I wrapped my arms around myself, tightly, and squeezed my eyes shut.

'Razi,' Anneh said, putting both her arms around me and rocking me from side to side. 'Don't be upset. Try to understand.'

'But … but … I'm Baba's eldest child,' I said opening my eyes to plead with her. 'And I'm your daughter; you're the Sultana. Your father was Sultan Ai-Beg. Baba says I am nobler in blood than even he. I was born to be Sultan.'

'And you would have been. It was *my* misfortune I had a daughter.'

I could feel my chin begin to tremble as a tight knot swelled in my throat. Biting down hard on my lower lip, I pulled myself out of my mother's arms. Don't you dare, I kept saying to myself, don't you dare be a woman.

I got up, thanked my mother quietly, and walked to the door.

'Wait,' Anneh called, and I stopped. Ilbari quickly brought me the folded veil. I stretched out my arms for it to be placed on them, like an offering on a platter, and brought it to my room. Azra lifted it from my hands with a rueful smile. She had probably known that this is what Anneh intended to give me on my birthday. 'Please tell Saras amca that I'll be going for a ride,' I said to her in a voice that was calm, as though my world had not just splintered into a thousand pieces. 'Also, tell him to send a message to Yakut to meet me in the minar in one ghadi. Oh, and Azra teyze, I will not be wearing the burqa today.'

Without a word, she took the folded green silk and, spitting something out with disgust, put the garment in the chest. Then she went to inform Hindu Saras.

Yakut was already in the balcony of the third storey when Saras amca and I arrived at the minar. I could see him from below, standing in one of the rounded flutings. It was Jumma, so there was no work at the minar. While Saras amca talked to the guards to secure the site, I quickly climbed the stairs and stepped onto the balcony. Yakut turned around and bowed.

'I heard it's your birthday. Congratulations, Shehzadi,' he said. 'Today you are especially welcome to the victory tower.'

I went to stand in the balustrade curve next to where he stood. In the Jami Masjid courtyard below, I could see a few people, although it was still early for the Jumma prayer. From up here, I couldn't quite see the hacked off breasts of the women on the sandstone pillars, but I knew they were there. How ironic it was that Musalmaan men were surrounded by them when they came to pray.

'Is something wrong, Shehzadi?' Yakut's voice broke into my thoughts.

I shook my head. Down below, two nobles had just arrived. I saw the veiled women accompanying them go in through the door of the women's apartment.

'I'm sixteen today,' I said.

'Mubarak.'

I moved from the railing towards the stairs.

'Where are you going?' he called.

'I want to climb to the top—the fourth storey.'

'No,' he said, sharply. 'It's not safe yet. The stairs are still being built. Besides, there's nowhere to go except up a few steps. Why do you want to go there?'

'I want to escape . . .' My voice had started quivering.

'What's wrong? Are you unwell?'

I shook my head and stepped down, although I didn't move away from the stairs. My chest felt heavy, and my throat was exhausted. I had been swallowing tears all day.

'Something's wrong. Tell me,' he said. Then he turned his head towards Saras amca, who had come up by now and was standing a few flutings away. 'Is the Shehzadi not well?' he asked. For the first few weeks of our companionship, Hindu Saras had attached himself to Yakut like a shadow. But, slowly, they had started to form a sort of reluctant camaraderie, and Saras amca had begun to keep his distance whenever Yakut and I met; although I had no doubt that he still watched his every move. He now rubbed his hand down his chin and then pressed his lips together.

Yakut, too, had become familiar with Hindu Saras' silent responses. 'Tell me,' he asked urgently. 'What has happened? Has someone hurt her?'

'I . . . I don't want to be a woman,' I said.

'What?' Yakut said, turning to me. 'I don't understand.'

'I'm Baba's eldest child. I'm his heir. But Anneh says that I can't be Sultan, because I'm a woman.'

He just stood there looking at me. 'I don't want to be a woman,' I said again, trying to make him understand. 'I want to be a man, like my brother Nisu. Anneh says that I must wear a veil now. She says,

I've grown up. I must hide myself in modesty. How can I be Sultan if I'm hiding myself? This,' I said, gesturing to my chest, 'this … this … I don't want to be a woman … like her … like Husni Begum. I don't want to distract men like she does. I want to sit on the throne of the Sultanate. I don't care about this. I don't want it.' Then, with fumbling fingers, I opened the folds of my qaba and lifted up one corner of the tunic and showed him the white muslin with which I had bound my breasts. I had had to send Azra on some errand to do it myself.

'Wha … are you hurt?' Yakut sounded confused.

I shook my head. 'I … I've tied it over my—you know … No one can say I'm a woman now,' I said, dropping my tunic and smoothing my hands over my flat chest.

It finally dawned on him and he gasped. His eyes darted from me to Hindu Saras, who just rubbed his chin and looked away.

'No, no. You can't,' Yakut said coming closer to me. 'You shouldn't.'

'Don't you see? With this I don't need a burqa to hide my modesty. No one will know.'

He looked at me and then away. His hands were acting very strangely, opening and closing, as though he was trying to grasp an answer from the air. Finally, he said, 'Allah will know. He has made you a woman. It's a gift from him. You must honour it.'

'Allah has made me a woman so that I will not sit on the throne. How can I honour that?'

'It's not Allah who has made that law. It's men.'

'Well then I hate men,' I said. And then the tears came, accompanied by loud sobs. They came and came. I couldn't stop them. He held me in his arms and let me shatter.

14

BUT I COULDN'T HATE NASIR. HOW CAN YOU HATE A BROTHER WHO gilds cowries with your name in gold—Razziat-al Din, and then lets you win every game of chausar, because it's your right; your name is on all the pieces? How can you hate a brother who stitches a leather binding with his own calloused fingers to keep your favourite book from falling apart? How can you hate a brother, who before taking any gifts from Baba wants to know if Razi got one, too? How can you hate a brother who on finding out that Baba intended to make him his heir, looks at you with eyes so penitent, it's as though he's begging forgiveness for all the sins of mankind.

No. You can't hate a brother like that. You can only wish upon him a Sultanate.

Nisu was beautiful. He looked like Baba—not in the way that I, sort of, look like Baba, but in a more precise way; the same arch of the eyebrows, the same angular ridge of cheekbones, the same sharp line from ear to jowl. It was as though Allah had taken exact measurements of Baba's face to create Nisu's. Even the depth of the vertical groove between his nose and upper lip was the same as Baba's, as if the pressure of Allah's finger there, where it touched the infant face in the womb to erase divine memories, had been precisely measured. The only difference between their faces was that while Baba's dark beard, touched with streaks of silver, was abundant, Nasir's meagre growth made him look like he was playing at being Baba.

He loved to copy verses from the Quran in Muhaqqaq, the most ornate of scripts, and he loved whittling wood. After completing military training, when he took up residence in the Green Palace, every available nook in his rooms became a miniature forest, teeming with lions, elephants, horses, monkeys and birds of all kind—tiny creatures that he had created in the precious leisure hours during training, his hands calloused and lacerated from wielding both weapons and the whittling knife. He used to have beautiful fingers, like a woman's, slender and tapering at the tips. I used to always tease him about that. I think that's why he stopped taking care of his callouses, letting them grow and harden so that they would redefine his hands.

A year after he completed his training, Baba sent him to take over the governorship of Lahore. I missed him terribly. Thankfully, I had Yakut and Altunia, but it wasn't the same. There is a different comfort with a brother. When Nisu was in Lahore, he would write to me—missives dispatched with reports he sent to Baba, written exquisitely in Naskh, the rounded characters faultlessly calligraphed, describing the city, the court and the people. He would also tell me how he was getting better at chaugan, which was my favourite sport, and that he would surely defeat me when he returned. That would make me smile and I would write back, telling him how that would be quite a feat, because I was already winning against, Altunia, who everyone knew was the champion chaugan player.

In one letter, Nisu invited me to visit him in Lahore. I was so excited. I even managed to persuade Baba to let me go. But before I could make any real plans, Baba sent Nisu to Awadh. He had received reports that the Hindu ruler there had massacred twenty thousand Musalmaan. Nasir was to destroy the infidels, to flush them out from whatever holes they had hidden in and not spare anyone. All were to be put to the sword, and their heads were to hang in every market square to make a show of it. But, by the end of it, there were so many put to the sword, their heads didn't all fit in the market square, so Nisu had them strung on ropes and hung in the streets of Awadh, festooned like flags in a festival—decapitated heads of infidel men, women and children, even infants newly born. Baba was proud of Nisu. He sent him orders to head to Lakhnauti, where Ghiyas-ud-Din Iwaz had suddenly rebelled. But Nisu was to first make a stop in Dilli for a few days. He was to be honoured by the Sultanate with a robe and the title of Malik-ul-Sharq—King of the East.

It was the month of Safar by the time Nisu got to Dilli, the month of whistling winds. The city was experiencing its first days of chill. Gardens were bare and the stone walls of the palaces were cold, but the tawakhana, the underground furnaces, that Baba had installed below the Blue and Green palaces to warm the rooms, hadn't yet been fired up. Every afternoon, the rooftops of the palaces became a patchwork of furs that the slave women put out to air. The black marble fountains in the garden no longer mushroomed with water, and no one sat in the baolis of the Blue Palace any more. That's where Nisu and I used to spend a lot of our time when he still lived in Dilli.

I saw him at the ceremony in the White Palace. He raised his eyebrows and gave me a half smile, as if to show me how nonchalant he felt about it all, but under the gilded robe of the King of the East, I thought I saw a tremor in his shoulders. He's nervous, I thought. I know how nerve-wracking it is to sit and face the entire body of the Sultanate's Dilli officials. After the ceremony, for the next two days, he was inundated by high-ranking callers and members of Baba's bandagan-i-khas, all congratulating him and swearing allegiance to him, and also by members of the Ulema, who wanted to kiss the hand that had dealt with the infidels in Allah's way.

On his fourth day in Dilli, I sent him a message:

> Meet me this evening at Hauz-e-Shamsi. How fortunate I will feel to see my favourite brother on this holy night of the new

> moon in such a sanctuary that the Prophet himself has graced. Come, sweet Nisu, and let me show you where the Prophet's own Al-Buraq has marked our dear Dilli to make it Dar-ul-Islam forever. Say you will come.

He wrote back:

> I will ride there after I attend the Maghrib prayer at Jami Masjid. I hear the reservoir is no more than a kos from there. Who knew that peace was only a kos away; my tortured soul has been searching for it everywhere.

He's become such a poet, I thought with a smile, looking at the beautifully rounded Naskh letters, reminded of the calligraphy homework I used to force him to do for me, while I practised writing my name in Tughra, the official script I would have to use to sign my name when I became Sultan. But when I read again the lines Nisu had written in his response, I noticed that the curve of the letters was a little shaky, and the mim in 'majruh'—tortured—was not quite legible. The Nasir I knew had a faultless pen. I wondered what had changed that. He must be out of practice, I thought, or, perhaps, just tired from all the battles and now the ceremonies. Whatever it was, Hauz-e-Shamsi would soothe him. It's just that kind of a place. Baba had it constructed after he had a dream in which the Prophet told him to build a water tank for thirsty travellers. 'Where?' Baba asked the Prophet. 'You will see,' the Prophet said, pointing east. The very next morning, accompanied by Qutb Saheb and a team of his maliks and jaandars, Baba started walking east from the Jami Masjid, searching every finger's width of land for a sign. About a kos away, they discovered it on a flat rock at the edge of the forest; it was a gentle semi-circular imprint of Al-Buraq's hoof, as though the Prophet's mount had rested there for just a moment, before ascending, taking the Prophet on his night journey to the seven heavens. The rock had faithfully recorded Al-Buraq's hoof print to strengthen the faith of believers. From the centre of the mark, a tiny rivulet was trickling out. And that's where Baba laid the foundation of the water tank.

After I received Nisu's response, I quickly called Saras amca to let him know I would ride to Hauz-e-Shamsi at sunset. 'Tell Yakut and also prepare Buraq,' I told him. Buraq was my new horse. Guzel was getting old, and although I still loved riding her, she tired easily. Besides, I wanted Nasir to see Buraq, an Arabian, fanaa black—the colour of the ego's annihilation—that Baba had gifted me when the reservoir was inaugurated. I named him Buraq; what other name could I have given him?

Nasir was already there when I arrived, standing, surrounded by his jaandars, in one of the four domed gazebos built in the four corners of the tank, his tall frame in a qaba of white makhmal, embroidered with silver, looking like a streak of moonlight in the sandstone setting sun. The moment I rode up and dismounted, he stepped down from the gazebo, but then remained where he was. I walked quickly to him and took him by his forearms, trying to peer at him through the veil. I hoped to look deep into his eyes, but his eyes were elusive; or perhaps, it was the fault of the netting over my own eyes.

'Nisu,' I said. 'It's good to see you again. How have you been?'

He nodded his head and then pulled his arms away. 'So,' he said looking around. 'This is all Baba's dream. He must've have wept when he found the imprint.'

'He did, but it was Qutb Saheb who actually spotted the mark. I wish you had been here. Three dozen men went searching for it, all barefoot. Baba made them all take off their shoes. You should have heard the jokes the women in the zenana made about the pained expressions on the faces of the men. When they return from battle, they're smiling, even though their bodies are sieving blood, and they couldn't bear to walk ten steps without shoes, the women said. I came later to see it, after they had found the hoofprint. Many of the ladies also came. It was quite a show, palanquin after palanquin. And the people of the shahr came in hordes, all waiting their turn to see the mark. Do you want to see it?'

'Sure,' he said. 'Might as well.'

His lack of interest surprised me, but, disregarding it, I began eagerly walking to the pavilion near the front of the tank. He walked beside me, and we crossed the small footbridge together. There, I showed him the mark, encased in a small marble arabesque square. He went down on his knees before it and closed his eyes. Then he touched his forehead to the marble and stayed like that for a long time. When he got up, I noticed the sheen of moisture under his eyes. 'Let's go to the tower,' he said distractedly and began walking with long strides towards the marbled mosque with a two-story muezzin tower. I followed behind, as quickly as I could.

'Look,' I said, after we had climbed the tower and were standing in the second storey balcony. 'See for yourself.' There it was—one full kos of the clearest water, contained in a rectangular tank, lined with buffed sandstone, and four corner gazebos topped by arched domes inlaid with white marble. A couple of boats, painted blue and green, were bobbing at the bank. Across from us stood Qasr-e-Shamsi, a miniature palace of sandstone, its outer wall carved with repeated interlacing of squares and circles, and in its courtyard, a fluted white marble fountain.

'You should see all this on a spring night,' I said. 'Lamps everywhere and the water in the fountain sprouting thousands of silvery sprinkles. And see those bushes all around? They're rows of kachnar and latak chandini that bloom bright white and pink; their fragrance is something else. Azra puts them in my bath and also makes garlands and hangs them from my bed posts.'

'I won't be here in the spring,' he said, his voice flat. Something was definitely not right; I was talking too much, because I was excited to see him, but he wasn't talking at all. This was hardly the Nasir I knew. That Nisu used to be excited about everything. So eager to try anything new. This one seemed disinterested and distant—even from himself.

'Nisu,' I said, impulsively placing a hand on his arm 'Why can't you stay in Dilli for a while longer? You seem really tired. Tell Baba that you can't go to Lakhnauti. Tell him to send Rukn. He needs to do some real work. He's been living in Gujarat like a Sultan.'

'Show me the boats,' he said, ignoring my words. 'Take me for a ride.'

We came down from the tower and, walking to the bank, I asked him the colour of the boat he would prefer, even though I knew he would pick blue. His favourite colour was green, but, whenever I was with him, he always picked blue.

'It doesn't matter,' he said, his voice impatient.

This time, I couldn't ignore the worry that squeezed my heart. I called for the green boat, and, as soon as we were seated and being rowed across the water, I asked him, 'What's wrong, Nisu? Talk to me. Did Baba say anything to you?'

He shook his head.

'But something happened, didn't it? Was it after you came here to Dilli? Or did something happen in Awadh?'

He kept looking unblinkingly at the gentle ripples near the bow of the boat. The sun was almost gone now; only a faint sanguinity remained in the water, like a washed-out blood stain.

'I can tell that you're distressed about something, and I'm so worried about you. I'm your sister. Why can't you tell me?'

'There's nothing to tell,' he said. 'It's just that I … it was … I don't know. I can't … I can't seem to forget it.'

'What? What can't you forget?'

He shook his head, as though trying to rid himself of whatever it was that was troubling his mind. Then he turned towards me with a wan smile, the first of the evening.

'It's nothing, Razi. Let's not talk about it. I'll be fine.'

'That means you're not fine now.' I took his hand in mine. He snatched it back. 'It's nothing,' he said, suddenly testy. 'Stop asking so many questions.' We sat in a tense silence for a while. Finally, he said, 'Can we go back now? It's getting really cold.'

Concern for him weighing heavy in my heart, I instructed the boatman to turn around.

As we drew close to the bank, I asked him, 'When do you have to leave for Lakhnauti?'

'Tomorrow.'

'Will you come back to Dilli? I mean, will you stay there, or will you come back home? Or does Baba want you to go back to Awadh?'

'I don't know. We'll see.'

'I hope you come back to Dilli, Nisu. I miss you. Besides, you're Baba's heir. You should be in Dilli, not campaigning all over the Sultanate.'

He gave me a sort of twisted smile—a contortion of lips really, and then turned his face away.

We were silent for the rest of the way. As soon as we disembarked, Nasir ordered the horses.

While we were waiting, a baby started crying somewhere in the distance—perhaps someone passing by. Suddenly, Nasir grabbed my arm, his fingers tightening in a death grip. 'What's wrong?' I asked him, but he wasn't listening to me. In fact, I think he wasn't even with me. His head was turned up and his eyes were scouring something up there, as though from one end to the other. I looked up to see what he was seeing. There was nothing there, except an empty expanse of half-light and darkening sky. 'Nisu, what's wrong?' I asked again, trying to pull my arm away. He let go of me and grabbed the hilt of his sword. Hindu Saras suddenly appeared from nowhere. I raised a hand to stop him. Nasir's gaze was on me now, but he wasn't really seeing me. His eyes were far away, and there was a terrified look on his face, as though he had stepped into hell. It was frightening. I was frightened. 'Nisu,' I called, grabbing his arm and shaking it vigorously. He suddenly sucked in air as though he had been underwater and had lost his breath. Then his whole body started shaking, and staggering, he almost fell against me. 'Yakut!' I yelled, hearing the terror in my own voice. He was there instantly, along with Sanjar, Nisu's companion, and they were both helping my brother.

Whatever it was that had invaded Nisu, left him as quickly as it had attacked him, and soon he was stable—stable enough to ride back to the citadel. He left for Lakhnauti the following morning.

In a few months, we received reports from Lakhnauti that there had been a pitched battle in which Ghiyas-ud-Din Iwaz had been soundly defeated. His severed head was paraded in Lakhnauti, and the people of the city were pleased to welcome Nasir-ud-Din, the Sultanate's representative. Along with the report came all kinds of valuables from Iwaz's treasury and also women, horses and elephants. Baba kept some of the animals and one concubine, and distributed the other women and jewels among his nobles.

While Dilli was still celebrating this victory, Baba himself received a very special honour, one that he had awaited ever since he became Sultan: the Khalifa's ambassador arrived from Baghdad to declare him the Khalifat's commander in Dilli and to confer upon him robes and titles: Yamin Khalifat Allah—Right Hand of the God's Deputy—and Nasir Amir al-Mu'minin—Auxiliary of the Commander of the

Faithful. Baba received the ambassador with great pomp and extended the celebrations for over a month. To mark the occasion, he even issued a new silver tanka, a coin with the Khalifa's name on it. Then he dispatched one of the robes and a red canopy to Nasir to officially declare him his heir to the Sultanate of Al-Hind. And so it was that even as Dilli celebrated Nasir's victory over Ghiyas-ud-Din Iwaz, it began to celebrate Baba's triumph. But then, it began to mourn.

Nasir died. Perhaps, he only lived long enough to receive the canopy, or perhaps he died from receiving it. Or perhaps, he was already dying when he came to Dilli that last time. The brief missive that came from Sanjar in Lakhnauti only stated his immediate cause of death:

> Shehzada Nasir fell ill from a fever of the brain that caused fits of delirium. The hakims administered medicine, but the Shehzada's condition worsened. He had a brief period of relief, but when the fever returned, it was fiercer, and, in a fit of madness, the Shehzada drove a katara through his heart. He passed into the care of Allah on Rabi' I 22, 626 H.— Inna lillahi wa inna ilayhi raji'un. Indeed, to God we belong and to God we shall return. May the Sultan of Al-Hind and his family find solace in the name of Allah.

Included in the dispatch were verses Nasir had written in his last days of lucidity:

> When death hangs festooned
> Behold, eyes! Behold, memory!
>
> Icy shadows tear at my flesh
> Dozakh, what fear I your fires.

Sleep has become red-hot rods
Eyes, when will you go blind?

And this, perhaps, the last, the most lucid of all.

Make no tomb, nor edifice for this, my body
It deserves only a pit, roughhewn and rocky.

15

AH NASIR ...

His death broke Baba and left something leaden in me.

Baba wept for months. It was only after Nisu's body was brought home, preserved with vinegar and aqua vita mixed with salt, myrrh, and wormwood oil and finally buried, that Baba's tears stopped. But, by that time, the few strands of precious silver that streaked his hair had become as prolific as base metal.

And I, weighed down by the guilt of somehow having willed Nasir's death, couldn't even sink into the pure sorrow of grief.

But, for both Baba and I, building a tomb for Nisu, exactly as he wanted it, was healing. About ten kos east of the citadel, Baba found a hillock and had that dug out like a cave—a pit roughhewn and rocky—and in that we laid Nisu's body to rest. Then, a year later, when the grief of his passing began to settle into the hum of our lives, Baba had an octagonal plinth and dome of chiselled rough stone from a quarry in Dilli constructed over the grave. To protect it, he also had a small fort built around it, whose arched gate of marble was decorated with verses from the Quran in Kufic characters. And, in Muhaqqaq, the script that Nisu loved, were also words honouring him as the king that he was: 'King of kings of the East. May God forgive him with his indulgence and make him dwell in the centre of paradise in peace.'

Standing in the vertex of one of the balustrade's flutings on the fourth storey of the completed minar, facing Dilli, I opened my arms wide and leaned over to embrace the city I've loved since Baba brought us here when I was six.

'Move back, Shehzadi,' Yakut said urgently, reaching out a hand but not touching me.

'Sometimes when I stand here, I feel like my arms have become stone, like the walls of the qila, encircling the farthest limits. There,' I said to him, pointing in the direction of Nisu's fort, which had come to be known as Sultan Garhi—the fort of the Sultan. 'Have you seen the arched gate? The marble of it is luminescent. I hope that one day when I look at it, it'll bring me peace. Right now, its new-marble shine hurts my eyes.'

Sorrows never pass; do they? They congeal in your blood like tiny shrapnel, sometimes pricking the heart, sometimes the eyes, and sometimes the very breath you take. Unlike joys. You experience a joy, and then it's over; even in memory, it doesn't evoke the same emotion. Sorrow bursts alive every time you remember. And there is so much to remember about Nisu.

'You know,' I said to Yakut. 'When we moved from Badaun to Dilli, Nisu cried every day that the caravan was on the road. When I asked him if he missed his friends in Badaun, he said, "No. I'm crying because I left my favourite kite behind." He never forgot that kite. Even when he got so many other kites in Dilli, it was the one he left in Badaun that he always remembered. That's how I feel. I'll never be able to leave him behind. No matter what happens; it's him I will remember.'

'I know what you mean,' Yakut said. 'What you leave behind is what you always carry.'

I looked at him, surprised. This was the first time he had actually said anything connected to his past, his childhood. 'You left behind a lot in Aksum, didn't you?'

He was quiet for a while, as though he was taking inventory of all that he had to forsake.

'Will you tell me about it? Please. Today, I need to know.'

He sat down in the circular fluting next to mine and leaned back, his head rising above the line of balustrade, the silhouette simply a curvature of the same fluidity.

'I don't have many memories of Aksum,' he began. 'And what I have is also fading away. You know, like painted pictures on a wall.'

'What was it like, your Aksum?'

'It's a land between the River Nile and Qeyyih bahri, what people call the Red Sea. When I was little, our father used to tell us stories about Aksum's golden age when King Anubis ruled. Back when the Prophet was not even born. Lots of farms, but it also has trading ports, some of the best on the trading routes, like Adoulis. Then Islam came into the land and took over the Qeyyih bahri and the Nile, and Aksum became somewhat isolated from trade links. The people of Aksum moved deeper inland, almost into the Adwa Mountains. And then came Gudit. She was a Jewish Queen and a bandit. She and her band of robbers attacked and burned all the churches and spread terror. The people of Aksum retreated even further into the mountains. And that's where they settled—at the foot of Adwa, between the Nile and Qeyyih bahri.

'Do you miss it?'

He thought about this for a moment and then said, 'I think I do. But I don't know what I miss; maybe our camels, maybe my mother's presence. But the day I was abducted, I remember that day clearly. I was with my older brother, Theo. But that wasn't his full name. He had another name; I can't remember it. My mother called him only that though—Theo. I can still hear her calling him as we played on the banks of Lake Tsana. "Theoooo!" She used to round the end syllable and stretch it—you know like a pebble bouncing and skipping over still waters; maybe all the way across to where the lake joins the Blue Nile. She never calls me in my memories, but sometimes in my dreams, I hear my lost name—Fikreyesus—a hollow echo, like something inhuman is trapped in a deep, dark tunnel. I wake up from these dreams with my chest pricking; it's like a memory is trying to pierce itself out.'

'Tell me about Theo.'

'There's not much to tell. I don't remember too many things about him. He was a couple of years older than me. Sickly. I remember he used to cough a lot. I was stronger; bigger than him. The day I was taken, Theo and I were unloading sacks of dried frankincense resin. We used to harvest it from an island in the lake. Suddenly, Theo fell in the shallow water at the bank, face down. It was so strange. There we were, chattering away. I was lifting the sacks out of the tankwa, our papyrus reed boat, while Theo tethered the boat, and then suddenly there he was—face in the water. The boat started to drift away. I didn't care about Theo. I was more concerned about the boat. "Don't lose the tankwa … Secure it before all else. Don't you dare come home if you've lost the tankwa…" That's what our father had ingrained in us. If we damaged the boat in anyway, he'd beat us. So, you see, of course I wasn't worried about Theo, I needed to catch the boat before it reached deeper waters. But, as I waded into the water to get it, a fishing net fell on me and I was hauled out.'

'Do you know who it was?'

'Probably slave traders from Arab; there were three of them. All I remember is them looming over me. I was probably wriggling and writhing like a fish-net full of stone loaches, because they kept holding me down. Once they had me under control, they pulled off the fishing net and tied my hands behind my back. Then they stuffed a filthy rag in my mouth. Vile; smelt like dead fish. The next thing I remember is waking up in the hull of a cargo ship, shackled to the floor, nose to nose with another boy. Actually, there were three other boys there, about my age, all from a tribe called Sandawe. That's all

I really learned about them. Couldn't understand a word of what they were saying. They sounded like click beetles. Have you ever seen those?'

I nodded. 'They click when they jump to straighten themselves. Isn't it?'

'Yeah. Except the hold of that ship was so full of sacks of frankincense tears, there was no room for any of us to jump high enough to right ourselves. We just lay there, nose to nose, till the sweet, slow fragrance of frankincense began to sicken us. Back home, we used to burn frankincense in our church, but very sparingly. It's an expensive incense.'

'Church? You were a Nazrene?'

'My parents were. I guess, I was too.'

'So, where did they sell you?'

'In Yanbu al-Bahr, the Spring by the Sea. It's one of the wealthiest ports in Arab. I'd heard about it from my father. He used to call it a fairytale land. It looked like it. When we docked there, and they hauled us out, I thought that we had sailed into heaven. All golden sands and palms trees. Mountain peaks in the distance, peeping out from the mist. They tied up our hands with one rope, from one boy to the other, and marched us, single file, to the centre of town into a market that was set up in a circle of stalls. I was so fascinated by everything that was being sold there, I forgot that I was part of the merchandise. I still remember the displays: bright blue lapis, stained glass beams, silk draperies, jars of frankincense and myrrh and also rose and sandalwood and musk. And there were barrows and barrows of huge saddle-red groupers. I've never seen so much fish.'

He stopped talking. I waited for him to continue, but his gaze was caught in the distant past. 'Who bought you?' I prompted.

When he looked at me, his face seemed more relaxed and there was even a slight smile on his lips. I felt grateful that at least this part of his memory was a happy one.

'Babak,' he said. 'A merchant from Baghdad. He saw me standing on the stone platform, probably gleaming and glittering from the coconut oil they had rubbed on me, and paid fifteen dinars.'

'What was he like? Was he good to you?'

'He fed me well and beat me only occasionally, but he was a pious Musalmaan and he couldn't abide by my Nazarene beliefs, so he named me Jamal-ud-din, and I became a Musalmaan.'

'Was that hard? I mean, to give up your belief ... ?'

Yakut shook his head. 'I was eight. All I understood was that instead of kneeling before Our Father, I had to kneel before someone called Allah. In my mind I still recited the Lord's prayer, but with a little difference: Instead of saying, Our Father, who art in heaven, I began to say, Our Allah, who art in heaven, haloed be thy name, thy kingdom come, thy will be done on earth, as it is in heaven.... I knew these words I recited in Ge'ez were probably not what I heard Babak murmuring, but I reasoned in my mind, how different could Allah be from Our Father? Fathers are fathers, Musalmaan or Nazrene.'

The simple logic of this eight-year-old was so reminiscent of the boy I had met in Guzel's stable, I felt like I knew him back then, in Baghdad. 'You mustn't have stayed very long with Babak, because when I met you, you were only a few years older.'

'That's right. Babak was a brisk trader. Everything was come and go; whatever helped him turn a quick profit: frankincense and myrrh from Aksum, paper from China, gold and glass from the Byzantine, ivory and spices from Al-Hind. But he didn't buy me to sell me. I worked in his stables and took care of his three camels and two horses. In Aksum, my father had two camels. I still remember their names—Jember and Zema. Sometimes at night, I can still feel their coarse warmth against my cheek. Jember, means "sunset" in my language. He had a gold sheen—like the colour of sky where it meets the waters of Tsana at sunset. And Zema—my father purchased her when I was about four. Her grunts were so drawn out, starting low and rising to a pitch, it was like she was singing, so my mother named her Zema, which means "melody" in my language.

'But in Babak's stable I learned very quickly the difference between camels and horses. He had a cook and general helper, an indentured slave called Yazid. He used to work in the stable in between cooking meals. He was really good at cooking. I loved his barads—they're fired dough drops dipped in honey and rosewater. Just delicious. He always passed me a couple more than my share. But I think he knew about horses and camels even more. He's the reason I got to like Babak's house. Everyone used to call him Yazidi because of the way he looked; he was sort of round-bodied and mostly bald, except for these tufts of grey hair over each ear. He would wear this skull cap that covered just the bald pate, and with the hair sticking out on either side, he looked like a fat bird with tiny wings. I learned a lot about horses and camels from him. A camel is like a woman, he used to tell me. Affectionate, emotional, curious; but it's lazy and unpredictable. It's also mean-spirited when it's hurt. A horse—even a mare—is more like a male, out to prove himself. It's smart and responds to commands quickly. It's also loyal to a fault, unless abused.

'"But, in a precarious situation, watch the horse and trust the camel," Yazidi advised me. "The horse will panic; the camel will think."'

'So that's how you know so much about horses. You knew exactly what I needed to do with Guzel,' I said to him.

He smiled. 'If I'd stayed with Babak longer, I would have learned more.'

'Babak is the one who took you to Al-Mansoura, is it not? I remember you telling me and Altunia about Al-Mansoura.'

'Yes. It was him. He used to do most of his trading in Al-Mansoura, and I used to go with him; you know, to take care of the camels and horses in the caravan. Then, one year he decided to branch out into the new business of artificial pearls. Do you know what those are? Have you ever seen them?'

'No. But I've heard about them. I've also heard the story about how one day a man from Al-Chin opened up a mussel with a spatula and placed a tiny wooden idol of their prophet inside it, just to see what would happen. And when he opened the mussel months later, the idol was covered with nacre, like a pearl. Isn't that how the Chin-e merchants began making artificial pearls, using their prophet's idol, a spatula and mussels? Is this story true?'

Yakut laughed. 'I don't know if that's true or not. I only know that the business of fake pearls has made Chin-e-men very rich. Everywhere—Byzantine, Arab, Misr—women are crazy about these pearls; they can make any woman look like a queen. In Al-Mansoura, I used to see women decked out in them. They wore them everywhere—around their neck, wrists and even embroidered into the hems and necklines of their tunics. I've also seen pearls on shoes. Babek had heard about how much these fake pearls could sell for, and he was determined to get into the business and make a fortune for himself. He wanted to buy them in Al-Mansoura and bring them to Yanbo and sell them at a profit. But, as it happened, when he got to the grand market of Al-Mansoura, he realised that he had underestimated the price. That year the Chin-e-men was charging 400 silver tankas for a bag of forty pearls. This was much more than Babek had planned for. So, he sold me. He figured he would make more profit from the pearls. A merchant from Al-Hind bought me for one hundred tankas. His name was Osman. Two days later, I carried his luggage to a ship docked at Domyat and we sailed to Al-Hind and arrived at Barugaza port, and from there we made our way to the grand city of Badaun, where the Sultan, your father, was governor.'

'Go on. How did Baba acquire you?'

'I think I've told you this story before,' he said, still smiling.

'Tell me again,' I said.

'It was during Eid al-Fitr. Wali Iltutmish was returning home from the Eidgah in a large procession. It filled the streets, from corner to corner. No place to even walk. Osman had come to see the procession and he had taken me along. I was standing to one side, holding Osman's horse. Suddenly, there was a commotion; someone's horse had bolted. People began shouting and screaming. There was so much chaos, I can almost still hear it.'

'You know, I remember that procession, or maybe I'm just remembering Eid processions in general. Baba used to take all his children on these processions. We would all dress up in our best clothes and ride on the elephant. But I don't have any memory of a horse bolting. I wish did, though. I would have liked to know you back then—hero-like,' I gave him a toothy smile. 'I am willing to bet you caught the horse.'

'Of course,' he said, flashing a smile back. 'When I saw the bolting horse, the horse that I was holding became the magical horse of Shehzada Feroz—you know, from Alf Layla. Yazid used to tell me these stories. I jumped on the back of my magical horse and went flying after the runaway, and I caught up with him. Then I swung from my own horse onto the runaway's back and had him under control in no time.'

'Were you rewarded?'

'Yes,' he said with a laugh. 'I got whipped—forty lashes.'

'What?' Without realising it, I put a hand on his arm. He had never mentioned this before. 'I'm so sorry.'

'It's alright. I deserved it.'

'No, you didn't. You probably saved lives that day.'

'I also left Osman's horse wandering around when I jumped onto the runaway. Osman was not happy.'

'Was it bad; the whipping?'

'Probably,' he said, looking away from me, and, after a long pause, added, 'I don't really remember. It's a strange thing, getting whipped. I think the fear of the whipping is worse than the strike itself.'

It was obvious to me that, for some reason, he remembered that whipping all too well. I wanted to ask more but didn't quite know how. Finally, I just said, 'I've never been whipped. Not even in military training.'

'That's because you are perfect in every way, Shehzadi.'

'No,' I swatted his arm, attempting playfulness. 'I was spared by someone's dark designs. It's a long story. I'll tell you another time. For now, tell me more about your whipping.'

'What's to tell? I mean, a whipping is a whipping. Most caravan campsites are set up with whipping posts where slaves get whipped every day. There's actually a trick to bearing the pain: take the first few strikes full on, like a man. Let the leather strap brand you with fire. And then let the initial pain fill your mind. Every strike after that is simply absorbed by the pain. And then, there's no new pain. Do you remember I taught you this trick when you stepped on a nail in the minar?'

I nodded. '"Breathe," you told me. Since then, I've never taken my breaths for granted. How did you learn to do that?'

Yakut didn't answer my question. Instead, he said, 'New slaves think if they pass out, they won't have to bear the pain. An experienced whipper knows when the slave has passed out, and he'll stop till the slave regains consciousness, and then the whipping will continue, and the fool will have to bear the pain all over again. The best thing is to just get it over with.'

'It was bad, wasn't it, the whipping Osman gave you?'

'It was a long time ago,' he said, turning his face to look into the distance again.

I got up and slid beside him in the circular fluting. There was barely room for the two of us. He squeezed his big body together to make space for mine. 'What are you doing, Shehzadi?' he asked, his voice strained.

'Nothing. I just want to sit with you. And, maybe, see the scars from Osman's whipping. It marked you, didn't it? Will you show me the scars?'

I thought he would deny my request, but he only said, 'It's dark. You won't be able to see them.'

'There's moonlight,' I said. 'I can see.'

He sat still for a moment and then quietly got up, removed his qaba, and raised his tunic. The moonlight glided on his back.

In the Sultanate's treasury is a sword called Mauj-i-Darya—waves of a river; it's the crown of all swords. It's made from steel eggs imported from the Deccan and then smelted in a crucible for weeks. After the crucible is broken, the blade is quenched horizontally in a mixture of glass and oil, and then it's heated and quenched again, this time, vertically, with its tip down and soaked all the way. When the blade is finally allowed to dry, it has ripples on it, like wind-tossed waves. That was what Yakut's back looked like—waves of a river. I've seen the Mauj-i-Darya only once. Baba showed it to me. It's so valuable, it could be worth half of all of the Sultanate's jewels.

Getting up, I stepped closer to Yakut, and then ran my fingertips on the ripples on his back. His skin quivered, as though a breeze were passing through it.

'Are all these from that lashing alone?' I asked in a hushed voice.

'Probably,' he said, his voice uneven. 'Osman's man was vicious. He tore skin with each lash. If he had just thrown a bucket of brine water on my back, I would have healed quickly. The sting of brine is worse than the whip, but the salt stops the infection.'

'Were you whipped in the tabaqa during training?'

'Of course. Every trainee gets whipped; it's part of the discipline. But you know that whipping is different. There are rules; the leather can't break skin. Your father is very strict about this.'

'How did you heal from Osman's whipping?'

'I was lucky. It was actually under your father's care. He purchased me on the same day and sent me to his hakims. The Sultan is a kind man.'

I felt gratified hearing him say that.

'How did Baba finally acquire you?' I asked, laying my cheek on his back.

He took one deep breath, and when he released it, his whole body shook.

'I don't remember that clearly. I was probably only half conscious. But I had a dear friend in Badaun: Saif-al-din. The Sultan had purchased him from an armourer that very day. He was in court to witness my entry into the Mamluk world. Saif told me I was brought into court by my master. The Wali had seen me chase the runaway and had commanded Osman to present himself and me. When the Wali asked him how much he wanted for me, he said he didn't want to part with me. He said I was very good with horses, and that he needed me in his stables. Your father said to him, "He'll now work in my stables." Then he asked Osman again to name his price. "He's invaluable." Osman replied.

'Your father removed a gold ring and threw it to him. Along with that Osman took a bag of one hundred silver tankas. After Osman left, your father asked me my name. Apparently, I mumbled, "Fikreyesus." But he couldn't hear me, and when he asked my name a second time, I said it was Jamal-ud-din.

'"A good Musalmaan name," he said. "And now you will be Jamal-ud-din Yakut—the sapphire. Because you are precious to me like a sapphire."'

'Yakut,' I said softly, my cheek still resting on his back.

He moved, so that I wasn't touching him anymore, and rolled down his tunic. Then, turning around, he pulled out the black string that he always wore around his neck. A bright blue sapphire and a small wooden cross were strung on it.

'Who gave you this?' I asked, touching the cross. The wood was warm from his body.

'My mother.'

Sometime later, Hindu Saras came to tell us that it was time to go. As Yakut guided me towards the stairs with his hand on my arm, I felt a tremor in his fingers.

'Are you okay?' I asked.

He nodded. 'Just …annihilated.'

16

'THAT'S EXACTLY WHAT I'M SAYING, RAZI. EVEN A SMALL WOUND CAN kill you, if it isn't treated properly.'

I come awake. 'What? What did you say?'

'I said, I need to know where all your wounds are, even the smallest one. Can you please show me?'

I am fully awake now. For a moment I was somewhere else, but now I'm aware that I'm lying in the dungeon of Tabarhind and talking to me is Altunia. I vaguely remember him coming in and shaking me awake, holding a torch near my face. I also remember that he asked me something, and I responded, but I can't remember what it was that we talked about. Behind my eyes are memories of that night on the minar when Yakut let me see his scars. Was I talking in my sleep? Did Altunia hear me talk about Yakut in that state? I try to raise myself, but I can hardly even manage to look up. Sinking back into the floor, I close my eyes. My body is on fire, and my right leg feels like it's going to explode.

'Don't go back to sleep, Razi. You need to stay awake. Keep talking to me.'

Remnants of anger lurk in my mind. 'Go away,' I want to scream at him, but the voice that comes out is no more than a raspy bleat.

'You should have told me you were wounded this badly. I think you've stopped bleeding from the wound in your side, but I'm certain some other wound has festered. You're burning up. Tell me where your other wounds are. I've sent for my hakim. He'll be here soon, Razi.'

I try, once again, to lift myself, and this time, I am able to push away from the floor and sit, leaning heavily against the wall.

'Don't … don't do me any favours,' I mumble, trying to hold my body from slipping to the side.

'I'm doing it for my own sake.'

I want to tell him to go to hell, but it's too much effort. Finally, I just allow myself to fall back down and close my eyes.

Yildiz! That's Baba's name for me that day—Star. I'm wearing a dark blue qaba embroidered with silver stars, each one streaking its glittery starlight across my body. I'm sitting in the howdah with Baba, on his elephant's back that is covered in dark red brocade studded with multi-coloured stones, as large as birds' eggs. Baba's robe is also blue, but it appears gold, because there is such a profusion of his names and titles in gold thread on his garment that the blue underneath seems just an illusion. I'm the only one sitting with Baba. Nisu and the others—Rukn, Shazia and the three-year-old Aisha are on another elephant. I think Nisu has been given the responsibility to take care of them. He's their elder brother, and he takes the responsibility very seriously. But I'm special; I'm Baba's star. I sit up tall like Baba, and smile at the crowd around us. We're in a procession—maybe it's Eid-al-Fitr—a grand procession; as though the White Palace has been turned inside out on the street. There are noblemen on horseback all around us. Soldiers are marching to the rhythm of kettledrums, their lances so tall, they could dip in the gold pot of the sun. Some are holding red and green banners with tails that float right across the sky. There are also many more elephants, fitted with gold howdahs. A muezzin, sitting in one of them, calls, 'Allah-hu Akbar,' and a nobleman in another is throwing silver coins into the street. Children are running between the elephants' legs, their little fingers trying to collect the coins. Scared they'll get crushed, I pull on Baba's sleeve to get his attention and show him the children. His forehead is glistening with sweat, but he's smiling. Maybe he's enjoying the cool air from the whisks that are fanning him on either side. I point to the children. He nods at me and continues smiling. I don't think he understands. I'm worried about the children and search for them again, but they are lost in the crush of people. So many people; it's like the whole shahr is there, and everyone is dancing, singing and throwing petals in the air. Horsemen are circling the procession, shaking silver sprinklers over the crowd, misting the air with rose water. The fragrance of roses, the soft dribbles on my face … I close my eyes and raise my face to catch more sprinkles. A drop falls on one eyelid and trickles down my cheek; then another one, and another one. A river of tears. Someone is sobbing—convulsive, deep sobs, drawn from the pit of grief. They're washing Baba's dead body in the other room. They're cleaning out all his impurities with water mixed with sidr leaves, then with camphor and then a third time, completely clean. They're laying him on the floor; three pieces of white cotton to wrap him. They're covering him from shoulder to calf in the qamees and placing his left hand on his chest and then the right on top of the left. They're turning his face to the Qibla. They're wrapping the middle of his body in the izaar, and then, finally folding the lifafah over his whole body. Now, they're tying ropes around the lifafah, just over his head and under his feet, and one around his middle. He's gone. This thing—this six-foot long bundle of white cotton—I don't know it. A violent squall blows through me. I run out wailing and shrieking. They're pulling at my arms, my shoulders, drawing me back. I break their hold and run to the men who are lifting him on their shoulders. I rip off my veil and claw at my face, drawing blood. I'm being dragged away. They're taking him. I'm screaming and screaming. The whole palace is howling along with the ululation of hired wailers. Around me, a swarm of black veils.

'Razi?' A soft hand on my forehead. I open my eyes. Altunia is bending over me. 'Are you in pain?' he asks.

I prepare my mind to take stock of the throbs off pain. But there are none—nothing—only a beautiful numbness. I rest there for a long moment and feel a sigh escape my lips. Then I shake my head in response to his question.

'Good. You were screaming. I thought you were in pain.'

I open my eyes and say indignantly, 'I don't scream,' but my voice is a mere whisper.

He smiles. 'Perfect. Now I know you're really feeling better. The hakim says the worst is over. You've had a fever for many days. Your leg wound festered. You had an arrowhead lodged in it. But he has extracted it and poulticed the wound. He has also dressed the gash in your side. He said the bandage you tied on it saved you from bleeding to death. But it was a clean wound. Rest now.'

I let my eyes close again. Sleep is drawing a veil behind my eyelids. Such solace.

I'm in the graveyard behind the Jami Masjid, sitting near an open grave. There's a body wrapped in a white kafn lying at the bottom of it. I take up a fistful of soil and open it over the grave, but instead of layering the kafn, every particle of soil cuts a hole in it and, even as I watch, the fabric shreds from the face. It's Yakut. Horrified, I quickly gather another fistful and release it over his face. When I look again, its Baba's face I see—contorted, as though in pain.

I wake up. I'm alone. There's sunlight. I realise that I'm not in the underground dungeon any more. I'm in an above ground cell. It's tiny, but there's fresh hay on the floor and a window grate, through which sunlight is streaming in. Altunia has had me moved. Wounds never heal in dungeons. He must really want my recovery. I close my eyes and try very hard to garner anger.

After they buried Baba, I couldn't sleep for weeks. Night after night, I lay in bed, but my feet paced the ground near Baba's grave. I was filled with so much anger, I didn't know what to do with it.

Once his body had been prepared for burial and the Fatiyah had been read, the men, like a silent flood of white, had poured out of the mosque, carrying Baba's body to the open area behind the Jami Masjid, where a two-guz hole had been dug. Not allowed to accompany the procession to the burial, sitting in the sanctuary of Azra's arms in the masjid, dry-eyed, I imagined them lowering him into the ground. I imagined his spirit—that had left his body to go and visit heaven and hell, that had watched from above when they had washed his body and wrapped it, that had accompanied them to the masjid and to the grave—finally returning to his body. I imagined the angels Munkar and Nakir—their faces blue, eyes jet black, shoulders as wide as the graveyard—pulling his soul out of his body and propping it up to test his faith with three questions: Who is your Lord? What is your religion? What is your faith about Muhammad? Ready to beat him with their hammers as heavy as sin till Judgement Day, if he answered incorrectly. I had no doubt that Baba would know the correct answers to these questions. His iman, his salat, his shahadah were true. But if only the angels would ask him one more question: What is your faith towards your daughter, Razziat? His answer would make him a sinner, and the hammer of the Denied and the Denier would strike him again and again, till eternity. 'Baba,' I said to him every night. 'I don't wish eternal torture upon you. But you know that you wronged me.'

Turning on my side, I face the window and watch the dust particles in the streaming sunlight. Once, when I was little, I had asked Baba how they were so illuminated. 'It's because around them there's only darkness—like a star in the night sky.'

'Yildiz,' I whisper, and all the other names slip out from my lips: Guzel, Inci, Zafer, Mehtap, Ozur ... No one calls me by these names any more.

17

BABA RETURNED FROM HIS CAMPAIGN IN BAMIAN ON A LITTER. BUT, perhaps, Bamian was only a flashpoint; perhaps, his body had already been harbouring its own enemy since his campaign in Gwalior. The fort in Gwalior is a stronghold that the Sultanate can't afford to have mutinous, because a lot of trade routes pass through Gwalior. It also provides easy passage to Bundelkhand, from where we acquire most of our war elephants. My grandfather, Sultan Ai-Beg, had defeated the Hindu ruler of Gwalior three decades ago, and since then that monarch had been paying tribute to the Sultanate. That's why when his successor, Mangal Dev, rebelled, Baba had no choice but to lay siege to the fort. It was one of the longest sieges of Baba's warrior life. For eleven months, the rebel's stronghold withstood it, while Baba's pavilions remained erected below the fortress. Hoping to negotiate with Mangal Dev, Baba continued to send him envoys, certain that the diminishing stockpile of food and water in the fort would eventually persuade him to surrender. What Baba didn't know was that the Hindu ruler, while pretending to consider each new term of negotiation, was having a secret tunnel dug under the fortress, and, one night, he, his family and all his nobles escaped through it. When Baba discovered this, he stormed the fortress in a fury, but by the time his men were able to ram the fifteen guz gate, all the Hindus had fled from the fort; only the Parsis remained—seven hundred of them. Baba ordered an execution of all seven hundred, in front of the Sultan's pavilion, right before his eyes. The people of Gwalior needed to know the price of joining forces with rebels and challenging the Sultanate and the might of Islam.

When Baba returned to Dilli from Gwalior, it was in a furor to gather another force to storm two more Hindu strongholds—Malwa and Ujjain. He raided their coffers, killed hundreds and thousands of infidels and destroyed their temples, especially those that were known for their antiquity, so that the infidels could see that nothing, not even their ancient gods could withstand the Din Panah, the Defender of the Faith. From Ujjain, he even brought back to Dilli a life-sized gold statue of Raja Bikramjit, that used to stand in the centre of the city, and the black stone from the cave temple of Mahakaal, that the Hindus believed to be thousands of years old. He had these thrown into the treasury, to be valued as no more than war booty. Then, within a few weeks, he left again, this time for Bamian on the Sind River, to fight the infidels there.

Just as Baba was preparing to begin his march into Bamian, a strange sickness invaded his body. It started with a fever, which made the soles of his feet numb and his fingertips tingle. The royal physicians couldn't understand it, so the astrologers were summoned. They saw evil omens hovering over the Sultan and advised him to postpone the Bamian campaign and return to Dilli. By the time Baba began his journey back, the numbness had already spread to his hands and feet. He arrived in Dilli, on a litter, a few days after the Shab-e-Barat fast, the day on which Allah descends to the lowest heaven and offers forgiveness for sins. On this day, Allah also records for the year who will be born and who will die.

In Dilli a slew of physicians examined Baba and prescribed treatments: massages, hot and cold compresses, poultices, herbals teas. But the paralysis in Baba's body kept creeping up, higher and higher, a finger's breadth every day, like slow-moving mortar in his veins. Nothing seemed to work, not even a talisman to counter the evil eye, if it was, indeed, some malevolent gaze that had struck him like a cartouche of paralysing needles.

Husni set up Baba's sick room on the top floor of the Kushk-e-Ferozi and took care of him herself. She also began to closely monitor every person who came to his rooms, not just serving girls and hakims, but also Junaidi, Baba's chief minister, and the Chihalgani. She had already assumed full control of the zenana five years ago, after my mother passed away. Now, Baba's sickness elevated her to heights she had only dreamed of.

Anneh had lain in bed for over a year, not speaking, hardly able to move, her bed a hellish torture, because her body had become ridden with sores. Towards the end, she stopped recognising people, even me. The only one who evoked a twinge of recognition in her was her serving lady, Ilbari. When Anneh died, there was grief in the zenana but no sorrow, except for Ilbari's. As for me—I was relieved. I had begged Allah every day to end her suffering. Baba was away when she died, quelling a rebellion somewhere. When he returned, he held me close to his breast, quietly, without tears, without a word. I wondered if he too were remembering that time in Badaun when she had almost died, and, holding me in his arms, his sobs had racked through my body.

To manage Baba's condition, Husni also moved to the top floor of Kushk-e-Ferozi, into the Sultana's apartment. Having to occupy the same floor as her was like having a raging rash on my body. You try not to scratch it, but it still burns and itches and sometimes gets putrid with puss. I suppose I could have moved to the third floor, to the apartment she vacated, but that would have been even more galling for me.

In a perverse sort of way, I was also grateful for Baba's sickness. It kept him in Dilli. No more campaigns. He used to joke about it himself, saying Allah was turning him into a pile of stones to keep him in his Hazrat-i-Dilli. In the early days of his illness, while his body was succumbing to paralysis, his mind was still acute and nimble. He used to have his strong men carry him to court in a palanquin, but this was only till the paralysis was up to his ankles. When his legs became immobile, he took to his bed and handed over many of his daily duties to me, such as public court hearings and the weekly tours of the markets and factories. However, the meetings with maliks and amirs that his Amir-i-Majlis organised, he attended himself. These began to be held in the stateroom in the Kushk-e-Ferozi, where his jaandars would carry him and prop him up against velvet pillows, his motionless legs and futile hands hidden under silk blankets.

Every morning, before I left for the business of the day, I would come to talk to him and get instructions, and every evening, I would return to give him the day's reports. I timed my visits to match with Husni's zenana engagements, so that I wouldn't have to deal with her. When I came in the evening, Baba would normally be in his bed, settled against the pillows, his body massaged and washed and made as comfortable as possible. I would sit by his bed and tell him everything that had happened that day, and on days that I visited the shahr, I could hardly stop talking.

The shahr was a new experience for me. When Baba went on campaign, he used to assign the court and other administrative affairs to me, but the bazaar tours were still conducted by the Shahana-i-Mandi, the superintendent of markets. But now that it was apparent that Baba may never be able to go to the shahr, the weekly inspection of the key markets fell on me. I didn't mind it at all, because for me, the shahr became like a magic box that conjured up a new surprise every visit.

Dilli has spread like sadabahar—a forever flowering vine: sun or shade, rich soil or rocky, boxed in beds or wild in fields, cascading down walls or cropping up in crevices—once the sadabahar vine takes root, its many-hued blooms are unstoppable. First came the traders, then merchants began settling in, growing business networks and families at equal pace. Soon houses sprouted—thatched, mud, brick and stone, and people who lived in them required bazaars. There are now seven main bazaars in Dilli: Kanak Mandi, the grain market; Sabzi Mandi, where, every day farmers bring vegetables and flowers; Gosht Bazaar, the butchers' market, that sells all kinds of meats, from partridge to wild boar; Jawhar Mandi, the gem market, where you can buy everything from finely crafted ornaments and imported precious stones and jewels to ivory-handled swords and copper-engraved shields; Kumhar Gali, the potters' street, with its whizzing pottery wheels; and tucked away in the north corner, Jolaha Gali, the weaver's street, its air vibrating with ghuggi bird-like songs, as cotton carders strike bowstrings with mallets to clean the fibre; floating puffs of cotton and lint everywhere. And then there is Bereket, the square of abundance, where you can get anything and everything—bowls and basins, daggers and finger-protectors, silks and cotton, wooden toy animals on wheels and terracotta bird whistles, hemp sandals and leather boots, Turki carpets and Baghdadi velvet. And in the east of the markets, just before the lashkar compound begins, are all of Dilli's own karkhanas—the workshops of weaponry and ornaments, fabrics and dyes, metalworks and furniture. If it's not in Dilli shahr, it hasn't been created; that's what people say.

Many years ago, Baba had signed a farman to begin construction on a trade route that joined Hazrat-i-Dilli to Daulatabad—a highway that reduced months of travel to only about forty days. He also had wooden sarais built all along the road so that traders, from both land and sea could get a hot meal and a good night's sleep, or even a few days' rest. After this road was completed, all kinds of imports began pouring into Dilli: cotton from Shaliyat, silk from the southern town of Kayampadi, and gold and textiles from Dhavalgarh, whose Chalukya king was so weak, it was rumoured all his traders had left and come to Dilli. From the port city of Khambat, that had the best gold craftsmen, fine ornaments arrived every day and sold in the market for high prices. Every amir and malik worth anything wanted Khambat gold for himself and his women. There was also pink coral and honey-red cornelian and the finest pearls that came via sea to be sold per ratti and were used not only for ornaments but also for in-lay work in sword hilts and elephant howdahs.

Sometimes, I would see in the market, men from Al-Chin with their reed thin moustaches and narrow beards and hair secured in a bun with ivory sticks, wearing colourful silk tunics with embroideries of birds and blossoms. They came to trade white porcelain, jade, celadon and quicksilver, and also vermilion that the Hindu women wore in their hair parting. Once I told Baba about a quarrel I had witnessed between a Chin-e-man and a Hindu Brahmin; they had been arguing about the price of a celadon bowl. The Hindu was willing to pay the twenty jital copper coins for the bowl, the price the Chin-e-man was asking, but he would not touch it till it had been purified in his temple, yet he would not let the Chin-e-man come close to the temple. Finally, the deal ended without a sale, with both men hurling abuses at each other. I asked the Qadar Mulk, who was accompanying me, what was going on, and he explained to me that according to the Hindu Brahmin the Chin-e-man was polluted.

When I told Baba about this incident, he smiled.

'But, Baba, why does the Hindu man think that the Chin-e-man is polluted? I've heard that they're overly clean. They go to public bath twice a day.'

'It's not whether they bathe or not; it's what they eat that the Hindus abhor. But there's a lot the Hindu won't touch,' Baba said. 'He thinks it helps him keep his faith protected. But the Hindu is shrewd. The one thing his religion doesn't forbid touching is coin, no matter whose hand it comes from. The richest moneylenders of the Sultanate are Hindus. The interest they charge often adds up to more than the principal. Many of my own amirs are deep in debt with them.'

'That's why I've been urging you to declare the Hindus as dhimmies. Put them under the tax laws so that the Sultanate can benefit from their wealth. That way they will feel free to practise their religion, but also feel like they belong to the Sultanate, protected by their taxes, and you will have more authority to control the interest they charge. You, yourself, have told me so many times about the cycle of taxes—that people are happy to pay taxes when they see the benefits from them, and the Sultan uses those benefits to bring them greater protection and greater happiness.'

The smile that Baba gave me was so full of pride, it filled my dream with the promise of reality.

Sometimes our discussions veered off into matters of spirituality. 'To understand people, know what they seek in the hereafter,' he would quote to me the words of Qutb Saheb. 'No matter what a man does here, on this earth, no matter how lost he gets in worldly affairs, he is always seeking fitra, the innocence with which he was born, so that he can recognise that his search is only tawheed—the oneness that is Allah.'

I should have seen in Baba's inward gaze that he was slowly withdrawing from life. Qutb Saheb himself had passed away only a few months prior to the onset of Baba's sickness, during the time when he had returned to Dilli after the Gwalior campaign, exhausted in body and mind. During one of the gatherings at the dargah, the Sufi saint had gone into a trance and had never returned to consciousness. People said it was from the ecstasy of a verse about total surrender that one of his students had recited. Both Baba and I were devastated when we heard of his passing, and Baba went to attend his funeral. He told me later how there was no one to lead the prayer for his jenaza, because in his will, Qutb Saheb had laid down a difficult condition: only he who has never done anything forbidden and has never missed the Asr—the first prayer of the afternoon—will lead the jenaza prayer. Baba was the only one who could step forward. I think this last connection to his teacher had already prepared Baba for the other world.

'Promise me, Razi,' he said to me one day. 'You will build a grand dargah for Khwaja Saheb's tomb so that people will always remember his glory.' And in his next breath, he said, 'Promise me that you will build a simple tomb for me.'

Those days of easy conversation ended all too soon. Baba's condition worsened rapidly. When the paralysis began to spread beyond his limbs, the fever that was an occasional occurrence, became constant. Seeing him so reduced, I began to dread the inevitable. Then, one day, as I sat watching Husni supervise the masseurs, a guardsman announced that a Hindu hakim from Ajodhan sought permission to examine the Sultan. He had been sent by Fariduddin Ganjshakar. Fariduddin had been Qutb Saheb's favourite disciple, and he had taken over the leadership of the Chisti Sufi order after him. My father had also publicly acknowledged Fariduddin as the next in line. But Baba Farid, as he was called, was a gentle man. The constant reviling by custodians of the Sharia distressed him, so, Baba signed a farman-i-tughra and gifted him a land grant of the village of Ajodhan where he could live and practise his beliefs in peace.

The introduction letter that the Hindu hakim brought from Baba Farid called him a miracle worker. After examining my father, he informed us, 'It seems that when the Sultan developed a fever in Bamian, it was from an infectious germ that entered his spine. That has been slowly spreading, obstructing the channels of his brain that control muscles. The cure is simple,' he said. 'Sarvanga Swedna—passive heat therapy of steam and daily body massages with Sainvadi oil. But the Sultan's condition is severe, he warned us, clucking his tongue. Then, pointing a finger skyward, he added, 'It is all up to Him. His Will prevails above all else.'

Husni went to work right away. She had jars of the special oil prepared, which was a mixture of twenty ingredients from specific fruits, salts and roots. She also ordered the building of the chamber for heat therapy. It was a wooden cell built over an underground heating chamber in which water was boiled. Steam from the water seeped through the wooden slats of the floor and filled the cell. Twice a day, two strong men carried Baba's diminishing body, covered in furs, into the cell and placed him, bare-bodied, on a platform. For a quarter of a ghadi, Baba absorbed the steam, and then he was taken to his room to be massaged with the oil.

The treatment began to work; Baba started to improve a little, day by day. The evening his fever broke, and he felt a tingling in his legs, I offered five prayers. When I went to the zenana's mosque at sunset to offer the Maghrib prayer, I saw Husni there. Her head was fully covered, and her face was bare, devoid of any cosmetics. I saw her again for the Isha prayer, and then again for the Fajr prayer at dawn and the Zuhr prayer in the early afternoon. Five times that day, we prayed side by side. I realised that day that we did have something in common, after all: our love for Baba. My heart would always become rock hard when I saw her, but, that day, a little corner of it softened, if only for a while.

After Baba began improving, we resumed our daily conversations; although now he hardly ever discussed the affairs of the kingdom. He became reflective, or, maybe, he always was; I just never had enough time with him to discover that side of him. Lying propped up against the pillows, he talked about his childhood, his youth, his battles, his lessons learned—a life he had been storing like a treasure that he was passing on to me. Those were precious days.

One day, he told me how he became a slave. The story was already legend in the barracks, but I'd never heard Baba tell it himself. 'I was the youngest of four brothers. People used to say Allah had gifted me an appealing face and great intelligence. Our father loved me most. He couldn't bear to see me out of his sight, but that made my brothers jealous. One day, they asked our father permission to take me to see a herd of wild horses, but he refused. "Don't you trust us?" they asked, offended. So, my father let me go. They took me to the market and sold me to a merchant from Bukhara. By Allah's grace, he turned out to be Bukhara's Sadr-i-Jahan. He was a kind man. He treated me like a son and taught me iman and salat. But he had a relative who took me by force and sold me to another. His name was Jamal-ud-din Muhammad, but everyone called him Tight Tunic, because of the way he dressed.' Baba smiled at the memory of the man.

I smiled back and kissed his cheek. 'Then what happened?' I asked.

'Tight Tunic brought me to Ghazni. He told everyone in the market about the beauty of his two slaves—me and Ibeg, who was the other slave he owned; he was a Turki like me and handsome and brave. Sultan Gazi heard about us and wanted to purchase us both for one thousand gold dinars, but Tight Tunic refused. He'd been training us in weapons to make us soldiers, and he was sure he could get a much higher price. Sultan Gazi was so angry at being refused, he prohibited our sale to anyone in Ghazni. Tight Tunic then took us from Ghazni to Bokhara, again and again, but for three years no one made a bid, because no one was brave enough to violate the Sultan's order. Then, one day, your grandfather came to Ghazni after his victory in the Holy War in Naharwala, and he heard about the beauty of the two slaves Tight Tunic was trying to sell, a sale that Sultan Gazi had prohibited. Your grandfather saw us and loved us, so he begged the Sultan to reconsider. As you know, your Dede had excelled himself in Sultan Gazi's service, and the Sultan didn't want to refuse him. "Let the boys be taken out of Ghazni to Dilli, and they can be purchased there," he said. And that's how Ibeg and I became Sultan Ai-Beg's slaves. He bought us for one thousand jitals in Dilli.'

'That's why you love Dilli so much,' I said.

'Yes. Dilli was where my worth was realised.'

'And Ibeg? What happened to him?'

'Your Dede gave him a new name—Tamghaj—and made him amir of Tabarhind. I loved him like a brother.'

I laid my head on Baba's chest. I knew his sadness. Tamghaj was martyred, fighting with Baba against Yulduz. 'And you? When did Dede make you an amir?'

'After my victory in Pir Panjal. He made me a free man and gave me the governorship of Gwalior and Badaun.'

'Did you really behead so many rebels at Pir Panjal that the Jhelum became a river of heads?' I asked. I'd heard the story about how Sultan Gazi had been fighting the rebels of Khita and Khokar mountain tribes and, to help him, my Dede had brought his own forces from Hindustan, including his best soldier—my father. Baba had jumped into the mouth of the Jhelum and beheaded so many tribesmen that, for days, people downstream saw only bobbing heads.

Baba laughed softly. 'I know that's the story everyone tells,' he said. 'They don't know the Jhelum. No sane man can jump into its mouth at Pir Panjal and come out alive; not even I. But I did fight the tribesmen in the Jhelum, in the valley there, where Liddar flows. With Allah's grace, I fought a good fight and killed a large number of enemies. Their heads didn't quite flow down the river, but the rebellion of the tribes was squashed. Always remember, Razi, it's not how many men you kill in battle that brings you victory; but who you kill that will end the enemy's aspiration.'

'Is that why Sultan Gazi manumitted you? Because you fought so effectively with the tribes that they ended their rebellion?'

'Yes,' he said. 'Although, I must say that the valley did get littered with heads and the water did flow red.'

To see the little silver twinkle return to his eye made my heart soar with gratitude and relief.

'Tell me about the time when you got the message from the Turki nobles to come to Dilli and how you became Sultan,' I said. But I regretted the question as soon as the words left my mouth. Although I had never heard it from Baba, Anneh used to tell me that he rarely ever spoke about that time, especially in her presence, because it was her own beloved brother, Aram, who had taken the throne after my grandfather and was killed by the Turki nobles so that my Baba could be Sultan.

Baba remained silent for a while. Then he cleared his throat and said, 'It's the nature of thrones, Razi, to be won with blood. You know your uncle Aram Shah had been made Sultan, but some nobles of Sultan Ai-beg, who had reluctantly accepted his son's sovereignty, began to breed sedition, and the Sultanate broke into four independent states. It had to be united, and Dilli had to be secured, and only a strong man could do it. Your Dede had always wanted me to be Sultan. He thought me worthy; that's why he gave me his daughter—your Anneh. I was governing Badaun at that time. One day, I received an invitation from the Turki Maliks in Dilli to come and celebrate the Hindu festival of Vasantautsava with them and fly kites, which, as you know, is the tradition on that day. I had the master kite-maker of Badaun make me a dozen kites and I left for Dilli, taking my central division with me. When I arrived in Dilli, Vasantautsava was in full swing. The Dilli sky was coloured with kites, none of which belonged to the Sultanate's maliks. Instead, the citadel of Rai Pithora was ready for battle, ready for me to prove my mettle. Waiting for me to join him in the battlefield of Bagh-i-Jud was the Sipha Silar, the General of Lahore, along with his faction of amirs and their forces. Your uncle was killed. Many of his maliks lost their heads, and the others fled. And that's how your Baba became the Sultan of Dilli. But you must also have some memories of that time, Razi. Remember, you and your Anneh came to Dilli a month later?'

'I do remember that caravan. I was six, right?'

'Yes, you were born in Badaun. From the very first moment that I saw you, looking so solemn in your mother's arms, I could see your nobility. I was a humble slave; your mother was a shehzadi, Sultan Ai-Beg's own daughter. You were truly Ozgurluk,' he said. 'It was for your arrival that Allah had made me a free man.'

I laid my head back on his chest. His steady heartbeats were so reassuring. 'You used to call me Zafer—your victory,' I said.

'Ah, Zafer! Yes, I remember. Ozgurluk and Zafer.'

'But you didn't give me either of those names. Why did you name me Razziat, Baba?'

'Because when I heard about your birth, I felt completely razi—happy and content. Allah had bestowed his glory on me.' Beneath my head, I felt his chest expand. 'Did your Anneh never tell you this?'

I had heard the story many times, from both Azra and Anneh, but I shook my head.

'Let me tell you,' he said. 'I was inspecting a military camp in the outskirts of Badaun, when one of the eunuchs from the zenana came to tell me the news. I asked him if Turkan Khatun was well. "Yes, Wali," he said. "And the girl. Is she well?" I asked him. "The Malika has asked me to ask you if this news makes you happy," he said.

'"Tell the Malika, I'm razi," I said to him. And so, you were named Razziat. Besides, Ozgur is a boy's name. I was happy that Allah had given me a girl.'

18

ONE AFTERNOON, AFTER A BUSY DAY IN THE GRAIN MARKET, I WENT to sit with Baba, but I saw Husni there, and, along with her, Junaidi amca. Muhammad Junaidi was Baba's Nizam-ul-Mulk, his Prime Minister. It was in his lap that I had received some of my first lessons in statecraft. I called him uncle.

When Nasir, Rukn and I were children, every time Baba was in Dilli between campaigns, he would have a little play area set up in the corner of his meeting room, so that he could spend time with us, even while he conducted business with his men. Nasir and Rukn were happy with their toys, but I was more interested in what the grownups were discussing. Sometimes, I would climb on to Baba's lap, and sometimes on to the lap of whoever had come to see him. The one person who used to be a frequent visitor was Junaidi amca, and I always preferred his lap to Baba's, because he was a plumpish man with a cushiony lap. It was from Junaidi amca's lap that I began to observe Baba—how, no matter what was being discussed, the expression on his face remained the same, except when he laughed; then his whole face changed. His eyes crinkled, his cheekbones softened and his beard trembled. I noticed how, instead of sitting against the cushions, he sat up straight, with his legs under him, kneeling, as one would in prayer; how he kept his hands flat on his thighs, restrained. Many years later, I asked him about this posture, and he told me that it was important to assume the most non-threatening position when discussing issues that one felt strongly about. That's how he sat in his throne, and that's how I learned to sit in mine.

Sitting in Junaidi amca's lap, watching Baba's still hands, I remember being fascinated by the rings he wore. They were only on his left hand; on his index finger was a green Zamurd emerald, as big as a koel's egg, and, on his little finger, was an oval Padparadscha, the rare lotus-coloured sapphire that a visiting prince from the Aryachakravarti island kingdom had gifted him. I loved those rings on my father's fingers. Their contrast—the sheer green of the emerald and the pure femininity of the pink sapphire, like a lotus dipped in glass, against the battle-scars of his hand—it was a paradigm of beauty with which I began to measure all other things of beauty.

That day, when I came into the room, Junaidi and Husni were in a serious discussion with Baba. There were no guards at the door, which meant that they had been dismissed for this confidential meeting. I hesitated near the door, wondering if I should leave. But Baba saw me and gestured me to come in, announcing to the others, 'Here she is. My dearest daughter, who is worthier than any of my sons.'

The look that Husni gave me was so venomous, I was surprised it didn't turn my body instantaneously blue and make me foam at the mouth. 'But, Rukn?' she appealed to Baba. 'You called him home.'

'I am a sick man. I wanted to see my son. But that doesn't change the fact that he's an idler, lost in pleasures. How will he manage the affairs of the Sultanate? In Badaun I sent with him nobles who are capable of managing the estate. Without them, he would have ruined Badaun. No, no. I can't allow him to ruin the Sultanate by giving him supreme control. But Razziat?—she's intelligent and hardworking. In all the time that I have been away and now, during my sickness, she has been managing the affairs of the kingdom. And you know very well, she has also accompanied me in war and proved herself to be a brave and honourable warrior. I believe my daughter is more than worthy.'

'Al-Sultan Al-Muaz'am,' Junaidi spoke. 'Your son may be engrossed in pleasure at present, because he has not been given the responsibility of the Sultanate. Once he feels that weight on his shoulders, he will prove worthy of your faultless upbringing. Besides that, you have ruled in the way of Allah; your august presence has made this Dilli a Dar-ul-Islam. Surely, naming a daughter heir when an able son is present is not the way of Islam? Forgive my impudence, Al Mu'minin, but my mind poses this difficult question.'

Junaidi's words of betrayal cut me. I was quite aware that he was Husni's supporter. She was generous in her gifts to people she could use to her benefit, and everyone knew Junaidi's stables had acquired some of the finest horses in the Sultanate. But still, in all the years that Junaidi had shown me affection, I hadn't realised that in his mind I was no more than a mere female.

Then came Baba's response to Junaidi: 'A woman who is capable is worthier than a man who is not. Was not the Prophet's first wife a successful merchant? Were her caravans to Syria not far superior to those of all the Quraysh? Islam does not forbid a daughter's heirdom. I have made up my mind. Soon I will name her my heir.'

I was stunned—rendered immobile by Baba's sudden declaration. I had dreamed about this, but to hear it pronounced—it kept echoing in my mind like a gong: 'My heir!' 'My heir!' Then it hit me: euphoria! It made my body lawless, breaking all conventions of bone, flesh, senses, and breath. I couldn't breathe, and I couldn't control the trembling that seized my legs. I don't know how I managed to take the few steps to walk to Baba and sit down beside him. And I don't know if I managed to keep my face impassive or not. But I do know that my eyes became teary, because when I turned to look at Baba, his face was blurred.

I was vindicated. From childhood to that moment, whatever

calumny I had suffered at Husni's hands, whatever denigration from my military trainer, whatever disparagement from Anneh, and whatever disappointments from courtiers like Junaidi, instantly, they all became a thing of my past; forgotten, irrelevant.

Later, in my room, I lay on my bed. I seemed to have lost the ability to do anything else. Sometime during the evening, Jamila asked me if I needed my horse readied. I vaguely remembered telling Yakut earlier that I would go riding. In a corner of my mind, I felt a familiar urge to go to him, to tell him what I had heard, to share with him this stark happiness that I seemed incapable of concealing. It was, perhaps, for this reason that I didn't go to see him that day. I felt too exposed, even to myself.

The following morning, when I woke up, my world was newly minted. Sunlight melting in the veranda, jewelled dewdrops on the freshly planted flowers, fountains twinkling like cascading stars, the blue sky, the chirping sparrows, the spring breeze … had anything ever been this perfect before?

Unable to suppress the smile that was bubbling inside me, I came in from the veranda and told Jamila to get me dressed as quickly as possible. I couldn't wait to embrace my new world.

'Which outfit would you like to wear, Shehzadi?' Jamila asked.

'The new purple one,' I said. Baba had gifted me purple cloth that he had had especially ordered from Misr. It was terribly expensive because the purple dye was not available in Dilli, or even in Baghdad. The snails that they crushed to create the dye, only lived in the waters of Bahr-i-Sefid. Jamila had had the cloth made into a qaba for me, but I'd never had occasion to wear it.

I was choosing the jewellery to go with the purple, when Azra came huffing into the room. Even though Jamila and her team of slave girls had taken over most of Azra's duties, my old nurse was still called upon when important messages had to be conveyed to me, and Husni always considered her summons to be of extreme importance.

'She wants to see you,' Azra said, making a sour face with pursed lips, which made her look comical, as she had lost most of her teeth.

'Do you know what she wants?'

'Humph,' she snorted. She had stopped spitting, because, lacking teeth, she couldn't chew the areca nut any more, which used to be her ammunition. 'How would I know what Beauty wants?' she said.

I smiled at her annoyance. I had a pretty good idea what Husni wanted to discuss, and I was really not in the mood to listen. But after Baba's declaration, I knew that the situation with Husni had become volatile, and I had learned from experience that it was better to hear what she had to say and gauge her intention than be caught unawares by what she may be planning.

'Watch yourself, Shehzadi,' Azra warned, as I made to leave the room. 'Oh, and she's not in the zenana. She's in the Kushk-e-Sabz, with Shehzada Rukn.'

I paused at the door. This was an unexpected development, one that called for much more caution. Such machinations are known to lead to treachery. Coming back into the room, I asked Jamila to help me put on my veil, and I told Azra to inform Hindu Saras that I wished to ride to the Green Palace with bodyguards.

Saras amca met me downstairs with my horse. He had also brought along four heavily muscled jaandars, their sword hilts gleaming reassuringly. Even though it was such a short distance to Kushk-e-Sabz, and I could have easily walked, I rode. With my face concealed behind my veil, my tegh secure by my side, Hindu Saras and four of my strongest jaandars at my back, I felt ready to tackle whatever it was that Husni had planned.

The first thing I noticed as soon as I entered Rukn's sitting room, was him reclining on a gold-embossed chaise, as though he didn't have a care in the world. Or, maybe, he was just inebriated. Husni, on the other hand, was pacing back and forth on the Turki carpet. I also noticed that the guardsmen had been dismissed.

'Razi, my sister!' Rukn got up as soon as he saw me at the threshold, but when I paused at the door to beckon my men to also enter, his smile faltered and he raised his eyebrows in perplexity.

I hadn't seen Rukn since he was made governor of Badaun years ago. I knew he had come to Dilli a couple of times in between, but our paths hadn't crossed. I had heard that he spent his time with his many friends in the shahr, sons of noblemen and merchants, who patronised dens where women and wine flowed abundantly. He looked almost the same: a little like Baba and quite a bit like Husni. Stunningly handsome, perhaps even more so now, because the years had added depth to his features and breadth to his shoulders. The only visible change was the lines on his face, grooves that ran from his nose down his cheeks and into his beard, which was much thicker than I remembered it. He was wearing a dark green qaba with embroidery only on the collar and the edges of the wide sleeves. Underneath, his tunic was unadorned, but of the finest silk. His jewellery too was just as simple: a single strand of large, perfectly round pearls. The simplicity of his attire was his hubris of knowing he was good looking. But I knew he wasn't a vain man. One could even say that he was as nonchalant about his looks as he was about life.

'Are you well?' Rukn asked, recovering from his surprise at seeing my soldiers, and coming forward with his arms extended. I almost put my hands in his, but then I stopped myself. When we were younger, this is exactly the kind of prank he would play on me: extend his arms to take my hands, and, as soon as I reached out, he would withdraw, leaving me looking foolish.

When I looked up into his face, I saw the same playfulness in his eyes. Instantly, we were children again. He, the annoying younger brother, and me, the long-suffering older sister, pretending disregard of his stupid shenanigans. Smiling at him, I carefully lowered my hands to hover over his, and then, before he could try anything, I quickly brought mine under and clasped his.

He laughed. 'I've missed you, Razi,' he said.

'Welcome back, Rukn. It's good to see you, too,' I said. It really was good to see him. I had missed his antics, but more than that, I had missed his light-heartedness; not that his attitude ever infected me, but just knowing that there is another way to look at life lessened the severity of mine. For me, life is the battle of Karbala, which one has no choice but to fight, even if it may demand one's own sacrifice. For Rukn, everything in life was a choice, even battle.

'You can remove your veil,' Husni commanded. She had stopped pacing and was standing on the other side of the room, watching us.

I disengaged myself from Rukn and turned towards her, slowly. 'Actually,' I said, 'I prefer to keep it on.'

Her lips tightened. Then she turned sharply to my men and ordered them to leave. 'The Shehzadi is with her brother,' she stated.

Hindu Saras and the four bodyguards just stood where they were, as if she hadn't even spoken. I applauded Saras amca in my mind. To ignore a direct order from Husni; it took balls of iron, or, in his case, no balls at all.

I heard Husni mutter something, but I couldn't make out what she said.

Rukn sat down, reclining, with his legs stretched out and his arm resting along the back of the chaise. Husni started pacing again. I thought about sitting, too, but I didn't want to sit on the same chaise as Rukn, and the only other seats in the room were the large velvet cushions on the floor. They looked very comfortable, but I didn't want to be sitting lower than Rukn; so, I decided to remain standing.

'Let me just say, congratulations,' Rukn said. 'I heard.'

'What did you hear?' I asked him, keeping my voice casual.

'Don't pretend as though you don't know,' Husni hissed at me.

I ignored her and kept looking at Rukn, waiting for him to answer.

'That the Sultan, our father, told the Mushrif-i-Mamalik, the Secretary of State, to write a decree, naming you heir to the Sultanate.'

I couldn't prevent my sharp in-take of breath. My heart started hammering. Breathe, I ordered myself. Breathe! Then I began counting to ten in my head: yek, do, se, chahar, panj…dah. Slowly, the hammer in my chest stopped pounding and my breathing became somewhat normal. I gave a short nod to Rukn to acknowledge his congratulations. He suddenly sat up, alert. His eyes were looking out of the door. I turned my head slightly and saw that Yakut had arrived with four more jaandars, all fully armed. He stood at the door and bowed to Husni. 'The Sultan wishes to see Shehzadi Razziat.'

She waved him away. 'Tell the Sultan she will be there shortly.'

Yakut just stood outside the door, with the jaandars still in position.

That's two orders ignored, I thought to myself with a smile. Oh, Husni! Today is really not your day.

But, when I looked back at her, I was caught by surprise, because her face was now all gentleness and appeal. She walked slowly towards me and softly placed a henna-reddened hand on my arm. 'Come, my child. Sit with me,' she said and drew me down to the cushions. 'Your father is not well,' she began. 'The Ulema will strongly oppose him, and he, poor man…' Her voice quivered and her eyes filled with tears. 'He's not well enough to argue with them. You know that his condition is delicate, and he's in no state to fight any battles. You must make him change his mind, Razziat. If you love your father, then you must do this for him. Tell him that he must change his decree. Besides, think about yourself. This will make you unhappy, as well. You'll never be able to prove your worth to the Ulema, or even to your father's Chihalgani. We—you and I—we're only women. We'll never be considered as strong as men. We'll never be able to oppose their wishes. That is how it is, child. Do yourself a favour and save yourself the heartache. Go and talk to your father. Tell him you don't want this.'

She stopped speaking. She was probably waiting for me to say something. I didn't oblige.

'Rukn is the Sultan's eldest son,' she, then, continued. 'It may be that because he has been away for so many years, your father hasn't seen his accomplishments. But Rukn has been serving the Sultanate and putting his life in danger. He deserves to be his Baba's heir. It's his birthright. Think about the injustice.'

I turned my head to look at Rukn. He was sitting as before, his legs stretched out, his arm resting leisurely on the back of the chaise. He looked bored, like he always did. I couldn't really tell whether he was truly bored or just pretending to be. 'What do *you* want, Rukn?' I asked him.

His reaction was true to form. First, he shrugged, as if he didn't care. Then he said, 'Why not?' As if it were simply a flippant question that could be answered in a number of flippant ways: 'Sure, I'll be Sultan,' or 'No, I'm not really interested,' or, 'Maybe another time.' Something like that—noncommittal. But when he saw Husni glaring at him, he said flatly, 'I deserve to be Sultan.'

'Why?' I asked him.

'Why!' he exclaimed.

'Yes, why? Tell me why you think you deserve to be Sultan.'

'I'm Baba's son.'

'So? I'm his daughter and his eldest child.'

'Why do *you* want to be Sultan?' he asked. Another true-to-form Rukn response. Deflection. Answer a question with a question. It wasn't that he was an idiot; he was just lazy. He didn't want to do anything, even think.

'I'll tell you why Baba has chosen me,' I said. 'I care deeply about the people of the Sultanate. People in Dilli trust me, and I will do everything in my power to never break that trust. I also know how to manage the kingdom's affairs. I've had years of practice. I work hard, day and night, solely for Dilli, its people and the Sultanate. That's all I do. That's all I know how to do. The Sultanate is my life. Should I go on?'

Rukn surprised me with his response. 'That's exactly what I've been telling Anneh,' he said. 'I think you'll make an excellent Sultan.'

'So, you won't oppose Baba's decree?'

'I didn't quite say that…' he started.

'That question doesn't even arise,' Husni sharply interrupted. The looks she was giving her son were like cuts delivered with a honed dagger. 'Your selection is against Islamic law. If your father doesn't reconsider his decision, I'll have to go to Council myself and present the case.'

I got up and left. I didn't need to hear any more. Besides, Baba was waiting for me. With Yakut, Hindu Saras and their teams of bodyguards following me all the way, I rode back to the Blue Palace.

Leaving most of my entourage at the gate of the palace, I went upstairs to Baba's sick room. The only one who accompanied me was Hindu Saras, but I left him at the door, as well, when I went in. In any case, Baba's own personal guards were inside.

I was shocked to see Baba's condition. He seemed to have deteriorated overnight. The skin on his cheekbones was drawn taut, his eyes were sinking in dark hollows, and he was wheezing.

'What happened?' I asked the physician who was attending to him.

'The Sultan had a high fever last night. We're still trying to bring it down.'

'Why wasn't I informed?' I asked, trying to keep my voice calm.

'Apologies, Shehzadi. We informed Shah Turkan. She said she would inform you.'

I took a deep breath and waved him away. What I wanted to do was shout and scream at him: how is it that in this season of renewal, of peaching blossoms and budding kachnar, my father's body is withering away? Why isn't the blood coursing in his veins quickening with life? But, of course, it wasn't the physician's fault that my father was dying.

'Razi?' Baba's voice came thin and laboured.

'How are you, Baba?' I said, removing my burqa and going to him with a smile that almost brought me to tears.

He also attempted a smile, but it looked more like a grimace. 'I'm fine,' he said. 'Come, sit next to me.'

I did. I sat near his pillow, next to him, shoulder to shoulder. He leaned towards me till his head rested against mine. His skin was warm and clammy, and I could feel how he struggled with each inhalation and exhalation.

With a slight wave of his hand, he dismissed the physician and the guards and then said to me, 'I asked Taj-ud-din to write up a decree; you'll be my heir.'

'I promise I'll make you proud, Baba,' I said.

He nodded. 'Taj-ud-din is a good man. He'll support you. I have also given him a dossier of my Chihalgani. Let that guide you in your dealings with the men.' He stopped and took a deep breath, as though his lungs just didn't hold enough air for him to say more than a few words at a time. 'Yakut,' he continued. 'He'll sacrifice his life for you. I have taken this promise from him.'

'I know, Baba. But why are you telling me this? You're going to recover, and you'll rule for many more years.'

He shook his head. 'It's time for me to go, Razi. It's your time to rule.'

I put my arm around him and held him fast. 'No,' I said, burying my weeping face in his chest. 'No. Don't say that. I won't let you go.'

A shuddering breath passed through his thin chest. After a while, he said, 'What about marriage?'

'What?' I looked up into his face. 'Why are you asking me this?'

'Your mother … she wanted you to get married. I always put it off. Many asked me for your hand. I refused.'

I sat up. I could hardly believe what he was saying. I was aware of only Altunia's persistent pursuit. I had no idea that other men had also been interested. Who were they? Why did Baba refuse them? Why did Anneh not tell me? I wanted to ask him so many questions. I also wanted to ask myself: would I have said yes to marriage, if I had known? Shazia had brought up the question numerous times, and I had always said, 'No. I want to rule.' But this was before I knew that I had had suitors. Would knowing about them have changed things? Was I angry at Baba for not letting me choose if I wanted to marry? A family of my own, a husband, children; just my own little world, or the Sultanate—which one would I have chosen? For a moment, I didn't know the answer. For just a moment, a different world flashed before my eyes.

'Why did you refuse, Baba?' I asked him.

He waited a long time. I thought he would not respond, but then I realised that he was only hoarding breath to say what he had to.

'At first you were too young. Then, I couldn't bear the thought of losing you. Then Nasir passed away.' He stopped and drew in a breath. The exhalation came with a cough, which made him breathless again. Finally, when he was able to, he said, 'Maybe I'm a sinner for keeping you from having a family of you own. Forgive me, Razi. If this is not what you wanted, then I have done you a grave wrong. I never asked you. Do you want to be Sultan?'

And there was my answer. I ignored the sudden pinch of sadness in my heart. Putting my arm around Baba again, I hugged him. 'You did the right thing, Baba. You knew my choice; I always wanted to be Sultan.'

'Then know that a Sultan should never be subordinate to another. But the way of our world is such that a wife must be subordinate to a husband.'

'I promise you; I will not marry.'

He sighed and leaned against me again. It seemed to me that his breathing had become easier. We remained like that for a while—his head against mine—a fusion. 'You will make a good Sultan,' I heard him say. The trust in his voice swept away the vestiges of a different dream I could have dreamt.

That evening I told Saras amca that I wanted to see Yakut. 'Tell him to meet me in the qasr at Hauz-e-Shamsi; not the minar.'

Hindu Saras rubbed a slow hand down his chin and looked at me with a question in his eyes; it wasn't so much about what I was doing, but whether I was sure I wanted to do what I intended to do. That's the thing with people who know you well; they don't just know why you do what you do; they even know the questions you are asking yourself.

I looked away from him.

'I'll post additional sentries,' he said quietly and left.

Of course, Hauz-e-Shamsi would have people. I hadn't thought about that. Only the qasr, the mini palace built on a plinth beside the reservoir, was off limits to the public. The park itself had become quite a popular site, not just for travellers, who stopped for a rest and a cool drink of water, but also for the people of the shahr, who came with their friends and families to stroll along its flowered sides, take boat rides, and renew their faith at the hoof print of the Prophet's mount. I stored away that thought to share with Baba the next time I saw him. It would make him happy. As for myself—I was glad that Saras amca would get additional guards who would ensure our privacy. An audience was not really part of the plan I had for that evening.

He was so beautiful! When I saw him walk across the courtyard to come and stand at the open door of the sitting room, with the moon directly behind him, it appeared like he had just stepped down from its silvery centre.

I couldn't look away. I sat watching him, but I was glad I hadn't removed my veil. For what I needed to say to him, I needed the courage of the veil.

I gestured for him to come and sit, but he hovered at the door. 'How's the Sultan?' he asked.

I shook my head.

He came and sat beside me then and put his arm around my shoulders. I leaned into him and just sat absorbing his nearness. After a while, I said, 'Taj-ud-din will make a formal announcement next week.'

'That soon?' He removed his arm from around me and hunched over, holding his hands between his legs, his shoulders hunched. I didn't know what he was thinking. I wished he would talk to me. I wanted him to tell me what to feel. I wasn't sure what I was supposed to feel. He knew I had been waiting for this moment all my life; it was here, but at what cost? In my heart, I knew what I had said to Baba about never marrying had, somehow, changed everything between Yakut and me. But what had changed? I didn't know. 'Say something,' I said to him.

'Shah Turkan,' he said.

The incongruity of our thoughts almost made me laugh. This was a rarity; normally, we thought the same thoughts and had the same concerns. But how could he have known my heart that evening? He had not heard me make that promise to Baba. I, myself, had not known I would make such a promise, but his response helped me come out from the tunnel of my thoughts and lightened my mood. 'Shh,' I said, bringing a finger to my lips over the veil. 'Let's not talk about her today.'

'Okay,' he said, turning towards me. 'What do you want to talk about? The decree? Are you worried? You've been preparing for this all your life, and you've been managing the Sultanate's affairs so well during your father's sickness. You're ready, Razi. Don't doubt yourself.'

'That's not exactly what I wanted to talk to you about.'

'What then? And why here? Why not the minar?'

'You've never been inside this qasr. Have you?'

'No,' he said and looked around. I, too, looked at the room we were in, to see what he was seeing; I had had it lit with dozens of lamps. They sat on the floor, all along the walls, casting their light upwards, creating a golden oasis in the squinched dome of the ceiling, and setting aglow the arabesque ornamentations of bells and tassels on the walls … Nothing special, really.

'Very nice,' he said.

'I thought … we always meet in the minar. This is more private.'

'It also smells better,' he said, drawing in a deep breath. 'What is that?'

'Latak chandani. I asked Baba to have those planted around the courtyard. I remembered them from the caravan when we came to Dilli. Wherever we stopped, there were bushes of the plant all around the stepwells and the inns. I used to love picking the flowers and making garlands, like a necklace with hanging moon rays. Surely you must remember them, too.'

He laughed merrily. 'No, I don't. The soon to be Sultan Razziat seems to have forgotten that while she was making flower garlands, I was hammering stakes into the ground to erect pavilions. Do *you* remember the pavilions?'

'Of course. How could I forget? My pavilion used to stink all night, because Anneh and I shared it, and she had a bad stomach throughout the trip. Now if you had hung a flower garland or two inside…'

'My apologies, Shehzadi, for not saving your beautiful nose from that torture.' Yakut laughed.

'But seriously. I love these flowers. Do you know that Rai Pithora's wife loved them too? The women in the zenana tell stories about how he carried a garland of latak chandani when he went to claim her from her father.'

'Is that what you want, Shehzadi? To be claimed with a garland of latak chandani?' he asked with the hint of a smile.

'Well, you lost your chance,' I said jauntily, matching his mood. 'You should have made a garland or two during your times of leisure in the caravan.'

'I should have. But I was too busy watching cock fights and wrestling matches. The winnings were quite good; in silver, no less.' He looked into my eyes, mischief sparkling in his. 'Maybe if I had met you back then, I would have. On second thoughts, it's a good thing, I didn't. Seeing you in those bright sunny afternoons and deep orange sunsets … a princess amidst the white blossoms of latak chandani… imagine all the silver I would have never won!'

I leaned against him and put my head on his shoulder. 'I wish I had met you then. I didn't even know you were in the caravan. How come I never saw you?'

'I was in the rear with the other slaves. You were probably in one of the palanquins with the other royal ladies, or maybe riding one of the elephants with the Sultana.'

'Both. I used to sit on an elephant in the morning, and when it would get really hot, I would move inside one of the palanquins. I only have a few memories of that journey. I remember the palanquins were huge, like rooms. The men who carried them on their shoulders used to sing some sort of a song. Each line of it used to end with a "ho-hum". Something something—ho hum, it went. And their steps would match precisely with the rhythm. Another thing I remember, for some odd reason, are these large peacock feather fans that the women used to wave over us to keep us cool. And I remember watching my mother and other women playing pachisi and saanp seedhi. I can still see their henna-red fingertips moving cowrie pieces,' I said.

'What I remember is how huge the caravan was; hundreds of horses and elephants and hundreds of oxen drawn wagons. Armouries, kitchens and wardrobes. To me it seemed like a village on the move,' Yakut said.

'Maybe that's why it took us so long to get to Dilli.'

'A whole month. Ask my feet.'

'Was it very tiring? It must have been. Walking day after day, for a whole month in the Rajab sun.'

'My feet were so weary that if I could have cut them off and carried them on my head, I would have,' he said, smiling into my eyes. But I couldn't smile back. The thought of that little exhausted boy made me sad.

'Hey,' he said, sensing my shift in mood. 'I was just joking. It really wasn't so bad. In fact, I think I quite enjoyed it.'

'I wish I'd known you then,' I said again, rubbing my veiled cheek on his shoulder.

'But I was already beginning to know you.'

'What?' I raised my head and looked at him. 'Liar. At that time, you didn't even know I existed.'

He reached for my hand, tangled in silk, and brought it to his heart. 'My mother used to tell us about a Zar spirit that possesses people without them even realising it. It's bewitching. And once it possesses you, everything you do in life is through the alchemy of that spirit. Your presence in the caravan was already beginning to bewitch me. If I had been in Aksum, I would have worn a rabbit's foot charm to try to escape you. Once we arrived in Dilli shahr, which is magic in itself, how could I hope to escape the Zar?'

'I spread my fingers on his heart. 'Then, can you promise me something?' I said.

'What am I promising?'

'That you won't try to escape me tonight?'

He let go of my hand.

'I want us to make love today,' I said softly.

He didn't move away, but I felt his withdrawal—a little tightening of the muscles in the leg that was brushing against mine.

I took the corners of my veil and drew it over my head. Yakut turned his gaze away.

'Can you look at me?' I said.

He turned his head to look at my face. I saw in his eyes, the wistfulness I had seen once before when Baba had given him to me.

'Yakut, today can you forget the promises you have made to … to my father, or even to yourself?'

'Why today?' he asked in a soft whisper, letting me keep the secret if I so wished.

I didn't tell him that I, too, had made a promise and sealed a bargain. 'Does it matter?' I said.

He shook his head and got up. Walking around the room, he blew out each of the lamps, except for one, which he brought back to where I was sitting and placed on the floor before me. 'Will you let me look at you?' he asked, his voice lurching.

Yakut and I became lovers that night—a tryst that lasted about seven months. They would have been months of buoyant enchantment if they hadn't been leavened by the reality of the promise I had made to Baba. I felt like I was caught in a tempestuous game of saanp seedhi. Every time my dice brought me to a square of Yakut, I climbed the ladder to joy, and every time it brought me to a square of self-incrimination, I was bitten by a snake, and I slid back. But the greatest tragedy of those days was that I knew all along that no matter how many ladders I climbed with Yakut, the end for both of us could only be a freefall.

19

SO, I GAVE HIM NOOR. A DELICATE RAY OF MORNING SUNLIGHT—TALL and slender, with glowing, unblemished skin; her hair the colour of cinnamon, her eyes, brown tinged with gold. She was from the harem of one of the Khwarazm princes who had fled from the Mongols. A merchant from the ruined city of Herat had sold her to me for five hundred gold dinars.

It was a month after I became Sultan. In a special ceremony held in the Qasr-e-Safed, I promoted to high ranks many of the men who had helped me in my bid to expose Shah Turkan and dethrone Rukn. I bestowed on them Khila robes of honour, fiefdoms, fine horses, strong slaves and beautiful slave girls. To Altunia, I gave the most coveted of governorships—Tabarhind. To Yakut I presented the high position of Amir-i-Akhur (Master of horses) of Dilli and made him the commander of a thousand slaves. Along with these, I also gifted him Noor.

Yakut accepted all three with courtly grace and decorum, kissing the floor before my throne and then the back of my hand. He barely glanced at the girl.

'Amir-i-Akhur, Jamal-ud-din Yakut, will you accept this beauty from Herat?' I asked him again, quite aware that repeating the conferment was below the station of the Sultan, and that the other amirs and maliks in the assembly were probably flabbergasted, but

I wanted him to look at her. There was a perversity in me; I wanted him to acknowledge that I was giving him the most beautiful girl in the Sultanate, but I also wanted him to look at her beauty and be unmoved by it. I knew he had many other concubines; that had never bothered me. This was different.

He gave me an oblique look and turned to look at the girl. Then he knelt again, kissed the floor and my hand and then looked up, directly at me—just for an instant. 'You are most generous, Sultan. I accept the gift,' he said. What I saw in his face tore a rent in my heart. All day, dread trickled from it and pooled in my belly. I wanted to stem it but didn't know how. And I was afraid. I knew my gift would affect him, but I didn't know it would be a rendering. I needed to see him to explain. But explain what? That disguised in the gift of Noor was my apology of a consolation prize. But he had never had any expectations from me. What he felt for me was without conditions; yet, I felt that I owed him something. What we had between us was his utter surrender; in my meagreness, I exchanged it with a reward.

I didn't see Yakut for two weeks after that. He went on a hunting trip in Sanjay Van. Then I saw him in the Daulat Khana in the weekly meeting of the amirs. He looked like he always did, smartly dressed in his signature black silk qaba with silver embroidery on the sides, a sapphire blue tunic underneath the qaba, glistening against the dark skin of his neck. On his head was one of his blue turbans that he had been wearing ever since he found out that blue was my favourite colour. His face, too, looked the same—relaxed, forthright, the smile lines forever ready to crinkle. He was suitably decorous and respectful in his greeting, bowing over my hand to place a kiss, a mere brushing of his lips on the silk of my veil, barely looking at me. But then I was Sultan. He wasn't allowed more than an oblique glance in my direction.

After I had become Sultan, we had hardly seen each other; more so, because it was almost impossible for me to be alone with him. Gone were the days when the only people accompanying me were Hindu Saras and Yakut. I was now constantly surrounded by people; in public, a dozen bodyguards and a small force of soldiers; and in my rooms, a dozen or more slave girls, aside from Jamila and her own personal team. I could have dismissed them all at any given moment, but to do so, I now had to have a justifiable reason. Meeting your lover clandestinely certainly didn't count.

However, that evening, after I saw him in the Daulat Khana, I was willing to risk everything. I summoned Hindu Saras to go to Yakut and tell him that I would ride at sundown—by myself. 'Tell him to come to the minar,' I said. I had thought about calling him to the Hauz-e-Shamsi, but a meeting there always became a tryst; it was as though the qasr was a magical palace of love, and we owed allegiance to its spirit. That evening, I needed to see him away from the magic.

Hindu Saras didn't move. He looked at me thoughtfully, but his hand didn't reach for his chin.

'Is there a problem?' I asked him.

He shifted on his feet. I had never seen him do that.

'Hindu Saras,' I said, adding an imperial tone to my voice, something I rarely ever did with him. 'Is there a problem?'

'How many jaandars will you require?' he asked. 'The Sultan is going to the minar, a public place. Many people will see. The Sultan will require much security.'

I knew what he was trying to say. He was telling me that I was risking too much. If anybody saw me and Yakut together in a public place, without my entourage, tongues would wag. For a moment I thought of changing the location from the minar to the more private Daulat Khana in the White Palace. But dismissing the bodyguards there would be much more difficult. At least in the minar I could conceal myself in its sky balconies. 'Get as many trusted jaandars as you think are required,' I said. 'But they will all stand below. Make sure the area is secure.'

This time Hindu Saras did rub his chin, but he still hesitated for a moment before leaving.

It was a moonless winter evening. I rode an ordinary Turki horse I had never ridden before and wore a plain brown cotton burqa over my sable fur qaba. I also took the long way to the minar, through Sohan gate and along the south wall. Leaving the horse with my jaandars, I told them to wait for me at the north entrance. Then, led by the lamp Hindu Saras held, I climbed the three hundred and twenty stairs to the fourth storey of the minar. As I neared the top, my heartbeat increased, and not just from the climb. Hugging myself tight within the veil, I stepped out onto the balcony. But it was empty. He hadn't arrived yet.

Breathing more evenly, I sat down in the angular fluting, scooting to fit myself into the acute meeting of the two sandstone sides. 'Put out the lamp,' I said to Hindu Saras. 'And leave. I'll call you when I want to go back.' Then, pulling my legs up to my chest, I tucked the burqa under my feet. I must look like a little brown tent, I thought to myself and, for some reason, that made me feel better. It was as though I had finally managed to gather myself together—all the pieces that had scattered since Baba's death—all regrouped under this compactness of thick, non-descript brown cotton. In that moment, I almost forgot about Yakut. But soon the cold air began to seep in through the sides that I was holding down, and I grew impatient to see him.

I waited and waited. When he didn't come, I became angry. How dare he not come? How dare he disobey the Sultan's order? I tried to imagine scenarios of punishment—a public whipping, his magnificent back, furrowing blood; starvation in the dungeon, rats feeding on his flesh. But my mind refused to even visualise these. Then I became worried. It wasn't like Yakut to disobey my orders. Had something happened to him? A surprise attack by one of the other men? Maybe he was attacked on his way here? I had received reports about a gang of robbers that was hiding out in Sanjay Van. Maybe they had jumped him while he was on his way to me. All these thoughts raced through my head, while the night crept closer. At some point, I fell asleep.

When I opened my eyes, the sky was lightening. And there he was, sitting across from my netted eyes.

'When did you come?' I asked him.

He shifted onto his knees and bent and kissed the cold floor at my feet. His gesture, meant only to honour the Sultan in public court, disconcerted me. I also realised that I was no longer a tent; sometime during the night, my legs had slipped out from under the burqa.

'I came a little while ago,' he responded.

'Are you all right?'

'Yes.' He bowed his head, still kneeling.

'I was worried.'

He bowed again.

I waved a hand at him. 'Can you stop? Please. We're not in public.'

He got off his knees and sat back.

'Did you have a good hunt?'

'A wild boar,' he said. 'He was evasive.'

'Your arrows never miss their mark.'

'This time I missed. Malik Khan shot him.'

'You must have been distracted.'

'I was.'

We sat quietly for a while. But for the first time since I had known him, it was not a comfortable silence; it was ridden with turbulence, which I needed to quell, but I didn't know how.

'How are you?' I tried again.

'How do you want me to be?'

'What do you mean?'

'Do you want me to say that I'm deliriously happy—with Noor?'

'Are you?'

'What do you think?'

'She was just a gift, Yakut. Don't make such a big deal of it.'

'I'm the one who is making a big deal of it? Look at you. You've risked everything to come here to talk about her. I shouldn't have come.'

'Then leave,' I said, my voice cold and flat from the frustrated anger I was trying to suppress.

Without another word, Yakut got up. Then he turned around and left.

I didn't even get a chance to remove my veil.

Yakut and I stopped being lovers after that. We stopped making garlands of latak chandani to hang moonlight around each other's neck. We stopped waiting for each other in secret rendezvous, seeking each other in every whisper of the wind. We were terrified that in our estrangement, we had also destroyed that which we had had before we became lovers. But what we had before was fierce, and it fought hard for survival. To preserve it, we began to build an edifice around it—not brick by brick, but in large, desperate, impatient chunks of solid stone. It was very difficult at first, because I couldn't bear to look at him. Whenever he was near, my whole body would quiver, as though he were passing through me like a fever or a spirit. And I know I plagued his nights, because the shadows that pooled under his eyes were filled with the spell of my presence—his Zar spirit.

We never again met in Hauz-e-Shamsi. We still rode together, and sometimes even to the minar, but we never climbed its three hundred and twenty steps to sit in its sandstone sky balconies of circular and angular flutings. Most often now, we met in the Sultan's rooms in the White Palace. Eventually, we grew comfortable enough in each other's company again that I began dismissing most of the bodyguards to talk to him alone. But there was a sadness in our meetings. My heart broke every time I saw him, and I could see the pain of it in his lost smiles. And even though we brought ourselves back together, I never stopped missing him. There was a hole in my heart that even he couldn't fill. But, in a way, I think our shared sadness brought us closer. It was something we had created together.

20

IF THERE'S ONE THING I AM GRATEFUL TO ALLAH FOR, IT IS FOR keeping Shah Turkan oblivious to my relationship with Yakut. The tempest she created in my life before I took over as Sultan would have torn me asunder if Yakut had also been caught in her machinations.

As she had threatened to do, in that meeting we had in Rukn's room after Baba decided to decree me his heir, Shah Turkan called the Council. Timing her entry very strategically, she arrived only after all the men were seated, so that her grand entrance would capture everyone's attention. As she walked to the front of the Council chamber, the sensation of her swinging imperious hips and cosmetically illumined face flashed like lightning across the men. She was also dressed in red, the colour of a complainant, even though, this was not the public court of Mazalim. But I could see how the tight-fitting red silk tunic on her affected the men around me; there was a lot of shifting in the seats.

The years had treated her well. She still had a figure that would put any woman in the full blush of youth to shame. Her hair was still black, though not naturally. Unlike the other older ladies of the zenana, who concealed their greys in the red of henna, Husni used a formula that a Yunani travelling merchant had given her: leeches fermented in wine in a lead vessel. Her eyes were still clear and kohl-lined, and she still wore jewellery that moulded to her shape.

The only change was the addition of fine lines around her lips and eyes, but she wore those with haughty grace.

This was not the first occasion that she had come into court. Years ago, when Baba was still enamoured by her, he had given her an open invitation to attend public court. She would arrive on an elephant, announced by the Naquib-ul-Nukuba with a pomp that equalled the Sultan's and saunter down the assembly hall to the pedestal placed just below the throne. Watching her from the mesh of my burqa, observing Baba's court, I would sometimes wonder why I had to be veiled, while she was prominently visible to everyone. I even asked Baba once, and he countered it with his own question: 'Would you rather learn, or would you rather be distracted by curious eyes?' So, I put down her unveiled presence to Baba's indulgence and felt proud of myself for eschewing distractions.

But this was a different court, one to which she had never been before, but one in which I had often sat beside Baba, albeit quietly. This was the Court of Counsellors, who were specifically selected and invited for their expertise on the subject that was to be discussed. While Husni may not have been familiar with the protocols of this court, she knew exactly how it operated. I knew that she had sent invitations to many members of the Ulema and also to the Ahl-i-Kalm, the people of the pen, scholars of religious jurisprudence. In addition, she had invited those amirs and maliks that she favoured, those who were rumoured to have a special fondness for the good things. Husni's generosity towards her sycophants was boundless. The men she did not invite were Baba's special coterie of Chihalgani, because she knew they could not be recruited to her private cause.

I, too, had dispatched my own invitations, mostly to those Band-i-Gan whom Husni had not invited. Unfortunately, I had not yet received the dossier that Baba had promised to give me, so I had to go with my own gut feeling, and the gut feelings of Yakut and Altunia, my two pillars of support. I knew most of these nobles were intensely loyal to Baba and had also pledged allegiance to his heirs, but that was exactly why within their loyalty lurked the danger of rebellion. I had no indication which of his heirs they believed to be most worthy of the throne.

After she was given permission to speak, Husni stood up and faced the room full of men. I noticed that instead of her usual lofty look, she had an appearance of distress. Her shoulders were burdened with calamity and her face was marked with woe.

'I am here to appeal to the members of the Ulema, to the men of learning, and to the loyal servants of the Sultanate,' she began, her voice slightly tremulous, as though she was struggling to contain her emotional state. 'But before I say anything, I want to request you all to not see my appeal as an opposition to the Sultan and his wise decisions. Sadly, he is not the man he used to be. Sickness has clouded his mind. If Allah allows it, he will recover, both in body and in mind. My fear is that the decisions he makes in this state may cause him distress when he recovers. Therefore, in all humility, I see it as my duty to ensure that the Sultan does not make any decisions that he may regret, or those which may deprive him of Allah's grace. As you all know, the Sultan is considering naming his daughter Razziat as his heir. My question to you all is this: Can a Sultan name a daughter as his heir when he has able sons?'

The room was abuzz, as nobles debated among themselves. Having shot the first projectile, Husni commanded the room again. 'Noble servants of the Sultanate and protectors of Sharia law, as you decide this question, please do consider: if the Sultan's decree is passed, can you, the men of the Sultanate, see yourself receiving orders from a woman?' There it was, the most powerful of missiles.

This time, there was only silence, and it was acute. Men stared at Husni in fear, as though she had thrown scythes at them to emasculate them. No one dared even a glance in my direction; even the men who had come here at my invitation avoided looking at me. Husni's chest puffed in victory. She was done. That's all she had to do—a whisper of indignity to men, a suggestion of tears, and a display of her unnaturally tight bosom.

But I wasn't worried. Baba was still Sultan and his word was final. And I trusted Baba. I trusted him utterly. I also knew with utmost certainty that once he made up his mind, nothing could deter him—not Husni, not the whole body of religious scholars, not his own loyalists, and certainly not a contentious private Council. He had named his heir—me.

Three days passed. Every day when I saw Husni sitting with Baba, the cold underbelly of defeat slithered up my spine. But every day when I saw her disappointed face, my chest swelled with gratitude for Baba. In the meantime, Yakut and Altunia posted their own spies to keep a watch on all who came to see him. I think Altunia even began visiting Baba on a regular basis; I saw him on the fourth morning, coming out of his room. I knew he wanted to ensure that after listening to Husni's persistent coaxing and wheedling about Rukn, Baba wouldn't forget the logic behind naming me. Knowing that I had his and Yakut's steadfast support made me feel invincible, even though my faith in Baba itself was like a mountain.

That afternoon, I was in my room, enjoying a cool glass of rose sherbet, having just returned from inspecting the barracks and the new Mamluks in training, when Shazia burst into my room, panting. She shooed Jamila out and took me in her arms, hugging me tightly.

'What's wrong Shazi?' I said, my heart sinking, fearing the worst.

'Go ask him,' she said. 'Why did he do this?'

'What? What did he do? Who are you talking about?'

'Baba. He's changed his decree. He has named Rukn.'

For a moment her words just hung in the air, like tiny blots. When they descended, I was in pitch darkness. I couldn't move. I couldn't see anything. I was lost. The bright star by which I always swore had been extinguished. I should have instead sworn by the setting of the stars. 'Fala̲ oqsimu bimawa̲qiAAi alnnujoomi,'—I swear by the setting of the stars—the whisper of the Quranic words that escaped my lips was that breath which I had been holding for three and a half days.

'Go, Razi. You must ask him to explain why he did this to you.'

Slowly, carefully, I removed myself from her arms and stepped away.

'Go! Tell him to look you in the eye and give you an answer,' she persisted.

'What difference does it make now?' I asked. I could hear the cold ashes of dead astral bodies in my voice.

'What difference does it make?' Shazia screeched. 'What difference ...? The difference between becoming the Sultan and not becoming the Sultan. He can't do this to you. It's that bitch Husni. I can't believe that he's still letting her influence him.'

I turned away from her.

'You have to go, Razi. What are you waiting for? Go! You owe it to yourself.' Then, impatient at me, she grabbed me by the arm and dragged me down the hall to Baba's sick room.

They were both with him—Husni and Rukn. She was sitting on the edge of his bed and he was standing at some distance, talking to a physician. Shazi deposited me on the other side of Baba's bed, across from Husni. He was lying flat on the bed, the covers up to his chin. His lips were bluish, and his breath was torturous, wheezing in and out of his mouth, as though the passage in his throat had become needle thin. I gathered two pillows and put them under his head. Then I tried to raise him up by hooking my hands under his armpits, but his body had become dead weight. 'Leave him, child,' the physician came to me and said gently. 'He has no more strength to sit up.'

'Is he...?' I began but couldn't finish.

He nodded. 'Pray,' he said. 'Allah is merciful.'

I went down on my knees by his bed and leaned close to him. 'Baba?' I whispered. He slowly opened his eyes and looked at me. There was sadness there, but more than that there was a deep disappointment. That look still haunts me.

All evening and half the night, we sat by his bedside, listening to the whistle of his breath. Sometime during the night, Azra came to take me to my room to rest a little. I got up without a word and went and lay down in my bed, falling asleep almost instantly. In the early hours of dawn, a cry wailed through the palace. The Sultan had passed.

I got out of bed and dressed unhurriedly, carefully putting on my veil and adjusting its netting over my dry eyes. Then I went to his room. Most of the ladies of the zenana were already there, as were his children. Everyone was crying and lamenting. Husni was there too, wailing, tearing at her hair, her neat braids, tattered. Rukn was sitting by the bed, weeping into his hands. His shoulders were shaking. Shazia got up and took me in her arms. Her wet sobs soaked me, but they were all hers. I had no tears. All my grief had turned inwards. Inside of me, I could hear loud screams. Inside, I was tearing at my veil and clawing at my skin, wailing loudly, 'Baba! Baba!' My tears were also all flowing on the inside. I could feel their cloggy wetness in my bones. My grief had transmuted into disbelief at Baba's betrayal, and that was a private matter—only between him and I.

Soon, professional wailers arrived, and the sound of their ululations filled Lal Kot. The men then took Baba's body to be prepared for burial. I watched them, dry-eyed, as they wrapped him in three pieces of white cotton and carried him on their shoulders to the Masjid-i-Jami. Dry-eyed, I joined the women in the zenana of the mosque, and dry-eyed, I followed them as far as I was allowed, when they took him away to lower him into the ground.

I attended Rukn's coronation in mourning, dressed from head to toe in unadorned black silk. I walked with the procession of amirs and maliks to the Daulat Khana, the White Palace's assembly hall where Baba had been crowned Sultan. Rukn rode an elephant that was more ornately attired than any of the attendees: gold-plated howdah, red velvet back cloth studded with emeralds and pearls, bells around its paws and pearls around its neck. Heralds called out to clear the way for the new Sultan, and standard-bearers, flying banners of red and black, flanked him on either side, declaring him the upholder of justice. Soldiers bearing naked swords walked before him to demonstrate his might, and trumpeters on silver trumpets tooted his triumph. After the nobility filed into the hall, Rukn was announced. He walked through the room and came and sat in the Sultan's throne, his sandalled feet cavalier on a velvet stool. Then the Khalifa's black robe that Baba had received, was placed on his shoulders, over his own green robe, and he became the Khalifat's representative. After that, the triangular sharbush was planted on his head, and his titles were read out, sonorously, by the Amir-i-Hajib, the Master of Ceremonies: 'Al Sultan Al Azam Rukn Al Dunya Wa al-Din Firoz Shah.'

All the maliks and amirs, who were in Dilli, attended the ceremony and swore on the Quran their allegiance to the new Sultan. They kissed the floor at his feet and then his right hand. I saw he was wearing both of Baba's rings; the Zamurd on his index finger fit with ease, but the Padparadscha on his little finger, was a little tight, cutting into the flesh. Yakut, too, was there, following protocol. The only one who didn't come to the ceremony was Altunia. I feared for him. I worried that if his absence was noted, his life would be in jeopardy. But, at that moment, he was dearer to me than even Yakut. This thought now leaves me feeling cheated.

21

THEY SAY JINNS ARE HOVERING AROUND YOU ALL THE TIME; ALL IT takes for a jinn to make his presence felt is for you to think about him or to act in carelessness. I remember when I was little, every time I inadvertently hurt myself or broke something precious, Azra would say, 'It's the jinn's trickery.'

Even as I think of Altunia, I hear the door of my cell open and he walks in, looking as treacherous in his yellow qaba and turban as the fire from which jinns are supposed to be moulded.

'Oh good. You're awake,' he says, walking towards me, the hay on the floor crackling under his sandals. 'How are you feeling now, Razi?'

I'm lying on my back, and I don't bother getting up, but I turn my head away rudely.

'Are you feeling better? I got the hakim's report. He says, you are healing well.'

'Why are you here, Altunia?'

'I came to find out how you're feeling.'

'Why?'

'So that I can ask you to marry me.'

Thoughts of killing him run rampant in my mind.

'I'm serious.'

'Get out,' I say indifferently.

'I have something to tell you,' he says, pausing dramatically. I know he's expecting me to ask him, but I refuse to play his game.

'They've put your little brother, Muiz-ud-din Bahram Shah, on the throne of Dilli.'

I turn my head sharply to look at him. He certainly has my attention now.

'It's true.'

'He's barely sixteen.'

'So what? You know he won't be the one ruling. They will.'

'The Turki nobles?'

'Who else?'

The matter of fact way in which he has given me this news tells me that he's known about this. It's all part of a grand plan. I wonder again what is Altunia's role in all of this. He is no fool. What promises has he received in exchange of his treachery? 'So, what did you gain?' I ask, sitting up. 'You kidnapped me, but obviously not to kill me. What's your motive? If you want Dilli's throne, then keeping me alive is the wrong move. You know that as long as I am alive, I'll fight for my Sultanate and kill for it, even you—especially you.'

'I don't want the Sultanate.'

'Then why did you do this?'

'I already told you. To save your life.'

I shake my head. I want to search his face for an explanation, but he's standing against the sun, and I can't tell what he's thinking. 'You want to know why I did it?' he asks. 'Today, I'm going to tell you.' He walks away to stand leaning a shoulder against the wall below the grate of the window. 'They were going to kill both you and Yakut. It was already planned. Saif-ud-Din, Kabir Khan and some of the other older nobles were behind it. I found out by accident. Remember, at your last Council meeting, you invited all the senior amirs and maliks and also the governors?'

I don't say anything; I want to hear what he has to say without any affirmations from me.

'That afternoon I went to the public bath near the lashkar. Some of the noblemen you had invited were there, and I heard two of them talking. They were in the cooling room and I happened to be in the adjacent room. When I heard the words "Habshi", "shameless" and "unveiled", I had no doubt that they were talking about you, so I dressed quickly and was waiting outside the room when they emerged—it was Kabir Khan and Aetkin. They were uncomfortable when they saw me and tried to avoid my eyes, but I managed to convince them that I was on their side. I said they had my full support in whatever they were planning. I wanted to find out more. They called me to a meeting in Aetkin's house that evening. There were about twelve maliks there. It was clear that they were unhappy with the reforms you are trying to bring about, but that was not the main topic of conversation; it was your consorting with Yakut. That was the reasoning they were going to present to the people of Dilli when they forcefully removed you from the throne. They already had a pretty solid plan: a few of the governors were going to begin insurgencies simultaneously, just as they did when Rukn was Sultan. Remember that? Remember how easy it was to destroy Rukn?'

I still said nothing, and he continued. 'Just like Rukn, you would have had to use most of your forces to quell all the rebellions, and the garrisons would have been drawn thin. Then, in subsequent battles, they would have first killed Yakut and then you, and put Muiz on the throne. With a diminished force, how long could you last? I reminded them that both Yakut and you were formidable in battle, and your forces were too well trained to lose. "You'll lose thousands of men, if not your own lives in these battles," I told them. They laughed at me. "Who'll be fighting," they said. "The strategy will be to retreat. The point is to scatter the Sultan's forces around the country to such an extent that she herself is easy to take out." That's why the plan was to kill Yakut first, because they knew that as long as he lived, he would protect you. But I got the strong impression that it was your ouster they wanted, more than your death. So, I decided to test my gut feeling, because if my hunch was right, I knew I could save you.

'"Why take her out?" I said to them. "Why not just take her captive and throw her in the dungeon?" "Fine," they said. "As long as that Habshi is gone. He's too dangerous." You know, he was never one of them, Razi. They respected him, but they never accepted him. And you know that he made no attempt to become one of them either. Then, to make matters worse, you went and made a public display of your affection for him. You let Yakut touch you in public. They were convinced you were having an affair with him. Can you imagine their outrage? The Ulema were probably red in the face. And the nobles—they were already resenting taking orders from a woman; imagine what they felt at the thought of submitting to a Habshi, if you had married him. You took it too far, Razi. They couldn't tolerate it. They were hatching plots to take you both out. While you were happily meeting with your philosophers, scholars and poets, and going riding with your Habshi, they were huddling together in their secret rooms devising ways to kill you both.'

I wasn't surprised by most of what Altunia was telling me; but it angered me to have an innocent moment turned into something sordid. 'To set the record straight, I did not make a public display. The incident you're obviously referring to was completely innocent. I felt faint and Yakut helped me off my horse. There was nothing else to it. And don't you dare insult me by suggesting that you saved me from them. What made you think I needed saving? I was Sultan. I am Sultan. I know how to take care of myself and my Sultanate. I can't run my Sultanate dictated by ridiculous notions of right and wrong set by a few men who think they know better. It's the people of Dilli I care about. And I know my people were happy. I used to see it on their faces every day.'

'Yes. The people were, but not the religious leaders. And not your father's Turki nobles, whose power you were intent on reducing. Day by day they felt their influence diminish. What did you expect them to do? I even warned you, but you didn't listen. So, I did the only thing I could. I removed you from the disaster that was waiting to happen and took him out of the equation. They would have killed him anyway...'

A niggling doubt works its way into my head. 'That rumour about me and Yakut—did you start it?'

'Of course not,' he says. 'Don't be ridiculous, and don't insult me, Razi. I don't know how that started. But I can tell you that it considerably worsened things. I told him to stay away from you. He chose to ignore me.'

'The choices were all my mine, Altunia. I don't know why the two of you always thought you could run my life.'

'I know this is making you angry,' he says, 'But you wanted to know why I did what I did, so I'm telling you. Knowing what they were planning, I tried a strategy to save you and it worked. I told them I could take you both out in just one battle. But the condition would be that you would not be killed. They agreed to that.'

'Did you also tell them why you were going to keep me alive?'

He doesn't answer me at first; instead, he comes and stands beside me again and looks at me intently. 'Yes,' he finally says. 'I told them the reason. I told them I was going to marry you.'

'Oh, I see. Razziat brought under control by the great Altunia.' I spit at him.

'That's the impression I gave them, but you know that I would never do that. Once you marry me, you can do whatever you want. I'll never stop you. In fact, you can even take Muiz to war.'

My breath catches. His words strike me like little shafts of hope. But I'm so leery; I don't trust him.

'And if I say no to marriage?'

'You'll remain Tabarhind's prisoner.'

I knew it. The lying bastard.

'Sorry,' he says moving away from me, the mass of his body blocking the sun and throwing the stream of sun particles awry. 'My love is not selfless like his, Razi. It needs to possess; it needs to bind. I can't be happy in just loving you like he did. That's just who I am, but it doesn't make my love any less. You believed his love; why can't you believe mine?'

I shake my head at the irony. 'I was never going to marry him, Altunia.'

He becomes very still, and the fearful suspicion I've had since he kidnapped me, wriggles up my spine. 'Is that why you killed him? Because you were jealous of him?'

'What? No, no,' he says vehemently. 'How can you accuse me of that, Razi? I loved him. No, I didn't kill him because I was jealous. I killed him so you could live.'

Suddenly, I'm suffused with grief. And then the tears come. I don't bother wiping them. Carefully lowering myself, I turn on my side and face the other way, letting the tears trickle down the side of my face into the dirt.

'Go, fight them, Razi. Take your Sultanate back.'

I hear him walk to my side again.

'I have a proposition. Can I tell you what it is? Will you listen? Can you look at me? Please, Razi.'

I want to ignore him, but I can't. With my face still wet and my eyes still streaming, I straighten myself and sit up against the wall, facing him.

'You know the extent of my force. I'll give it you. Use it to fight Muiz. I'll even gather all the nobles who support me. And I'll send out my spies and get all the information you need. I took you out of the war, and I'll put you back in it.'

His words filter through the stream of sunlight, and, like little particles of light, they infuse with my tears, creating shimmering mirages.

'What do you say? We can do this. Together, we can fight them. Let's battle Muiz.'

Muiz. Shazi's brother. My little half-brother, who used to ask me for tips to better his archery and fencing. I try to imagine him on the throne of Dilli, and I remember when I saw him last, just a few weeks ago at a competition in the maidan. He won the sword-fighting contest, and I rewarded him with a beauty of a horse. Muiz, who was almost murdered by Shah Turkan.

22

THE FIRST MURDER IN KUSHK-E-FEROZI WAS OF MY YOUNGEST HALF-brother, Qutb. He was only four. Someone crept into his room at night, slit his nurse's throat, and scooped out his eyeballs with a dagger. Little adorable Qutb who used to hide behind his nanny's legs every time he saw me and then peep at me from the side, shyly calling me 'Zabla', his version of Razi and abla—elder sister. When they found him the next morning, he had bled to death, his eyeballs hanging on his cheeks. His mother, Safiya, was my age. Nisu had sent her to Baba as a gift from Lakhnauti after he defeated Iwaz. She was a beautiful woman, with skin the colour of roasted wheat and a voice that seemed to come from within the husks. She used to write verses. I loved spending evenings with her, listening to her recite her poems. One couldn't help but fall in love with her. It's no wonder that Baba was enchanted by her. A day after Qutb, Safiya, too, was killed. They allowed her a day of mourning for her son, and then they slit her throat while she slept.

After that, others began to show up dead. Two of Baba's concubines' bodies were found in the baoli below the Blue Palace, gutted, their entrails floating out of their bellies like reeds. Then one of the eunuchs found a slave girl's body stuffed into a sack, sitting outside the door of the lady she used to serve. Soon after, a seamstress' body was discovered inside the tailoring room, strangled with her own tape measure. Next, a eunuch, a bodyguard of another royal lady was found cut into pieces, strewn all over the second-floor courtyard. It was as though the Shaitan had come to play games of blood and the Blue Palace was his playground. Terror spread like unleashed evil, and a palace that used to be boisterous with life became deathly quiet. No more slave women running up and down the stairs on this errand or that. No more little feet pitter-pattering in the corridors. No more excited squeals, pained wails or bratty tantrums. No more rivals standing in their decorated doorways, bickering about trifles. Women now sat huddled together in each other's rooms, holding their children fast to their breast, doors shut tight. And, at night, the eunuchs, standing guard outside the doors, shook with fear of whatever it was that lurked in the dark.

I, too, grew afraid for all the women in the zenana and especially for those whom I loved dearly: my sisters Shazia and Aisha and all my little brothers—Muiz, Jalal, Shihab, Masud and Ghiyas. I worried too for Nisu's wife and mother, and my maids Azra and Jamila, along with the other women who served me. I wanted to protect them, but I didn't know how, or from what. All I could do was stay awake at night and keep a vigil in the third and second floors, an unsheathed sword in my hand, Hindu Saras at my heels.

The lack of security in the floors below shocked me. I noticed that instead of an increased guard, the number of eunuchs on night watch had been considerably reduced, and when I asked of the chief eunuch's whereabouts, since it was he who assigned these duties, no one seemed to know. I was even more shocked to discover that Shah Turkan had moved from the Kushk-e-Ferozi to Qasr-e-Safed a few weeks after Rukn had become Sultan, and had taken up residence in the Sultan's rooms. But outside her apartment in the Blue Palace stood two eunuchs on guard, to give the impression that she still resided there.

Finally, I sent an urgent message to Saif-al-Din, the Wakil-i-Dar, the amir responsible for the Sultan's household, asking him to increase the guard at the zenana's main gates and also to assign more eunuchs at the chamber doors of all the royal ladies. I also demanded an update on the investigation.

His response came many ghadis later:

> Shehzadi, I will bring the matter to the attention of the Sultan, when I see him at the next meeting of the amirs. As for the investigation, the Sultana herself is overseeing this.

I could hardly believe it. As Master of Household, it was his sole responsibility to take care of the zenana. He had full autonomy to pass any orders that he saw fit. He didn't need Rukn's permission. All he had to do was inform Shah Turkan, who oversaw the zenana's affairs. Had Rukn changed the rules? Had Shah Turkan given up her control of the zenana? It all seemed improbable and very suspicious. In any case, I wrote back to him:

> The matter, as you know, is of utmost urgency. There is extreme fear in the zenana, and the decision cannot wait till the meeting of the amirs. I demand that the Wakil-i-Dar act on it at once.

I waited all afternoon for his response, in vain. Then, I sent an urgent message to Yakut and Altunia, telling them to meet me in the strategy room of Qasr-e-Safed . But when I arrived at the White Palace with my jaandars, the guards wouldn't let me enter the room. 'By orders of the Sultana Shah Turkan,' they said, bowing their heads in apology.

My first instinct was to storm the palace, but I stopped myself. The time was not right. The priority at that time was the zenana and its safety. 'When Malik Altunia and Yakut al-din arrive, tell them I am waiting for them in the weapons' training room of the Green Palace,' I told the guards and turned around.

When Yakut and Altunia arrived, they were already fuming about my curtailed access to the Qasr-e-Safed . 'I had heard that Shah Turkan has laid claim to the entire top floor of the palace,' Yakut said. 'But I didn't know that she is not allowing even you to enter. Do you think Rukn is aware of this?'

'What difference does that make?' I said. 'Shah Turkan is the unofficial ruler of Dilli. After Rukn passed the farman and gave her the Sultan's official stamp, she has the same authority as him. She's finally able to make Qasr-e-Safed her own private domain. That's what she's always wanted.'

'I know most of those ass-licking nobles who are helping her,' Altunia said. 'Did you know, Razi, that she buys that loyalty with money from the State's treasury?'

'So I've heard,' I said. 'But I haven't called you here to talk about Shah Turkan's dealings. Do you know what's been happening in the zenana?'

They shook their heads. I wasn't surprised. Whatever happens in the zenana remains within the walls of the zenana—that's how it has always been. The ears of the Kushk-e-Ferozi are tuned both inwards and outwards, but its lips are only allowed to open inside the palace. If any tongues wag outside, they are cut off.

When I recounted to them all that had been happening in the zenana, they became like a pair of angry lions. Yakut visibly expanded his chest and stepped closer to me in a protective stance, while Altunia pulled out his sword and snarled, 'Who has become weary of his head?'

I tried to calm them down. 'First, let's please make the women safe,' I entreated. 'And then we'll find out whose head needs to be lopped. I've sent urgent messages to Saif-al-din, but his responses are so lackadaisical. I'm sure he's been instructed. My only hope now is Rukn. Can one of you ride to him?'

Rukn had moved out of Dilli a month after he became Sultan and had taken up residence in Gilukheri, an area a few parasang east of the shahr, on the banks of the Jamuna river. He had had a hunting lodge rebuilt into a royal palace and moved in there with his wife and concubines. He only came to Dilli for meetings and other business that needed to be conducted in the Daulat Khana. In any case, most of the Sultanate's business was now being handled by his mother. Rukn himself was too occupied with his other pursuits. The official word was that he was busy acquiring war elephants, but I had no doubt that the purchasing of elephants required wine parties and dancing girls to woo the mahouts. In fact, I had been informed that he was giving away huge land grants to the mahouts. Rukn had always given generously, so this news did not surprise me.

'What do you want us to say to him?' Altunia asked.

'Get him to sign this.' I handed him an appeal I had already written, requesting him to order an increased guard at the Kushk-e-Ferozi's gate and additional eunuch soldiers inside the palace.

'What if he refuses?'

'He won't,' I said with a certainty I did not feel. The truth was, I, too, wasn't sure if Rukn would sign or not. I only hoped that despite his mother's influence, Rukn would honour my request. We may have been contenders for Baba's throne, but we had never been enemies. Also, the Rukn I used to know wasn't heartless.

'I'll do it,' Altunia said. 'I'll get him to sign the order, but you have to move out of Kushk-e-Ferozi.'

'What? No, I can't. How can I leave the palace? The women need me.'

'I agree with Altunia,' Yakut declared. 'You're not safe in Kushk-e-Ferozi.'

'Are you both not listening to me?' I said. 'I can't leave the women. They're terrified. Besides, where will I go?'

They looked at each other, as though they would find me a place to stay, if only they could sync their thoughts. 'The qasr at Hauz-e-Shamsi,' Yakut said suddenly. 'We'll post soldiers all around it to make it secure.'

'Brilliant, my man,' Altunia said and slapped him on the back. 'Shehzadi, get ready to move your things to that qasr right away. Please.'

'I'm not moving,' I stated. 'And I'm thoroughly insulted. You don't think I'm capable of taking care of myself?'

They looked appropriately shamefaced, but they had the audacity to exchange a look and then shake their heads.

I was exasperated. 'Will you both just pay attention to the matter at hand?' I said. 'Someone is killing the women in the zenana. We have to find the killer. And the best way to do that is for me to remain in the palace. Stop worrying about me. And believe me, I'm safe. I'm untouchable. You know, no one will dare hurt me. Besides, you forget, I have Saras amca. He's all I need. These days he's sticking to me like glue from the chir tree.' I turned to look at Hindu Saras, who was standing guard at the door. He gave a brief nod, and that seemed to satisfy my friends.

Rukn signed the appeal without question, and that very day, the guard at Kushk-e-Ferozi was doubled—at the main gate and inside the palace on each floor. Altunia and Yakut went home and readied their own personal guards, to be deployed at a moment's notice. They also posted their own spies outside the palace, and I noticed two new eunuchs outside my own door. Because Hindu Saras accepted their presence, I knew they were trustworthy. The truth, although I hated to admit it, was that I, too, had started peering into shadows and looking around corners, every time I stepped out of my rooms. The additional security was comforting.

The incidents ceased and an uneasy calm settled in the zenana. Gradually, a modicum of normalcy returned to the palace. The women went back to some of their routines of beautification, embroidery and gossip, although when evening came, the corridors outside their rooms still smelled of fear. The laughter of children began to replace the silence, but even those tinkling sounds were tremulous.

I relaxed a little, but didn't stop making enquiries. One day, sitting with Nisu's mother and some other women, I asked them if their maids had noticed anything out of the ordinary.

'You know what all those women had in common?' Mariam, one of Nisu's concubines, said. 'Shah Turkan.'

I looked at her sharply and brought a finger to my lips. Then, dismissing all the serving girls, I shut the doors. 'What do you mean?' I asked her.

She replied in a lowered voice, 'All the women who were murdered were specially hated by Shah Turkan. She hates all of us, of course, but her hatred towards those women was particularly vicious. They had all done her some sort of wrong. Safiya replaced her in the Sultan's affections—she and her son, dead. Zara discovered the secret formula she used to blacken her hair. When Shah Turkan found out that she was the one who had told the others, she confronted Zara and warned her that she would regret it. Zara laughed at her. Now she's dead. And Samira—she was just too pretty. Everybody said so. She used to walk around flaunting herself. She even told her seamstress to tighten her shirts and make them just like Shah Turkan's. We used to say to her, "Watch yourself. Don't try to compete with Husni." She would laugh and reply, "She's an old woman. I'm younger and far prettier." Now see what her pretty looks have brought her.'

There was no proof for all this, but what Mariam said made sense, especially when one considered the brutal way Shah Turkan had been executing her orders in the zenana. She was decreeing punishments that surpassed the harshest verdicts passed in the Mazalim court. She had cages built behind the Kushk-e-Ferozi in which she threw slave girls without food and water for mistakes as small as a smudge on her clothes. If it wasn't the cage, then it was the kubash, the baton that her own eunuch, Shuja, wielded on the women with diabolic delight. For lying, nostrils were slit; for being caught flirting, nipples were pierced; and if some girl was caught speaking so much as a word of disrespect against Shah Turkan, her tongue was chopped off. But all these changes in policies of the zenana had the stamp of the Wakil-i-Dar. There was no proof that Shah Turkan was behind them, or that she had ordered the killings.

Then Muiz was almost killed. One afternoon, in a practice game of Chaugan, I was teaching him and three of my younger brothers how to keep a firm seat on the saddle, while swinging down to strike the ball, when Muiz's horse stumbled and came to his knees, flinging Muiz over his head. He was so still, I thought his neck was broken. When he began to mewl, I breathed with relief. 'Be still,' I hushed him, smoothing my hand on his forehead. 'Don't move a muscle.' Muiz was taken on a litter to the Kushk-e-Sabz and examined by the hakims. He was fine; just winded.

My grandfather, Sultan Ai-Beg, had been killed in a Chaugan accident. His horse had fallen, with him still in the saddle, and the saddle horn had bruised his heart so badly that he had died shortly after. But my Dede's fall had been a true accident; his horse had tripped over its own hoof in a Chaugan manoeuvre that Dede knew very well carried immense risk. Muiz's fall was made to look like an accident, but I was sure it wasn't. When Yakut examined the horse, he discovered that it had been struck on its right foreleg joint with a blunt object and the joint had become inflamed. The manoeuvre I had been teaching my brothers required the horse to have strong forelegs. And even more proof was the saddle horn; it had been sharpened. If Muiz had fallen under the horse, as my grandfather had, the horn would have pierced some vital organ.

When Yakut told me this, I recalled the accident that had occurred during my own training, and this left no doubt in my mind about who was behind Muiz's fall. But all of it was still conjecture. If I were to take this matter to the Sultan's court, what proof would I give?

And then I found the proof—proof I wish to Allah I hadn't found. My old nurse, Azra's body cut into three portions; her head, her torso and her legs, lying in the garbage heap outside the kitchens. I was in the riding range, where I spent a lot of time now, when Hindu Saras came to tell me. For the first time in my life, I saw him weep. I rode back to the Kushk-e-Ferozi on a precipitous rush of grief and rage, but, as I neared the palace, where I was told the body was still lying in the garbage, my courage faltered. When I finally saw her, I just collapsed on the ground, right there, in the midst of Kushk-e-Ferozi's heaps of waste, the smell of rotting vegetable peals and animal offal in my nose. Sobs racked through my body in wave after wave of sorrow. I was inconsolable. I was orphaned all over again.

That night, Nisu's mother slept in my room. Deep into the night, there was a discreet knock at the door. When Jamila cautiously cracked it open, Hindu Saras, who was on guard outside, stepped in with a girl. Her head was covered with a dark shawl. 'Listen to her, Shehzadi,' Hindu Saras whispered and slipped out again.

The girl stood, shaking in every limb, holding one end of the shawl over her nose and mouth.

'Don't be afraid,' I said, drawing her to a floor cushion. 'No one will hurt you, I promise. Tell me what you can. But first tell me who you are.'

'I ... I work in the kitchen, Shehzadi. My name is Zehra,' she said in a voice that was hardly audible. 'Today at dawn, I was cleaning out the stoves and I went outside to throw the ashes. There was a man there. I quickly hid myself. But I saw him. He was … he was …' She started crying; low, plaintive moans emitted from her throat and tears streamed down her cheeks, trembling at the edge of her chin.

'Shh,' I said, laying a hand on her head. 'Can you tell me what he was doing?'

'He was … he was emptying out a sack on the garbage pile.'

'What was in it?' My own voice broke. I knew the answer, but I needed her to say it.

'Azra teyze. In three pieces.'

I sucked in a breath. 'Did you recognise the man?'

She nodded. 'Sultana's kasap,' she whispered.

I knew who she meant. Shuja: Shah Turkan's eunuch, her enforcer, the man I knew everyone called kasap—butcher.

I thanked the girl and told Jamila to keep her in the apartment and find her a bed. Then I stepped out of the room and asked Hindu Saras if he knew where Shuja would be at this time. 'Come with me,' he said.

On soundless feet, we descended the stairs, all the way to the ground floor, and went to Shah Turkan's eunuch's quarters. Inside the dark sleeping area, we saw the forms of at least a dozen men on the floor, almost shoulder to shoulder. We couldn't make out any faces. I nodded at Hindu Saras. He tiptoed to the left of the sleeping forms, and I went to the right. He began twisting necks with his bare hands, as I slit throats with my katara knife. Within moments, all twelve were dead.

23

'IF THE LAL MURG CALLS, IT'LL BE TOO LATE.' JAMILA WOKE ME UP with this cryptic message two mornings after the incident of Shah Turkan's eunuchs. It wasn't even dawn yet. 'It's from Jamul-ud-Din Yakut,' she told me. 'The guard said he's been waiting many hours to convey it to you. He wants a response, right away, before you go riding.' I went riding at dawn every day.

I repeated Yakut's message in my head. It rang a bell, but I couldn't quite remember its meaning. Then it came to me, evoking decade-old memories. This was a game him, Altunia and I used to play—a game of deciding a meeting place through a code that only the three of us would be able to decipher. It required putting together clues: naming a place that can be identified with elements of nature; stating a time that can be identified with a symbol that connotes that time of day; conjugating the two together to define the exact time and place. From Yakut's message, I understood the time—before the cock crows, meaning before dawn—but I had to rack my brain to figure out the place. Finally, I remembered: the ruined temple, which the locals called Yogamaya near the Chaumukha Gate. We had discovered this temple together when we were children. I hadn't been there in years.

The temple was one of the twenty-seven that had been destroyed by Sultan Ai-Beg's soldiers, and its pillars had been removed and reinstated in the courtyard of Jami Masjid. When the three of us found the ruined temple, it was already disappearing in the overgrowth, mostly, prickly acacia bushes and also shrubs that the local people called vishtendu—full of vish—because its yellow fruit that ripens in the summer is very poisonous. And, growing at will, between these shrubs, as though defying the venom, were the red cockscomb—Lal Murg. The courage of these flowers is what had inspired us to use it as a code for the place.

The temple was probably built long ago, during the time of Anangpal Tomar, Rai Pithora's grandfather. By the time we found it, all that remained of the main temple was a plinth, crumbling sandstone walls, and pieces of a collapsed dome. In Rai Pithora's time, the temple used to be within the walls of the original Lal Kot, but Baba's new wall had left the temple outside the citadel.

The locals have a legend about the goddess who used to be worshipped in this temple. It's a fascinating story. In fact, the reason I had gone looking for it with Yakut and Altunia was because I had heard the story from one of the Hindu slave girls:

> The Hindu god Krishna had an evil uncle who had imprisoned his sister and her husband in his dungeon, because an astrologer had foretold that his sister's child would be his destroyer. Every time the sister gave birth to a baby, the evil uncle came to the dungeon and smashed the infant's head against the dungeon's stone wall and killed it. The sister's eighth baby was a boy—the Hindu god Krishna. And when he was born, something miraculous happened. The chains that bound the sister and her husband fell off, the dungeon gates flew open, and all the guards fell into a deep sleep. The father then put the baby boy in a basket and, carrying him on his head, left the dungeon, which was built on the bank of Jamuna River. The waters of the river were swift and rising high, but as soon as the father stepped into the river, the

waves not only lowered but also created a passage for him. The father waded all the way to the village of Gokul and went into the house of the chief of cowherds there. This man's wife had also given birth that night, to a baby girl. Krishna's father exchanged his son with the girl and brought her back to the dungeon. When he placed the baby girl in his wife lap, the chains locked on their wrists again, the dungeon gates shut, and the guards woke up. In the morning when the evil uncle came, he grabbed the baby girl from his sister's lap and flung her against the wall. Here, another miracle happened: instead of falling to the floor, dead, the infant girl vanished into thin air. Then laughter came from Jannat and a deriding voice said to the evil uncle, 'He who will destroy you still lives, and it isn't I. I came to earth to protect him so that he can destroy your evil.' That was the goddess Yogamaya.

I loved this story. I loved how the little girl goddess thwarted the oppressor. When Yakut, Altunia and I found the temple, I searched for her idol. I knew the Hindus give faces and bodies to all their gods, and I wanted to see the face of the goddess who challenged evil and laughed at it. But all we found was a hole in the ground, where the idol had, most probably, stood. Later, when I asked the slave girl what had happened to the idol, she told me that there never was one. This temple was the spot where Yogamaya's head had fallen, and it had turned into a black stone, like a symbol of her power. So, people had installed the black stone and that is what they worshipped as the presence of the goddess. Who knows what happened to the stone when the temple's structure was destroyed. It probably got lost in the rubble. That made me so sad. I couldn't bear for this story of the goddess to be lost.

'Tell Yakut I'll be there,' I said to Jamila that morning, after I had deciphered his message. I wondered why he had called me to this place that we hadn't visited in over eighteen years.

It took me a while to find the temple. The vishtendu had spread abundantly. This early in spring, the fruit was just budding, but its huge lance-shaped leaves spread like a green army. And hiding between the leaves, like battle-ready soldiers, was the waist-high prickly acacia, which poor Buraq had to bear. After all these years, there was hardly any sign left of the Lal Murg; it was probably choked out by the vishtendu and the acacia.

I saw Yakut before I saw the temple. He had cleared a path and was sitting on the edge of what looked like the ruined plinth. Stopping at a distance from him, I got off Buraq, handed his reins to Zafar-ud-din, the bodyguard who used to accompany me on my early morning rides, while Hindu Saras got his few hours of sleep. Telling Zafar to remain there till I called him, I walked to Yakut on the path he had cleared and came to stand before him.

'I'd almost forgotten this place,' I said. 'I wouldn't have been able to find it if I hadn't seen you.'

'The minar is not safe anymore,' Yakut said without preamble. 'No place is. Shah Turkan has spies everywhere.'

His tone was serious, so I removed my veil and sat down beside him. He had once told me that one of the things he hated most about my veil was that it prevented him from seeing my reaction to what he was saying. 'It's frustrating to talk to a piece of cloth,' he'd said.

'What's happened?' I asked him.

He didn't speak for a while; just sat there, looking at the deluge of green around us. His hands were clenched in his lap, and he looked as though he was trying to suppress words, so that they wouldn't rush out of his mouth.

'Tell me,' I urged softly.

He took a deep breath and then started talking—slowly, almost conversationally: 'Last night, as I was leaving the citadel, I thought I would check on Piyari. She threw a shoe a few days ago which, we discovered, was not just a dropped shoe; a bit of the hoof wall had also fallen, and the nail that still remained had caused the hoof to bruise pretty badly. I'd given the shahana a recipe for a poultice of wheat bran and salts. I thought I'd check on her, to see how she was healing, so, I went to the stables. As I drew near, I saw three men; I recognised two of them: one was the new slave from Arab, who has just been assigned to the royal stables; the second was Gul Shah, Husni Begum's man. He takes care of her horses. But I couldn't recognise the third man; I don't think I've ever seen him in the citadel before. I saw Gul Shah hand this man a bag of coins and then head off towards Chaumukha; the other two skirted around the stable and headed towards Bhind Gate. I had a bad feeling about the whole affair, so I followed them. They started in the direction of the minar, but then they veered off south, toward the open area there. Do you know the place I'm talking about? Not the training maidan, but the stretch further down to the side that's overgrown with weeds and bushes; the one that hardly anyone goes to—except you. You're the only one who rides through it every morning to get to the trail along the north wall.' He stopped and looked at me. His face was ravaged.

'Go on,' I said.

'One of them went to the bushes on the side and brought back shovels, and then they started digging. They dug out a three-guz wide hole. Then they covered it with a net of leaves and twigs.' He paused and looked at me again. 'You know what that means, don't you, Razi?' His voice shook a little.

I placed my hand on his.

'I kept seeing you lying in that pit, broken.' He sucked in a breath. 'If you'd gone riding...'

'But I didn't. I came here—because of you,' I said slowly. I moved my fingers to the inside of his wrist and held them on the pounding pulse there.

'You were wrong, Razi!' He yanked his hand away and stood up. 'You were wrong. You said you were untouchable. You're not untouchable.'

I tried to take his hand again, but he kept slapping it away. I'd never seem him like that. 'I would have broken every bone in those men's bodies and buried them right there in that pit. But then what? She would have just found another way. Hindu Saras, Altunia and I can't watch you all the time. She's not going to rest till she's removed you from her way. You know that,' he said.

I sat quietly. What could I have said? I knew his concerns were very real. Ever since I had found out that Husni was behind the murders in the zenana, I had been wary of every shadow.

'I'm going to kill her,' Yakut words interrupted my thoughts.

'No. Don't even think about it,' I said sharply. 'She's too heavily guarded. Her men will kill you before you even get close to her. Yakut, you have to promise me that you won't attempt anything. Promise me!'

'Then what do you want me to do, Shehzadi? Sit on my hands while she sends out men to murder you? I've got to do something.' He began pacing back and forth and then picked up a rock and hurled it with such violence, I heard it crash through the acacia.

'I'll go to Gilukheri I'll talk to Rukn.'

A bark of laughter shot out of his mouth. 'Sure,' he said. 'And he'll send a sweet message to his mother to stop trying to murder you. And she'll send you an abject apology.'

Perhaps the situation was, indeed, as hopeless as he made it out to be. Rukn was too preoccupied with the instability in the upper ranks of his maliks and too impeded by his own addictions to do anything. Besides, his mother was managing the Sultanate for him; why would he do anything? In the early days of being Sultan, Rukn had actually shown real promise. He had made a few positive changes, not with the sword, but with strategy. He had shaken up the status quo and put this own team of Mamluks from Badaun in key official positions, replacing many of Baba's Shamsi slaves. To counter their dissatisfaction, he had offered them land grants. But, within the first month of his rule, our younger brother, Ghiyas-ud-din, whom Rukn had appointed Governor of Lakhnauti, rebelled and refused to send to Dilli the revenue that he was collecting in the Sultan's name. Rukn spent precious months quelling that rebellion. Soon after, there were reports that three of the maliks who had initially supported Rukn and whom he had appointed as governors of key fiefs—Badaun, Lahore and Hansi, had also rebelled and refused to send in revenue. With no revenues coming from these wealthy fiefs, Rukn began using the reserves in the State's treasury to not only run the administration but to also counter these rebellions. There was also the troubling fact that Rukn was wasting most of Dilli's tax collections on elephants, wine and women. In fact, his obsession with elephants was just out of control. I'd heard that he'd paid ten thousand silver tankas just to ship a hundred elephants all the way from the kingdom of Dambadeniya. By the time the animals crossed the ocean and made their journey through the Deccan, a few dozen had perished, and the remaining that had arrived in Dilli were so gaunt and exhausted, they had needed weeks of expensive care to recuperate. And then he'd given away large land grants to their mahouts. The nobles in Dilli were not happy, and neither were the citizens. To deal with people's dissatisfaction, Rukn had started touring around the shahr on his elephant, showering coins on them, like some magnanimous alms-giver. He just didn't seem to understand that people didn't want alms—a few coins tossed in their faces like they were beggars. They needed hospitals, roads and parks. They needed safety and crime control. To make matters worse, his mother, Shah Turkan, who was supposedly taking care of administrative affairs, only cared about securing her own power, and for that she freely used Dilli's treasury as her own private purse. And, while her cronies' houses became more opulent, their stables more pure-bred and their attire more bejewelled, the people of the Sultanate bore the burden of increased taxes.

Yakut was probably right. Rukn would do nothing. In fact, if he continued as Sultan, the treasury would soon be depleted. And then what? More taxes. More dissension. In just a few months, Rukn and his mother had brought Dilli to the point of destitution. What if the Mongols attacked? The very thought sent shivers through me. I had been hearing about the Mongol threat almost all my life. That was a worry Baba, too, had lived with all his life. Genghis Khan had lurked in the outlying areas of Lahore for over a decade, attacking the surrounding regions, looting and destroying everything in his path, threatening to invade Dilli. After he had died, Ogedei Khan, his son, had razed the Khwarazm Empire to the ground and had been camped near Peshawar since then. What if he turned his eyes towards Dilli? We would not be able to withstand his advance. Without funds in the treasury, how would we furnish a force?

'So, what do you want to do, Razi?' Yakut asked.

'I've got to save the Sultanate,' I said, standing up and looking to see where Zafar had gone. I needed to get back right away.

'Yes. But first you have to save yourself.'

'Yes, yes,' I said, impatiently. 'I'll do that, too. I think I know how to stop her and Rukn.'

'What are you going to do?'

'Tell the people of Dilli exactly what's happening.'

'And then what?'

'Then I'll let the people decide their own fate.'

He shook his head. ' I think we're talking about two different things here. I'm talking about your safety. What are you talking about?'

'The same thing. Don't you see? If Dilli is safe, I'm safe.'

'Sit,' he said, pulling me down so that both of us were seated on the edge of the resilient plinth of the goddess' temple. 'Tell me what you have in mind.'

24

MY FOOTSTEPS FALTERED AS I STEPPED DOWN FROM THE NARROW staircase of the women's apartment into the main courtyard of the Jami Masjid. There, surrounded by pillared goddesses in erotic dance poses, their breasts and noses slashed by righteous swords to shame them, I straightened my shoulders and lifted my head. I was covered from head to toe in a red burqa. But, underneath the full veil, I was terribly conscious of the thrust of my breasts against the silk—thanks to Yakut.

When I had discussed my attire for that day with him and Altunia, Yakut had said, 'Remember when you first started wearing the veil? You wanted to hide all signs of femininity?'

'Yes,' I had replied. 'What are you trying to say?'

'I think this may be one of those times when you want to de-emphasise that you're a woman. I've seen you in the red silk burqa. It accentuates your shape too much, especially when you pull back your shoulders and stand straight.'

I could hardly believe that Yakut was suggesting that I bind my breasts. I knew he was nervous. In fact, he and Altunia were both so nervous, they made me nervous. Together, they were like an anxious mother sending her teenage son into his first battle.

'I absolutely agree,' Altunia had added, his face completely devoid of the naughty grin that normally lurked in the crater of his cheek whenever he talked about women's attributes. 'But what does Yakut mean, de-emphasise? I understand why you have to wear red, but what can you do to hide your ... you know what I mean. Is there something you can do?' he had asked curiously.

'I can hunch,' I had said quickly, responding to Yakut's concern and ignoring Altunia's question. 'I won't pull back my shoulders. Besides, what happened to gaining strength from convictions, not convention? Remember, that's what you told me?' I had reminded Yakut.

'When you do something as unconventional as this, conviction loses all ground.'

'Actually, I think this time both convention and conviction will work in my favour,' I had said. 'Let them see that they are dealing with a woman. Let them know that I hide nothing, at least nothing that convention allows.' I could see from their frowns that my words had added to their nervousness, but they had stopped objecting any further to what I intended to wear.

The three of us had met on the steps of Anangtal on the same afternoon that Yakut warned me about Husni's plot to kill me. Sitting bundled in our furs, shivering from the water's chill in the month of increasing cold, we had developed a plan. The deep-walled Anangtal was the safest place to talk, because no passerby could see us or hear us from above. Also, no one ventured into the tank in the cold weather. Anyway, we had Hindu Saras guarding it. And with the wind whistling through the zigzag of steps, even the walls became deaf.

Our plan was simple: I would address the congregation after the Friday prayers. I would appeal to their sense of justice, to their loyalty to Sultan Iltutmish and the Sultanate, and to their own welfare. And then let the people decide.

We had also argued about what would be the best venue for me to make the appeal. Altunia had suggested that we invite the men to the courtyard outside the Kushk-e-Ferozi, and I address them from the veranda of the fourth floor. 'That way, you'll be a more difficult target for marksmen.'

Yakut had visibly blanched at the thought of me being an open target. 'Qasr-e-Safed,' he had stated emphatically. 'Do it indoors, in private council, surrounded by nobles and thoroughly guarded.'

'No,' I had insisted. 'Jami Masjid. After the Jumma prayer. Right in the midst of the congregation. And alone.'

'And by alone you mean with Hindu Saras protecting you, of course. Right?' Altunia had asked.

'No. I mean, all alone. Not even Hindu Saras. They must see me alone—unprotected—the victim of injustice, the mazamil petitioner.'

'Impossible!' Yakut had declared loudly in a resounding voice. 'I won't let you do it.' Altunia and I had both looked at him in surprise. He never made such bold, possessive statements.

'This is my decision,' I had said. 'So, you can either help me carry it out, or you can back off.' I hated when they treated me like a helpless woman who wasn't capable of rational thought. 'Think about it,' I said more calmly this time. 'Jami Masjid is the perfect place. The congregation will already be present; we won't have to gather an audience. People will have just finished offering prayers; they will be thinking pure thoughts. No one is wicked in the masjid, especially on Jumma. And the most important factor: the Jumma congregation is not just nobles; it is most of Dilli's citizenry—ordinary men and women. It is their support I seek.'

And so, the Friday prayer at Masjid-i-Jami it was.

Once that was decided, we needed to make sure that the men would be prepared to give me a proper chance to say my piece. We needed supporters in the congregation, and to solicit this support the three of us had carefully put together a list of men to whom I would either write letters or pay a personal visit. The two people on my list, whom I personally approached, were the Sufi fakir, Qasi-ud-din Zahid and Malik Taj-ud-din Sanjar.

Sheikh Zahid was a reclusive man of god and rarely stepped out of his hut, but when he did, people thronged around him. He alone was able to rally hundreds. I, myself, had a very special connection to Sheikh Zahid. When I was born, Baba had invited him to Badaun, and he had predicted that I would one day be a great Sultan. That is why, when I went to request him to come to the Jami Masjid on Jumma, it seemed that destiny itself was leading me. After hearing what I had to say, Sheikh Zahid promised me that not only would he come to the Jumma prayer, but he would also help recruit supporters. This is what I had hoped for. His presence and support would validate my appeal.

Taj-ud-Din Sanjar, who was the other person I visited, was Nisu's old companion. When I was a young girl, I was enamoured of him and used to make excuses to spend time with Nisu, just so I could be within the same circle of air that Sanjar breathed. I never said anything to Sanjar—just watched him from afar with love-sick eyes, but I'm sure he knew. When Baba sent Nisu to Lahore, he sent Sanjar with him as his commander of armies, and he remained a loyal companion and advisor to Nisu, as long as my brother lived. When Nisu died, it was Sanjar who was by his side, and it was he who brought his body back to Dilli. After that he remained here, commanding two of Baba's garrisons. He was greatly respected by the other maliks. At the special Council that Shah Turkan had called, he had strongly opposed her claim for her son's accession. That's why I knew I could count on his support.

The other contacts on our list were personal and trusted friends of Altunia and Yakut. And, on Altunia's advice, we had also included a few prominent religious leaders who he knew were opposed to Rukn, because of his flagrant disregard of Islamic laws. Yakut and Altunia used their own spies to deliver the letters to all these men.

The letter didn't say much, in case it was intercepted; it simply said:

> Shehzadi Razziat requests your august presence at the Masjid-i-Jami on Jumma. After the *Salaat-ul-Jumu'ah*, she will address the congregation.

Everything else that I wanted to say would be in my verbal appeal—it all depended on that.

We had taken all aspects of the plan into account. But we knew there were eventualities that we could not control: what if the men listened but did nothing? In that case we would have set ourselves up as seditionists. What if the members of the Ulema took offense and had me taken into custody? What if Shah Turkan discovered the plan before we had a chance to implement it and had her own men planted in the mosque to counter any dissension? What if she had some concealed sharpshooter waiting to take me out in the courtyard, even before I got a chance to speak? I also had another fear that, I am certain, was only mine. What if everything *did* go exactly as planned? Was I ready for the consequences? There were too many what ifs; and even a tiny bit of a loose thread could unravel the whole plan. I had to, purposefully, push aside all these unanswerable questions so that I could concentrate only on the planning.

And then, there I was—my femaleness hidden under five guz of red fabric, my head buzzing with a painstakingly prepared appeal, my belly aflutter with nervousness—walking past the pillars and into the open courtyard. Once there, I couldn't stop myself from taking a quick look around. I was so exposed, away from the sanctuary of the pillars. Instinctively, I glanced back at the gates of the mosque, where I knew Yakut and Hindu Saras were standing, concealed, watching me, their eyes following my every step. Altunia was stationed outside Chaumukha gate, his men hiding in the localities around the mosque, ready to root out any impediments to our plan. Yakut, on the other hand, had had his men preemptively seize the masjid's kotwali, so that no policemen from that station could even attempt to interfere in the goings on that were soon to occur in the mosque. Standing there in the courtyard, I could almost feel the tension in all three men.

I walked as far as Anangpal's iron pillar, and then stopped again. Beyond it was the stone screen through which was the main assembly hall of the mosque, and I could see the line of bent backs of the men in supplication. Once I crossed the iron pillar and stepped through the screen, there would be no turning back.

When Nisu, Rukn and I were young, we used to love playing the game of victory and defeat predictions that the iron pillar's legend promised: standing with your back against the pillar, hugging it backwards, if your fingers meet, you will be victorious, and if they don't meet, you are surely doomed to a defeat. Most often, our little arms were hardly capable of wrapping around the pillar; however, every once in a while, by some miracle, our fingers would touch. At that time, just to be the one with the winning hands was a victory. As the years went by, my competitors at the pillar became Yakut and Altunia, and, more often than not, they, with their long, boyish arms would win, and I just ended up begging them to pull on my arms to force my hands closer together. I wasn't at all averse to cheating fate to attain victory, especially because I had realised that defeat had implications that were too agonising to bear.

Before going on any campaign, Baba always used to stop by my room to kiss me. 'Victory or Death, Razi?' he would always ask, jovially, as though picking the correct answer was all there was to determine his fate in the battle. I, too, would play along with him, pretending to take a moment to consider both answers, and then, inevitably declare, 'Victory!' I knew very well that the game, if indeed it was a game, was really not about his losing or winning. The choice was between glory here on this earth or glory in the after world. I loved him so dearly, how could I ever choose the latter?

That day, however, as I stood before Anangpal's iron pillar, victory and defeat were truly on opposite sides: winner takes all, and loser dies, not to be glorified in the afterlife but to burn in the hellfire of breaking conventions. I felt such an urge to wrap my arms around the pillar and test my fate, but all I did was free a hand from my Burqa and briefly skim my fingers over its cold, black metal. 'Victory or Death?' I asked in a whisper. Then I glanced back at the main gate again to share one last moment with the co-strategists of this game of fate, before I stepped through the screen to the other side. It was time to present my case and await my fate's verdict.

The men in the congregation were standing now, shoulder to shoulder, their backs to me, facing the Mihrab, offering the last prayer. I stood just at the entrance of the prayer hall, waiting for them to finish. When they turned to each other in greeting, that would be my cue. 'Noble Sirs,' I would begin, to draw their attention. But when I tried to recall what I would say after that, my mind suddenly drew a blank. I couldn't remember a word of the appeal I had so carefully prepared. My knees started shaking and my heart started pounding. In that instant, I was that man—a sinner, who in the afterlife, stands before grim angels. They demand his soul to come out and face the wrath of Allah. And, he, petrified, tries to hide in his body. But the angel of death is relentless. He draws out his soul, like pulling out an iron skewer through wet wool, tearing veins and sinew. And his soul is damned.

Standing there, terror-stricken, facing in the direction of Mecca, I closed my eyes and appealed to the Merciful One: if my intention meets with Your approval, then show me Your mercy, and if what I am doing is wrong in Your eyes, then strike me dead. And realisation dawned like a heavenly light: I was not that man—that sinner. If, indeed, I was to face the angel of death, my soul had no reason to hide. When the angel commanded my soul to come out and face Allah, it would flow freely from my body, like water from a pitcher. I was not a sinner. I was a fighter, righteous in my cause.

By now, the final prayer was complete, and I stepped forward with resolve. 'Noble sirs,' I called in a voice as steady and piercing as the North Star. All heads turned towards me. For several moments, the only sound in my ears was the beating of my own heart. Then a low murmur rustled through the mosque. I saw Sheikh Zahid begin to move toward the centre of the crowd, and the men to whom he had spoken, starting to gather around him. I noticed, too, that many of the citizens were slowly inching towards Zahid Saheb. From where I was standing, I also had a view of the arabesque screened women's hall, and I could see excited movement within. It was happening exactly as I had envisioned, and seeing it actually occur filled me with courage.

Drawing air into my lungs, I pulled back my shoulders and said more loudly: 'Noble sirs and gentlewomen of Dilli, I am Razziat al-Din bint al-Sultan Iltutmish.' I paused. In the hush that followed, I could gauge the enormous implications of my presence. Drawing another breath, I continued. 'I come to you as a petitioner today, on behalf of the Sultanate, on behalf of the people of Dilli, and on behalf of the women and children in the zenana.' Every man was now looking at me, fully attentive to what I had to say. I took another deep breath. 'Your justice and your wisdom were commendable when you chose my brother, Rukn-ud-Din Feroz Shah as the heir of Sultan Iltutmish, May Allah grant him peace. But Rukn-ud-Din has not honoured your wisdom and justice. He is a weak Sultan, unable to defeat the Sultanate's enemies. And to make matters worse, instead of taking care of Dilli and her citizens, he is squandering away its wealth on expensive elephants, mahouts, dancing girls, and wine servers. The wealth he is spending is yours—your heritage in the Sultanate's safe-keeping, built with your money, from the taxes you pay. If he is allowed to continue thus, before long Dilli's treasury will be empty and the Sultanate will be destitute. There will be no more coin to build roads, hospitals, schools. No resource to pay salaries. And without soldiers' salaries, how can Dilli sustain a fighting force? In such a situation, if we are attacked, if Ogedei Khan, the Mongol who awaits in Peshawar for just such an opportunity, turns his infidel forces towards Dilli, Dilli will not be able to defend herself. Our beloved city will be razed to the ground, our sons will then become slaves of infidels, our women will be raped and sold by them as prostitutes, and our children will be put to infidel swords.'

I paused to look around. There was horror on the faces of many of the men.

'That is not all,' I continued. 'It is also not hidden from you that while the Sultan remains immersed in his own pleasures and employs his garrison to quell the ever-growing rebellions, the Sultanate is being run by his mother, Shah Turkan, who has moved from the zenana and is living in the Daulat Khana of Qasr-e-Safed. I am fully aware that you have been suffering her oppression from unjust farmans of increased taxes—money that she takes from you in the name of the Sultanate. What you probably don't know is that she doesn't use that money for the running of the Sultanate; she uses it for bribes to aggrandise her own power. And now she has also let loose terror in the zenana. You may not know this, but every day innocent women and children are being brutally murdered in their sleep by her men.'

'Is this true?' 'Can this be true?' Disbelief passed from one mouth to the other.

'It is indeed true,' I stated. 'Every day we find royal ladies, their serving women, and their children hacked to death, only because Shah Turkan bore them some grudge. Every day, the zenana is filled with wails of mothers, and every day we send our loved ones, wrapped in shrouds, to the graveyard. Shah Turkan is even killing all my father's children. Two weeks ago, my little brother Qutb-ud-din was merciless blinded, and he bled to death. He was only four years old. A day later his mother was also murdered.' I paused to let this horror story sink in and then added, 'Surely, Allah will not forgive us for the sin of doing nothing to prevent these wicked acts. How will we face the angel of death, when he demands that we account for our sins? What answer will we give, when he asks why we let innocent children be killed before our eyes?'

The outrage that was brewing was palpable now. Faces became grim and bodies shifted impatiently to take action.

'Shah Turkan wants to wipe out my father's line,' I continued. 'She is killing all his sons, one by one. Last week, my brother, Muiz-ud-din Bahram Shah almost lost his life in a treacherous plot, but, by Allah's mercy, he escaped. And just three days ago, my own men unearthed a plot that was being hatched to kill me. Noble sirs, if my man hadn't discovered the grave that was dug to bury me alive, I would not have been standing here before you today; you would have been preparing my jenaza. But Allah is merciful. Through his grace, I am here, before you to beg for justice.' Once again, I paused. I needed to make sure that each man in the assembly was not only listening to me but was also willing to be persuaded by me, because the words I was going to utter next would decide whether I would receive victory or be condemned to death.

'As you may remember,' I said, carefully establishing the fact that what I was going to say was not new. If they were reminded that they themselves had debated about it, they would be more likely to accept that it was still a debatable point. 'I was my father's legal heir. He had Malik-i-Mamnoon, Taj-ud-Din, draw up a decree stating this. It was no secret. Many of you, his nobles, knew of his intention. But, before the decree could be read in court, Shah Turkan had it changed to put her son, Rukn-ud-Din, on the throne. My father was too sick to protest. Now I plead for justice! I was the heir my father selected, because he knew I was the most deserving. Many of you have also witnessed with your own eyes that he was not wrong. My fair judgments in public court, my dealings with merchants and farmers, my management of the treasury and development projects are all testimony to my worthiness. After my brother, Nasir-ud-Din passed, May Allah grant him peace, it was I that my father saw as his successor. If you want to honour my father, the great Sultan Iltutmish, then honour his wish. If you want the Sultanate to be restored to its glory, then honour his wish. If you want your own lives to be happy, freed from the burden of undue taxes, then honour his wish. If you are true to your faith, then honour his wish. I plead to you in utmost humility to give me a chance to prove myself worthy of my father's trust and also yours. If I fail, I will gladly submit to your justice. I myself will come and stand before you to be publicly beheaded.'

I stopped speaking. My heart was pounding again, but not from fear. Exhilaration was quickening my blood. But the congregation was silent. The moment was building into a reckoning: Victory or Death! I was ready.

25

JUSTICE CAME LIKE THE WRATH OF ALLAH AND SWEPT THROUGH Lal Kot.

After presenting my appeal to the congregation, I had walked out of the masjid with carefully measured steps; one of the longest walks I have ever taken. All the way across the courtyard, my back had tingled in the awareness that behind me, I had left an active battlefield. Once I was out of the gate, I swung onto Buraq's back, and retrieving my sword from Hindu Saras, spurred him. The three of us rode at break-neck speed to the palace compound, where Altunia would join us.

When we had discussed the plan, the most glaring factor that was missing in it was the outcome. We had no idea what to expect or how it would end; this course was so unchartered. In the best-case scenario, we hoped that the Turki amirs and maliks, who supported me, would gather the men, garner support, and call for action. I would then be invited to command a force and head to Gilukheri to depose Rukn, with or without a battle. It all depended on how he reacted. This was the perfect time for a takeover, because the bulk of the Sultan's armies were deployed in three different rebellions: Muhamad Salari's in Badaun, Saif-ud-Din Kuji's in Hansi, and Ala al-Din Jani's in Lahore. Only one small garrison of soldiers remained in Gilukheri. We had also hoped that, in the meantime, some of the other senior nobles in Dilli would organise a legal case against Shah Turkan and charge her with the crime of murder.

But we had planned for the worst, in case those against me set up a case of sedition and came after me. Yakut and Altunia had wanted me to wait in my room in the Blue Palace, my door guarded by Hindu Saras and four other jaandars, till we knew, with certainty, how the congregation had reacted, while they themselves spread out with their men in the maidan near Bhind Gate, prepared to fight—to death, if need be. But I had refused to hide in my room. 'If this will result in a battle against us, then I will fight it,' I had told them. 'And I will fight it to win, even if it means death. If you wish to die in defeat, you are on the wrong side.'

When we rode into the courtyard of the White Palace, we were ready for a dirty meleé. We strapped on our hand-to-hand weapons: swords, pikes, knives, daggers, maces and axes in preparation.

What came through Bhind Gate was not organised nobles on horses, but a rogue wave of ordinary citizens, a frenzied mob, much more pell-mell than we hade envisioned: carpenters, weavers, cobblers and farmers, carrying whatever they could use as a weapon—hoes, rakes, hammers, butcher knives and staffs. These were the men I had addressed in the masjid, but there they had appeared timid, civil; now they had transmuted into something feral, pushing their way in through the gate, waving their fists and weapons in the air, shouting, 'Free Dilli', 'Justice!' And the loudest shout of all, 'Kill her!' All we could do was step aside.

They stormed Qasr-e-Safed. Slashing and striking at whoever came in their way, they barged in through the palace gates, leaving a trail of severed limbs and chopped heads in the gardened courtyard and splattered blood on the bright white walls. After they entered the palace, mayhem broke out in every corner: screaming men and women came fleeing out, tripping on body parts, slipping in puddles of blood, adding more of it from their own cuts.

Then suddenly shouts erupted from inside the palace and a group of men exploded, like a roaring blaze, onto the third-floor veranda. One of them was holding up a severed head on the point of his sword, blood dripping down the blade, bits of flesh hanging from it, black braids swinging on either side. Shah Turkan's oppression was over.

The trance in which Yakut, Altunia and I had been caught, broke. 'Protect the other palaces,' I yelled to them and, spurring my horse towards the entrance of the White Palace, rode up the blood-slick stairs to the third-floor veranda. The men who had killed Shah Turkan were still there, still impassioned, still shouting loud slogans of freedom. The burly, full-bearded man who had Shah Turkan's head on the tip of his sword was still dangling it over the balustrade, calling raucously to the mob below.

'Enough,' I called loudly. The shouting stopped, and all the men, including the one who was holding the sword, turned to look at me. I inched Buraq a few steps towards them, glaring at them through the mesh in my veil, willing them to look into my eyes, making sure they saw my hand hovering near the hilt of my sword. I saw their grips firm around their own bloodied weapons. Behind me, I felt Hindu Saras move closer to me and my jaandars tighten their grip on the hilts of their naked weapons. I held up my hand in an imperious gesture, mostly to stop my jaandars from making a move. 'I am Shehzadi Razziat!' I said. And then I waited. Slowly, the men lowered their weapons. The man with Shah Turkan's severed head, lowered his weapon and, grabbing one of the braids, planted the head on a stone spike in the balustrade. Then, all the men bowed their heads to me and left the veranda in silence. I heard one of them slip on the stairs and tumble all the way down.

Urging Buraq forward, I came to the balustrade and addressed the mob below: 'Citizens of Dilli,' I called. But the crowd was still in a furore. I called again, more loudly, 'Citizens of Dilli!' Slowly heads began to turn towards the veranda, and shouts began to subside into a low rumble, and soon, I had everyone's attention. 'I am Razziat bint Al Sultan Iltutmish. I am grateful to you for giving me the justice I sought. Now let us stop the bloodshed and embrace peace. You have fulfilled your duty to Dilli and to the Sultanate, now let me fulfil mine. Go home. I promise you, I will not let you down.'

For many moments the crowd remained in a tense standstill. The only movement was from Yakut and Altunia, whose horses pranced on the edges. Then feet began to shuffle, and, gradually, the men began to stream out of the gate. Soon, all that remained of the mob was the smell of blood.

The organised unit of nobles we had hoped would support us, did finally arrive—about two hundred or so of them, with their personal guards, led by Sanjar. They came riding through Bhind Gate and then drew to a sudden halt before the battle-wounded Qasr-e-Safed. By this time, I had come downstairs and was directing men to bring water from Anangtal to begin the clean-up. Altunia and Yakut were riding around, cordoning off the area around the qasr so that none of the women and children from the zenana would come this way. Shah Turkan's head was still sitting on the balustrade like a grotesquery to ward off the evil eye.

None of the nobles asked what had happened. After a battle, no one asks such questions.

Sanjar told me about the force that they were preparing to oust Rukn. 'The troops are gathering in the lashkar,' he told me. 'We will march into Gilukheri, but first we have to fight Junaidi and his men. He has garnered support from some maliks and will prevent us from reaching Rukn-ud-Din. They are stationed between Dilli and Gilukheri.'

'How many?' I asked.

'About a thousand,' he said.

'How many in Gilukheri?'

'Six-seven hundred, at the most. The Sultan's own personal unit. As you know, the rest of his armies are headed to Badaun, Lahore and Hansi.'

I took command. Asking Sanjar to gather his men and meet me on the bank of the Jamuna, I collected my own men and headed that way. Once we were all there, I split us up, keeping one unit with me to fight Junaidi and his supporters and sending the other to Gilukheri. I didn't want that wily old man to have the advantage of warning Rukn, while he kept us engaged in battle. As it turned out; the battle was over in no time. My men killed Junaidi's maliks and most of the soldiers, while the others fled, along with Junaidi himself. We followed him for a while, but when he escaped into the hills, we let him be. He wasn't worth the pursuit anymore. Then, as planned, I brought my unit back to Dilli to wait for word about Rukn.

They brought him to Dilli on the back of an oxen cart, chained in a cage. Handsome as sin, even in his ruin. The austere simplicity of his clothes was torn to shreds, his sun-yellow turban lay like a soiled rag around his neck, and his face was bloodied and wrecked. I had to look away. They threw him into the darkest dungeon in the citadel. His wife, Sajda Begum, was brought to Dilli in a palanquin and sent to the zenana. She was five months pregnant with his child.

When Rukn died two weeks later, I had been Sultan of Al-Hind for ten days. Before the formal announcement of his death was made, Yakut came to the Kushk-e-Firozi to inform me. When he said the words, a strangled breath, like a hiccough, escaped my throat.

'What do you want to do?' Yakut asked me, gently.

'Bury him with honours. He was my father's son.'

Before Yakut left, I asked him if he had seen Rukn's body.

'Yes,' he replied.

'Is he still wearing my father's rings?'

'I think so.'

'See that Sajda Begum receives the Zamurd. And bring me the Padaparadscha.'

26

ANNEH USED TO SAY DAYS OF HAPPINESS PASS SO QUICKLY, YOU DON'T even notice them go by, but days of sorrow make you count each ghadi.

Three and a half years passed. Years in which I certainly counted many ghadis, but the days that went by unnoticed are what, I hope, tarikh will remember about me. When I think of the past three years, I think of the people I used to see in the streets of Dilli. Whenever I toured and wherever I went, my people lined the streets, smiling, waving, the elderly calling out blessings, the children shouting excitedly, 'Sultan Razziat! Sultan Razziat!' Often, I would tell the mahout to halt the elephant so that I could speak to them, and they could speak to me. 'Are you happy?' I would ask. Sometimes, they had legitimate complaints: dried wells, cheating produce vendors who tampered with weights, careless night watchmen who fell asleep on the job, leaving the streets unsafe... But, more often, they would shyly invite me to their celebrations—a marriage, the birth of a child, Eid, Vasantautsava, Deepavali. I had my man record the complaints so that they could be dealt with, and for the celebrations I dispatched gifts of cradles lined with velvet, silk wedding veils, platters full of kebabs, crates full of rose sherbet, and baskets full of mangoes—congratulatory items to show my people I shared their joys as an equal—but never gold or coin as charity from a Sultan to her subjects. My people were happy. I know, because happiness is unmistakable; it shines in the eyes, it sits in the corners of lips, it smooths out the lines of the forehead; it even erases the shadows behind wrinkles.

And they had every reason to be happy. I built more schools, more parks, more hospitals—things to improve my beloved city. I passed a farman that the Sultanate respected all religions. Most of all, they were happy, because I stabilised the economy and reduced taxes by increasing trade. I appointed new overseers for Dilli's numerous karkhanas which produced goods that we traded as far as Baghdad and Al-Chin. The first item I put in trade was sheeshum wood, which grows in Dilli's forests. It is such a hardy wood that it never warps, and it is equally suited for the first training bow, as it is for furniture. I also opened new factories for sword-making, silk and cotton-weaving, leather-tanning, pottery, metalworking, as well as woodworking. Now Dilli has no less than one hundred and fifty factories, some that have existed from my father's time, and many more that I started. I also invited craftsmen from Al-Chin, through whose know-how in mechanical devices we were able to install pulleys and mills in Dilli's factories to make them more efficient. And to ensure that the goods Dilli produced could be safely traded, I strengthened kotwalis all along the highways and increased the salaries of the policemen.

A karkhana that I am particularly proud of is papermaking. I wanted Dilli to produce enough paper to copy the books that scholars from Baghdad have been bringing to Dilli since my father was Sultan—books of astronomy, Al-Jabr, theology and medicine; also books of Farsi and Arabic translations of Yunani philosophy and Hindu epic tales that my own scholars have translated from Sanskrit. I wanted to create a Bayt al-Hikma in the Daulat Khana, similar to the famous House of Wisdom in Baghdad. My beloved copy of the *Shahnameh* that Nisu so lovingly bound for me in leather now sits in a satin-lined box in this room.

But what I believe would have been my greatest achievement, sadly, did not reach fruition, or rather, it wasn't allowed to. I was working to alleviate Dilli's water shortage. The region doesn't get enough rain and wells often dry up. Baba used to talk about building more tanks, but he was so busy with his campaigns, he couldn't implement a sustainable scheme. The solution came to me last year in the form of Kasim ibn Mahmud, an engineer from Baghdad. He was a towering man, almost as tall as Yakut, except that his shoulders were hunched over, as though to shorten the distance between his eyes and the books he was always reading. He had travelled to lands as far away as Byzantine and Misr, and, that too in hemp sandals, which he himself braided. He came as a visitor to Dilli, but after he saw Hauz-e-Shamsi, he requested an audience with me.

'Allah's grace is boundless,' he said to me and to an audience of a dozen of my noblemen in the Daulat Khana. 'But it is we, His people, who must devise ways to receive it.'

'Explain yourself,' Khwaja Muhazzab, my wazir, said.

In response, Mahmud pulled out a roll of parchment from his satchel, unrolled it and laid it before us. On it was a diagram of a seqiya, the oxen-powered water-raising machine we use for farmlands and neighbourhoods.

'Agha Mahmud, I'm sure you have seen in our city many such seqiya to draw water from water tanks,' Khwaja said to him.

Mahmud pulled out a second scroll and laid that on top of the first. On it was an elaborate diagram of a series of cascading roof layers from which water flowed to an underground tank, fitted with large tunnels that emptied into a series of baolis connected to seqiyas.

'I am a water muhandiz. I create engineering plans to harvest rainwater,' he explained. 'This,' he said pointing to the diagram, 'is a system that shows how rainwater can be collected and stored so that it can be used in periods of dry weather.'

I hired Agha Mahmud for a salary of three thousand silver tankas a year and housed him as the Sultanate's guest in the Kushk-e-Sabz. Within a year he designed and built a system of large reservoirs in Dilli that collected every drop of rain that fell during the rainy season, and then distributed it to small tanks across the region throughout the year.

I wanted to apprentice Dilli's brightest young people with an inclination for engineering to Agha Mahmud, so that they could learn about water machines, and even after the Baghdadi muhandiz left, continue his work and help build similar systems in the Sultanate's other territories. My dream was to have Dilli's own cadre of engineers who would begin to experiment with new designs. With this pilot program, I hoped to start a whole system of education and mentorship, for both young men and women. I wanted to infuse the trading culture of Dilli with learning, education and advancement.

However, in a special council meeting, when I proposed to extend Agha Mahmud's contract with the Sultanate to start the apprenticeships, most of my council men voted against it. I was baffled. How could they not see the benefit of having such a scholar and engineer lead us into the future? 'But we need him for the apprenticeship program,' I insisted. 'We need more engineers in Dilli to not only sustain what Agha Mahmud has started but to also develop schemes and methods that will improve how we live.'

There was silence in the circle of councillors. Some of the men shifted in their seats, as though the silk cushions against which they sat, had suddenly sprouted thorns.

'Khwaja Muhazzab? What are your thoughts?' I called upon my wazir.

'Sultan,' he spoke hesitantly. 'Pardon my candour, but the council members will consider extending his contract only on two conditions: no girls be included among the apprentices. And…and…'

'Speak your mind freely,' I told him.

'The Nobles also feel that the Sultan's dealings with him should remain restricted to work,' he finished, his eyes refusing to meet mine.

An uneasiness curdled in my stomach. 'Explain yourself,' I demanded, trying to keep my voice even.

Khwaja Muhazzab didn't respond. Instead he looked around at the other men. I, too, looked at the faces around me. They all looked discomfited.

Then Aetkin spoke: 'A thousand pardons, Sultan. I will speak what most of the maliks here want to say. They think that the Sultan is spending too much time in the company of this man from Baghdad.'

What he said was true. Many evenings after Agha Mahmud returned from touring around Dilli, selecting suitable sites, I invited him to the Daulat Khana, and we sat in the Wisdom House, talking and discussing matters unrelated to rain-harvesting. He was a great observer of people and places, and I enjoyed listening to him talk about his journeys. 'Discussing learning with scholars is not a new practice,' I said to the nobles. 'Surely you remember how my father used to spend much of his free time talking to guest scholars in the Daulat Khana. And, if you recall, I, too, used to join him.'

'With due respect, Sultan, when Sultan Iltutmish, May Allah grant him peace, was alive, you kept yourself veiled."

I was relieved to know that the council's objection wasn't to the advancements I was trying to bring about. I knew that my unveiling continued to rankle many of my nobles, and I thought it prudent not to press that issue. Besides, my desire to open up advanced education to girls was more important to me than nourishing my own mind, so I tried to bargain with them. 'I will take the council's concern about my private meetings with Agha Mahmud into consideration,' I replied. 'But I must insist on keeping the programs open to girls. They are as entitled to learning as our boys; are they not? After all, we allow them primary education in the school rooms; then why not further that effort? Did not my father, Sultan Iltutmish, afford me the privilege of the highest learning, along with my brothers?'

'Pardon the censor, Sultan, but the people of the Sultanate are afraid that the Sultan's programmes will make our girls too bold and immodest.'

'Like yourself.' Aetkin didn't say those words, but clearly that was what he implied. I knew that some of nobles disapproved of my ways, and the fear that they might see my behaviour as a bad influence on young girls had arisen in my mind many times, but I didn't want to acknowledge it. Also, short of hiding myself behind the veil again, I could see no solution to it. I tried to argue my case, but the more I argued, the more adamant the maliks became. Finally, I had to agree to both conditions, just so I could keep Agha Mahmud in Dilli and we could continue to benefit from his expertise.

However, my dream to create an engineering programme for Dilli under his mentorship was not to be realised at all. Kasim ibn Mahmud resigned his post and left Dilli. He didn't really give a reason; all he said was that he was needed urgently in Baghdad, but I got the distinct feeling that the urgency had been created in Dilli, not in Baghdad.

I was still smarting from this setback when I was ruined by a vicious rumour. One afternoon, Yakut requested a meeting with me in the Daulat Khana. As soon as I saw his face, I dismissed the guards. His upper lip was badly cut and his right eye was swollen and bruised in variegated colours.

'What happened to your face?' I asked him.

'Altunia's fist,' he said.

I couldn't help smiling. The three of us were past our thirtieth year, yet Yakut and Altunia sometimes still acted like boys, unable to control their impulses.

'Who won?' I asked, still smiling.

'That's not the point,' he said, his voice more sombre than warranted by a juvenile fist fight. 'He came to my house yesterday to defend your honour.'

'What does that mean?'

'That means people are talking, Razi. There's a rumour...'

I waved at him, dismissing his concern. 'There are always rumours. Ever since I became Sultan, people have been talking. Whatever it is, it'll pass. But what does that have to do with Altunia?'

'He came to ask me if the rumour was true. When I said it was, he punched me.'

'So, what is the rumour?'

'Remember two days ago, when we returned from riding, you felt faint and I helped you off your horse?'

I nodded. 'Go on.'

'They're saying that I put my hands under your shoulders and lifted you off the horse.'

'That's true,' I said and then realised that that was exactly what he was talking about; he had touched me in a way that was being deemed inappropriate. 'But that didn't mean anything,' I protested. 'I was feeling faint and you helped me.'

'You and I know this, but, according to the rumour, we are lovers.'

I almost laughed at the irony of it. When we were lovers, there was not a whisper about it, and suddenly now, years later, people were making us out to be lovers. 'That's ridiculous,' I said. 'Ignore it.'

'This is serious, Razi. You must take it seriously.'

'What do you want me to do? Stop seeing you? You're my Amir-i-Akhur. I have to deal with you every day.' Ever since I had become Sultan, Yakut and I had made an extra effort never to have any physical contact in public, not even inadvertently. I couldn't believe this innocent act was getting so blown out of proportion.

'Maybe for a few days, or weeks, we should stop meeting. Perhaps, it'll blow over, but at least, let's not fan it.'

'This is ridiculous,' I said again. 'I can't stop working, just because someone has raised some niggling objection. How can I do my job with them watching my every move with a disapproving eye? Today I stop dealing with you; tomorrow they'll tell me to stop going to the bazaars. Enough. I'm just going to ignore it; it'll blow away like a waft of foul air.'

Who knew then, that that waft of foul air would puff itself up into a gale and sweep away all that I had worked for and accomplished. In the past three and a half years, I have worked very hard to create a system that will sustain peace. And it did exist—from Lakhnauti to Dewal, for a while there was peace in the Sultanate. Peace—such a precious state, but it prevails until eternity only in Allah's universe, where the sun is not permitted to catch up with the moon; and the night cannot outrun the day; each just swims along in its own orbit, peacefully. In the human world, peace is as transitory as an exhalation of air. The sun clashes with the moon, and night overtakes day; because unlike in the planetary world, orbits in the human world must change for people to move forward.

My next step made peace even more perilous. I tried to replace the old nobles who formed Baba's cadre. He had treated his Chihalgani like sons, but now those sons were old men, and in their old age, they had become stubborn, rigid and opposed to change. I wanted to recognise new nobles of young and eager blood, who would bring in new ideas. I also wanted to phase out the system of small land grants, the iqtadari. This system not only fragmented Dilli's control, but it also bred greed in the iqtadars, who spent their four-year terms fleecing people and filling their coffers. Baba used to say the greedy have jaws like crocodiles—they don't let go; they tear apart. That's exactly what the old system was doing to the Sultanate. But, in every council I called to discuss these changes, I met with opposition, and, after every meeting, I came away feeling like the walls of objection got higher and higher. But I know that much of the opposition was not so much to the changes but to the simple fact that I am a woman who had dared.

I had known, even as I had put on the Sultan's sharbush and sat for the first time under the huma bird of the Sultanate's throne, that every day I would have to battle to accomplish what I wanted. I also knew I would lose some of these battles. But I had hoped that the ultimate victory would be mine. That hope is still alive in me. I still live, and my Sultanate—the Sultanate I dream about—is only a battle away.

27

IT'S A BEAUTIFUL DAY IN EARLY AUTUMN. THE SKY IS A TENDER BLUE, and a gentle breeze is rustling through trees that are just beginning to turn sun-gold. I am lying on a thick Turkaman carpet, against overstuffed cushions, in the marble veranda outside Tabarhind fort's Meheman-i-Khas, the special guest section of Altunia's palace. Behind me are the guest rooms, and in front of me is a waist-high wall of the veranda, allowing me a view of the citadel's farthest crenellated boundary walls; beyond it is the blue line of Darya-e-Satluj.

I have accepted Altunia's proposal of marriage. The first benefit of it is this change of accommodation, from prison cell to royal palace. How different my tiny stone cell, with a two-hand wide grilled aperture, was from this grand palace with marbled pillars, latticed archways and open verandas. The price I have to pay for it is perfidy to myself. I turn my head leisurely to look at the irony of my surroundings.

This is an old sandstone palace, probably not as old as Qasr-e-Safed, but, like the White Palace, old enough to show traces of its Hindu inhabitants, who lived here before it became the Sultanate' property. Some of the interior rooms still have doors with inlaid images of the flute-playing god, and some of the walls, as in Qasr-e-Safed, have small protrusions, where the elephant god's pot belly was not quite evened out when the carvings were plastered over. But I can definitely see Altunia's touch in the elegant renovations.

Tabarhind fort, though, is older than Lal Kot. When I was a child and Baba would bring us to visit Baba Haji Ratan's dargah, we would always stay here for a few days. I remember I used to be fascinated by the fort's formation; it was just so different from Lal Kot. Instead of corner bastions or gate projections, as in Lal Kot, the whole stretch of Tabarhind's walls is a series of rounded bastions, thirty-six of them, like massive rings, with short curtain walls between them. It was built this way to prevent the enemy from scaling the walls, because the rounded bastion is impossible to climb, but that older design also made it harder to defend the fort. Standing on the platform in the bastion, the archer can't strike at the enemy on the other side, because the circularity of it obstructs a straight shot. This is why new forts are built more like Lal Kot than Tabarhind.

On one of our visits here, Baba told me and Nisu the story of how this fort came to be so important for the Sultanate. There is a uterine connection, complete with birthing pains. Every descendent of royal or noble blood in the Sultanate hears this story from a parent or a grandparent. It's even taught during military training as a first lesson of a warrior's determination and how to turn defeat into victory.

Lying shackled in the cell, day after day, for five months, my mind became tethered to the story: Tabarhind used to be Prithviraj Chahamana's defence fort. He inherited it from his maternal grandfather, but he chose not to stay here. He lived in Ajmer, which was his seat of administration, and his cousin and feudatory, Govind Rai Tomar, governed Tabarhind. At that time, the lion-hearted Sultan Ghori was campaigning in Al-Hind and to challenge the Chahamana might, he stormed Tabarhind fort and seized it, sacking Govind Rai. Govid Rai sent an urgent message to his cousin in Ajmer, and Rai Pithora, knowing how formidable Sultan Ghori was and how fierce were his Turki warriors, marched to Tabarhind, bringing with him as big a force as he could manage: his own Chahamana army, Dilli's garrison, and many Ranas of Al-Hind. He met Sultan Ghori in the battlefield of Torwan. The Chahamana army was massive, with over a hundred thousand war elephants especially trained to crush the enemy. Sultan Ghori's force was only a fraction of that, but the Sultan himself was a lion, and he fought like one. Then a chance lance wounded him badly in the arm and he started losing a lot of blood. When a brave Turki soldier saw the Sultan slumping on his mount, he quickly shifted him onto his own horse and brought him out of the field. But without the Sultan in the battle, his soldiers couldn't hold off Rai Pithora and the Chahamanas laid siege to the fort. However, the Rai wasn't prepared for the grit of the Turki forces that Sultan Ghori had left in the citadel. They defended it like a wall of iron. For thirteen months they held the fort, while the Rai waited and suffered outside. Ultimately, because food and water supplies in the fort were exhausted, and the women and children couldn't hold out anymore, the brave Turki men had to surrender.

It was a defeat of circumstance, not warriorship, but a defeat nevertheless, and it wounded the lion-hearted Sultan; it was as though the lance had not struck his arm but his heart. Defeat was not in his make-up. For weeks, he didn't eat or sleep or change his clothes, or even go to his women. He just sat in his war room, strategising how he could overpower Rai Pithora's huge force with his own meagre army. Finally, he had a plan. Within a year he gathered his men and challenged Rai Pithora in Torwan again to reclaim what he had lost. The strategy that the Sultan came up with was deceptively simple: he divided ten thousand of his archers into four units and surrounded Rai Pithora's forces on all four sides. But the soldiers were instructed not to engage in any heavy fighting. In fact, they were told that if the Chahamana forces advanced, they were to show a retreat. Advance, retreat, advance retreat; it went on for days, till the Chahamana forces were completely exhausted. As they advanced one more time and the four units of the Turki forces retreated, a fifth unit that Sultan Ghori had kept hidden, suddenly fell upon the Chahamanas with a fury. Caught by surprise, Rai Pithora's soldiers were routed. Those who could escape, fled like squealing dogs, with their tails between their legs. The Rai himself jumped off his elephant and tried to flee on his horse. But the Sultan's soldiers caught him and took him to Ajmer. He was brought before the Sultan, and offered friendship on the condition that he accept the Sultan's overlordship. But that treacherous Rai rebelled against Sultan Ghori, and the great Sultan had no choice but to behead him. And that's how Sultan Ghori won not just Tabarhind, but, eventually, also Dilli. Victory was Sultan Ghori's creed.

'Zafer,' I say softly, remembering the name Baba used to call me sometimes. For the past two weeks, that's all I've been thinking about. How to turn my defeat into victory. That is the reason I finally accepted Altunia's proposal of marriage. I couldn't refuse his offer of Tabarhind's forces. 'No marriage, no military help,' was his condition. 'If I can't have you; you can't have the Sultanate,' he told me. I wasn't surprised at his stance. Nothing Altunia says or does surprises me anymore. It's as though the Altunia I knew never existed. Maybe even his promise to help me fight Muiz is a lie; but what if it isn't? I have to take that chance. I just know that I'll never forgive him for the way he has used my Sultanate to possess me. I wish I had the power in me to refuse him, but Allah help me, my Sultanate is dearer to me than even myself. And if the sacrifice I must make to win it back is to bargain myself, then so be it.

Ever since I accepted his proposal, how strange my situation has become. Most times, when Altunia comes to see me, red-hot rage still uncoils in my belly. But I suppress it. To achieve my goal, I need strategy, not rage; or better yet, strategy alchemised by rage. So, assuming an easy casualness, I pretend to tolerate him; I talk to him; I smile at him. On some days, I even allow myself to forget. On these days, we slip into the camaraderie we used to enjoy; he becomes the Altunia who used to make me laugh with his silly antics and shameless flirtations. But on these days of forgetfulness, sometimes, I also forget that Yakut is gone, and when I instinctively say his name—'Yakut, what do think?' or 'Yakut, do you remember?' an acute pain cuts through me. On these days, I want to grab any sharp object within reach and stab Altunia in the heart.

'Altunia,' I say, looking at him. 'Can I ask you a question?' He's sitting across from me, reciting verses in Farsi. Living here in Tabarhind, he's become quite a poet. But his couplets are too pretentious, too deliberate. I want to tell him that to be a poet you need to abandon yourself—surrender, as Nisu did before his wounded heart, as Yakut did before his heartache. In an earlier time, I would have told him so, without hesitation, but this Altunia—he doesn't even seem to know the meaning of surrender or heartache.

'Of course' Altunia says. 'Ask.'

'Did you never love him?'

He becomes very quiet. Then, he sits up straight and, looking deeply into my eyes, says, 'He was my brother.'

'Then how is it that you feel no remorse?'

'You have no idea how I feel, Razi. Just because I don't weep for him doesn't mean I don't regret what I had to do. But to answer your question: no, I don't feel remorse. And I think he, too, understands that. Wherever he is, he knows why I had to do it.'

'Why?'

'I bartered his life for yours. By killing him, I've given you a fighting chance. He would have wanted that, too.'

Perhaps, Altunia truly means what he says. And, perhaps, I should just stop questioning his motives. I've grown weary of the questions that constantly plague me. Now I'm just itching for battle, especially because my body has almost completely healed. The stitches in my belly are a mere welt of red, and the hole in my thigh is no more than an angry pucker of skin. The only visible sign of my wounds is a limp when I walk. According to the hakim, the infection from the arrowhead damaged some of the tissue in my thigh so much that it died. He said my limp may disappear in time, or it may not. 'Be grateful, I didn't have to give you a wooden leg,' he joked, instructing the slave girls to make sure I walk and move the leg every day. Some days, when the guilt of not having gone to Yakut's aid fast enough racks me, I wish the hakim had, indeed, given me a wooden leg instead of this whole, healed body. All I have to show for his death is this small limp, which also I may lose.

'I have a special gift for you today,' Altunia says, laying aside the binder of his verses.

I wait for him to tell me.

He calls out to his man and, within a few moments, I hear soft footsteps behind me, and my back tingles with a warmth, as though someone is enfolding me in loving arms. I turn my head quickly to see who it is, and a soft shout of joy escapes my lips. 'Saras amca!' My eyes blur with happiness. I make to get up, but he quickly walks to me, and, kneeling before me, takes my hand to kiss it. The back of my hand is wet with his tears. And suddenly my arms are around his neck and I am sobbing—deep, wet sobs drawn from a well that I thought I had sanded. He lets me cry, till nothing remains in me except hiccoughs, the reflex of sorrow. Then he gently pulls my arms from around his neck and lays me back against the cushions.

'How ... how did you know I was still alive?' I ask him.

He shakes his head as though to deny the very question of my being anything but alive.

'One of my men delivered a secret message to him,' Altunia speaks, beaming at me. For that moment, I forgive Altunia everything.

Later that evening, as the ladies come to fetch me for my bath, Altunia draws me aside. 'I have a proposition,' he says. 'It's not about control, I promise, so don't get upset. Just a proposition.'

'What is it?'

'When you come out of the bath, there will be a platter waiting for you with a marriage veil. There'll be another set of clothes as well,' he adds quickly. 'But if you feel ready, we can be married in two days.'

'So that's why you brought Hindu Saras here?'

'I won't deny it,' he says. 'But that's only one reason, Razi. All the other reasons combined are just that … I care.'

28

AT THE CRACK OF DAWN, ALTUNIA RIDES UP TO THE ZENANA IN Tabarhind Fort with a small group of his men and a band of drums and pipes, and like a brave-heart king laying claim to a land he wishes to conquer, plants a red flag with a golden crescent and moon just outside the palace door. He has staked his claim—to his bride; me.

All day I sit in the zenana's most opulent room, whose walls are elaborately patterned in ivory and silver ridged hexagons. Around me are hundreds of platters filled with gold coins and flower ornaments, mostly roses—a surfeit of fertility and wealth that Altunia is bestowing on his bride. Gold plated braziers, burning peat and fragrantly moist orange peels, gently warm the room, and hundreds of women sit in groups around me, chattering, giggling and singing ditties about sad partings and happy beginnings. They decorate my hands with henna ground in rosewater, the traces of callouses on my fingers hidden under delicate patterns of dragonflies to symbolise my transformation from maiden to married woman, and in the centre of each palm, the ancient eye to ward off evil. I sit, as though in a dream; I am the dream, but the dream is also about me. I am the protagonist in it, but I am also the detached observer.

When Altunia returns in the late afternoon, sounding his arrival with more drums and pipes, an old lady of the zenana gets up and makes her way to where I am sitting. A slave girl holds out a platter.

On it is the marriage veil, red, with flecks of gold. The colour red; it finally wrests me out of my dream state. Every moment in my life that has made me has been coloured red. Seeing it, neatly folded, served ritually on a platter to seal yet another bargain in my life suddenly makes me feel anchored. I'm ready. I'm Altunia's bride. The resolve of what I'm about to do is so rock solid, I almost stagger from its sudden mooring. The old woman picks up the veil and holds it up, its folds cascading open familiarly. I bend down a little to let her arrange it on my head. She takes me in her arms and calls me daughter. If this had been another citadel, another zenana, another moment, I would have been reduced to tears, missing my Anneh. But this is not marriage; it's war.

Many other women walk me downstairs where my groom, Altunia, awaits. I see him from behind the net of the veil. He has probably never looked more handsome, dressed all in gold—his qaba, his turban, his tunic; around his waist is a red belt studded with gems, and circling his neck are rubied gold chains falling in layers down his front, like blood red stones sprouting from his chest. His sword is swinging in a gold baldric, and he is sitting on a white Arabian whose fetlocks are adorned with gold bells and tail is streaked with strings of pearls. A beaded plume of victory sticks out between his curved pointed ears.

Altunia looks down at me and grins; the lopsided crater in his cheek is a naughty secret. For a moment, I have a crazy urge to grab his sword and slash his face. But then someone ties a blindfold on my eyes and women help me mount a mare. I know the ritual: the groom doesn't want his bride to see the way to his palace; he's afraid, she'll run back home if she knows. Oh, no, Altunia, I say to myself. Don't fear. This bride will not turn back. And, without a single objection, I follow Altunia, blindfolded, to his palace that is lit with a thousand lamps.

In the early evening, accompanied by Hindu Saras, I go to the masjid for the Yatsi Namazi. After it is read, the qazi states the terms of the marriage contract and establishes the mehr, the groom's obligation to pay his bride. I ask for just one gold dinar for the muqaddam, which is paid right away, and for the mu'akhar, the second part of the mehr, which is paid after the consummation of the marriage, I ask for his garrisons.

Technically, the military of a fief belongs to the Sultan, making it obligatory for the governor to make the troops available whenever the Sultan calls for them. But the troops of a fief also constitute its fighting power, and if the governor refuses to lend them to the Sultan, it is a declaration of insurgency. By asking for Altunia's troops, I am launching him into rebellion against Dilli.

For a moment, Altunia doesn't respond to the qazi's question: does he agree to pay the mehr? I raise my head to look at him and see the muscles in his face are taut and his jaw is clenched. I am vindicated. The gravity of what he's doing by marrying me has finally hit him: if he agrees to my terms, it'll be tantamount to him declaring war on Dilli. He's been wooing me with this offer for months. Now it's time to see if he will honour it. And if he says no, he will be the one refusing the marriage. His eyes seek mine behind the mesh of the veil. I stare back at him, offering no respite, daring him to answer.

'Qabool,' he says—accepted—but the tone of his voice is subdued.

Benedictions are called out, and Altunia and I are drawn into numerous congratulatory embraces. Then we head back to his palace, where we are led into the dining hall for the wedding feast.

Finally, the wedding is over. All that remains is the ritual of the nuptial bed. Twittering and giggling women pull me into a room to fuss over me. They remove my veil and straighten the ornaments around my neck; they pinch my cheeks to make them blush red; they sprinkle me with the essence of rose; and, jokingly, they demonstrate to me how to woo my groom with lowered lashes and a slanted gaze. Then, they carefully adjust the veil over my head once again and steer me out of the room towards the nuptial chamber. But Hindu Saras intercepts them. Drawing me away from the women, he stands looking at me with a question in his eyes. I know what he wants to ask. Am I happy with this marriage? He's been asking me this question, silently, ever since he arrived, and I've been avoiding his eyes. I know if I give him any indication that I'm unhappy, he'll sever Altunia's head from his body, even if he has to kill half the wedding party to get to him. I pull my veil up so that he can see my face and, bending forward, kiss him on the forehead. 'Trust that you raised a warrior,' I whisper to him. Then, dropping the veil, I walk to the women and allow them to lead me into the nuptial chamber and place my hand in Altunia's.

The warmth of Altunia's hand confuses me; it's the warmth of Yakut's hand. When he lifts my veil, I close my eyes. I am back in Qasr-e-Shamsi. The single lamp that is sitting on the floor beside me is illuminating Yakut's face. And the eyes that look at me are Yakut's. They're filled with so much love, I'll never want for more, as long as I live.

29

THE MORNING AFTER THE WEDDING, I AWAKEN ALTUNIA TO TELL HIM I want to inspect his troops and weapons. He doesn't open his eyes, but I can tell he's awake, because his face loses its laxity of sleep, and his body begins to recover from its early morning lethargy. His legs are still tangled in the white sheets, and twisted around the sheets is my red veil, like a long smear of virgin blood.

I have been up for hours. Dressed in a loose, unadorned tunic and salvar, I've been pacing the veranda outside this room, making mental lists, collating soldiery to weaponry, and tallying the pros and cons of battlefields between Tabarhind and Dilli. I've convinced myself that a pitched battle is better than to lay siege to the Lal Kot, because its storage capacity is so immense, it would frustrate a siege. But the truth is that just the thought of holding the citadel in Dilli hostage is turning the blood in my veins white. I've also decided that if there is to be a pitched battle, it must be the battlefield of Torwan, where Sultan Ghori turned his defeat into victory.

Now I need to assess the soldier-power in Altunia's garrisons to see how it matches up to Dilli's. But, most importantly, I need to determine if his troops will remain loyal to him when he declares war against the Sultanate. Of course, the question of whether Altunia himself will be loyal to me still remains. But the only way to test that is in the battlefield itself. It is only when I face Muiz will I know whether Altunia has my back or not. Till then, I have no other choice but to keep the illusion of Altunia's words.

'So, are you getting up?' I ask him again. 'I want to inspect the garrisons.'

This time, he sits up and makes to get out of bed. But then he suddenly stops and starts looking around for something. I see him grab his gold turban cloth from the floor. Holding that over his lap, he ties it around his waist, before standing up. His shyness is so unexpected, I can't help but smile, but I turn my face away quickly; I don't want him to think I'm softening.

'Just give me a ghadi to get ready and I'll take you to see the troops,' he says. 'Have you eaten?'

'Yes,' I say, lying. Food is the last thing on my mind, and I don't want him wasting time arranging it. 'I'll meet you downstairs in the garden.'

Tabarhind has always had a fairly large standing army. I recall that in the last assessment, the numbers were one thousand war elephants, triple that number of war-trained horses, an equal number of cavalry, both heavy and light, and twenty-five thousand foot soldiers. It's a considerable force, but not enough for what I have in mind. The Dilli garrison is almost double this size, and combined with the garrisons of other territories, the numbers can swell up to ten times. Of course, we will not know how many maliks support Muiz till we get confirmed information, which Altunia's spies are already gathering. But whatever the case may be, we will need to recruit more troops.

When Altunia arrives in the garden, immaculately dressed in shades of yellow with a sun bright qaba and lemony tunic—attire befitting a happy groom on the morning after the nuptials, I greet him with a question: 'How many troops are stationed in the lashkar?'

'Only the trainees are in the lashkar,' he says. 'They can be readied, if need be. Also, most of the elephants and horses are stabled there.'

'How about the maliks who are in your network?'

'I don't know how many of them are still sympathetic to you. We'll need to send letters. Maybe, Malik Izz-ud-Din Salari, Malik Karakush and some others.'

'That's good,' I say. 'What do you think about asking for help from the Khokhar and Jat tribes?'

'They're formidable warriors. But they're not easy to recruit. I know as a fact that they really don't give a damn about what happens in Dilli. We can try contacting them if you like.'

'I want to go and talk to them myself.'

'I wouldn't recommend it, Razi. Those hills are treacherous, and the tribesmen are not the friendly sort.'

'I want to leave in a week's time. Do you think you can have some fifty thousand silver tankas made available to me? I'll return the coin to Tabarhind. But, if I lose to Muiz, you'll lose it all.'

'You think I care about the coin?' he says. 'It's you I'm concerned about. Your goal is Dilli's throne. Why would you put your life in danger before you even go to battle? It's more than likely that other maliks may support us. I really don't like the idea of you going into the hills.'

Last night, after Altunia fell asleep, I lay awake planning, and the idea of recruiting Khokhars suddenly popped into my head. These tribes live in the hills, north of Tabarhind, along the Jhelum River. Baba had annexed the territory after the battle in Pir Panjal, and the tribes pay an annual tribute to the throne, but even Baba hadn't been able to bring them into the fold of the Sultanate. 'The hillman is unpredictable,' Baba once told me. 'Today, the tribes are allegiant to the Sultanate, tomorrow they may decide to rebel.' Sultan Ghori, himself had lost his life to their treachery. Even after he had defeated them and received their fealty, the Khokhars had murdered him. They had attacked his caravan at the camp in Dhamiak and killed him while he was prostrate during the Maghrib prayer.

The challenge of allying the Khokhar and Jat tribes is exciting my blood. If I can get them to fight for me, not only will this be a first for any Dilli Sultan, but also, to have them with me will mean having the whole of Punjab on my side.

Despite his misgivings, Altunia furnishes me with a small force of jaandars, soldiers and also scouts, who are familiar with the hills. In addition, he provides extra horses, pack horses and fifty household men. Two of the pack horses are laden with chests containing twenty-five thousand silver tankas each.

The night before my journey, as I lie in bed beside him, he suddenly takes me into his arms and holds me tightly. 'Promise you'll come back to me, Razi,' he whispers into my hair.

'Where would I go?' I ask, wriggling to get out of his hold. 'My heart is in Dilli, and now, it seems, the way to Dilli is from Tabarhind.'

I feel a heavy sigh pass through his body and his hold loosens a little, as though he realises it's not his arms that hold me. 'Just be careful. The hills are dangerous.'

The following morning, as I mount my horse and turn his head towards the North Gate of the fort, Altunia, on his own horse, trots beside me up to the gate. Then he stands and watches our little caravan stream out. I feel his eyes on my back all the way down the citadel's pathway, from where we will take the rocky road that leads to the mountains.

For days, we trek through steep and almost impenetrable terrain. I discover that the hardest part is to sit as upright in the saddle as the trees around us. The body instinctively wants to lean forward to parallel the incline. But the horse needs unburdened forelegs to make the climb. I never realised how punishing it is to go against the body's instincts. It takes my mind a few days to form this new relationship with the body and relax, although my stiffening leg has a will of its own. We follow the path that the scouts delineate through dizzying heights of blue pine and sloping deodars and oaks so copiously foliaged, they challenge the blue expanse above. Every evening, at sunset,we stop and set up camp in clearings that suddenly appear like glimpses of jannat; they're filled with thickets of speckled white birch and flowers so unearthly, even their names are other-worldly. The scouts name a few for me: bagh jandhra and brahm kamal and the purple amrata. The men erect tight, narrow tents within a circle of small fires that keep away bears and leopards, which, I am told, abound in these mountains. I hear them in the night, sometimes too close, their roars often followed by the piercing screech of monkeys and langoors, and the hysterical giggle of hyenas. I've hunted tiger and wild boar in Sanjay Van from such proximity, I could smell their foul breath, but to hear the deep darkness suddenly erupt—the heart jumps into the throat every time.

Finally, we reach a plateau with sloping meadows of lush green grass, blue khuskhus, and streams gurgling with sweet water. Birdsongs of bulbul and myna lilt in the air and hiran and goral graze here and there, oblivious to our presence. Here, we meet the first tribal leader, Deva Raj, whom Altunia had described as the most level-headed of the lot. 'If you can get him to agree, he'll help you secure the others,' he had advised me.

As we relax after the evening meal in Deva Raj's simple, wood-planked house, he says to me, 'I remember your father. A sagacious man.'

I turn grateful eyes to him. He himself seems to be about the age Baba was when he passed, but I have a feeling that the deep lines on his swarthy face are deceiving. The honesty of his eyes, however, is unmistakable.

On meeting him, I had described the situation in Dilli and he had invited me to join him for the evening meal. 'I am my father's daughter,' I tell him now. 'He mentored me all his life. Therefore, I speak from his experience—an unstable Dilli brings instability to every territory connected to it.'

He smiles. 'An unstable Dilli means that we can once again bid for independence.'

I look at him, making no attempt to hide the distress his words cause me. He raises his hand and continues, 'But by being consolidated with Dilli, we, ourselves, have peace among us. Independent, the tribes constantly fight each other. So, yes, a stable Dilli is a stable Punjab. What do you need from us?'

I'm sure the smile I give him is wider than protocol dictates, but I don't care. Suddenly, I am full of hope. I feel certain that this small victory portends the battle with Dilli.

Over the next two weeks, while I remain a guest in Deva Raj's home, and my men camp in the meadow, he invites other tribal leaders. Most of them accept the invitation. Day after day, we negotiate terms, some of which are a hard bargain for me, but I find myself promising the leaders reduced tribute and subsidised prices on goods produced in Dilli's karkhanas. By the end of the month, when we begin our return journey to Tabarhind, I have a promise of five thousand foot soldiers and a thousand horsemen who will bring their own hill-bred horses—squat animals with sturdy legs and ferocious hearts.

On the way down from the hills, we are ambushed. We're taking a short respite in a clearing, when, suddenly, there is a downpour of arrows, like a cloudburst. When it seizes, five of my men are writhing on the ground. We lunge behind bushes and rocks, pulling our wounded with us, while returning the volley, not knowing at whom we're shooting. Around us are only trees, the lichen on their trunks glistening emerald in the filtering sun. And silence, the sudden suspension of sound—disquieting—heavy with the gaze of invisible eyes that we can feel trained on us. Even the birds have stopped chirping. We wait. Nothing. A horse whinnies. We wait some more. Altunia had warned me to beware of hostile tribesmen, who did not take kindly to intruders in their hills and of bands of robbers, who kill anyone for loot. But why now? Why didn't we encounter anyone on the way up, when we were carrying trunks full of coin? I wonder if our negotiation with Deva Raj has something to do with this. I intend to find out. Raising a hand to indicate to my men to stand down, I call out loudly, 'I am Razziat bint Al Sultan Iltutmish.' Then I add, 'I am Malika Altunia, Malik Altunia's new bride. Deva Raj is my friend and ally. Who are you? Declare yourself.' Even as my voice penetrates the silence, there's a flurried rustling in the trees. And they're gone. Around us, the air is light again, and somewhere a myna bird whistles sweetly to its mate. Whoever they were, they've left; whether in deference to Deva Raj, Baba, Altunia or me, I'll never know. Or, maybe, it was just the capriciousness of the hillman.

By the time I get back to Tabarhind fort, Altunia has received intelligence reports about Dilli, which he shares with me on the evening of my return. 'While you were in Tabarhind, the maliks and amirs who invited Muiz to become Sultan had a ceremony for him in the Daulat Khana,' he tells me. 'And, one of the first things your brother did as Sultan was create a new position of Naib, deputy of the Sultan. And guess whom he appointed?'

'Whom?'

'Ikhtiyar-ud-Din Aetkin.'

'I knew it,' I exclaim. 'The snake.'

'My spies tell me that Muiz created that position of naib on Aetkin's advice. But that's not the only news. After he became naib, Aetkin married your sister, Shazia.'

'What? No. That's not possible.' To say I'm shocked comes nowhere close to describing my disbelief. 'Your spies have made a mistake. Shazi would never get married again, and especially not to a snake like Aetkin.'

'She didn't do it of her own accord. Apparently, Aetkin forced Muiz's hand, who, in turn forced his sister to marry him. He must have had an eye on her for a while.'

My heart squeezes with pain for Shazi. 'Aetkin's days are over,' I say through clenched teeth. 'Soon his head will be no more than battlefield offal.'

'You won't see him in the battlefield. It turns out, soon after appointing him naib, Muiz tried to have him killed. But Aetkin fled from Dilli.'

'What? Why? Because of Shazi?'

'No. Aetkin reached too high. Thought he could equal the Sultan. He stationed an elephant at the gate of his palace, and he started arriving to court in a full procession, equal to the Sultan's. It seems your young brother is not so young and naïve after all. He dispatched two men to take care of him, and they attacked Aetkin outside the Daulat Khan with knives. Reports are that he was badly wounded, but he got away. No one knows where he went.'

'So, where does this leave us?'

'Well, Muiz is in full control now. And he seems to be managing affairs quite well. It appears that he's quite a smart strategist. He's allowed the maliks and amirs to keep their power, which means that they will lend him full support. And, by the way, news about you has reached Dilli. Muiz knows you went to meet the Khokhars. He knows you're getting ready for battle, and he has started his own preparations.'

Muiz would have found out sooner or later. It doesn't worry me; it only means that I must play my hand before he plays his. But it is still hard for me to believe that little Muiz is now the Sultan of Dilli; although I also recognise that it's not at all surprising. Even at fifteen he was such a determined young man, so different from Baba's other sons, and perhaps more like Baba than any of them. I'd never seen him in silks or embroidered clothing. He had the same aversion to flashiness as Baba did, but unlike him, he had a cruel streak. When he was a little boy and still lived in the zenana, Shazi used to tell me about his sudden bouts of rage and his vicious treatment of the slave girls. I still remember the horror on her face when she told me about a box he had, full of fingers that he had cut off from the hands of slave girls who didn't do his bidding. I didn't really know Muiz, except in the training ring, and there I only saw his courage and fighting spirit, which were already quite formidable. Hearing Altunia's reports, I am convinced that he will prove to be quite a challenge in the battlefield.

Soon, Altunia and I begin battle drills with the troops. I have begun to form a sort of partnership with Altunia, and, as the days pass, I allow trust back into our relationship. My greatest challenge is myself. I have to regain precision in my own skills that have become rusty in my idleness. My body, too, has to relearn soldiering; my arms tire after just a few hours of sword practice, my softened palms have forgotten the shape of the hilt, and my fingers are protesting their reacquaintance with the bow. These days, even my limp is more pronounced. And I miss Yakut like a lost limb.

At the beginning of the month of Rabi-ul-Awwal, about five months after I lost the Sultanate, I declare war on Dilli to win it back.

30

AT DAWN, JUST BEFORE THE SUN BREAKS THROUGH THE HORIZON, I stand in my pavilion near the field of Torwan as my ladies dress me for battle: silk tunic with ruby studded clasps of gold, and over that a red kazaghand, the padded overcoat fitted inside with chain mail. Then come the long overboots, and over them, metal plates to protect my legs. Next is the mighfar cap of chainmail that cascades to my shoulders, protecting my ears and neck. One of the ladies places a conical helmet on my head and ties a red turban around it, its tail hanging in the back over my single braid of hair. When I'm dressed, Hindu Saras comes into the pavilion to give me my weapons: the round, bossed shield on my back and a holster fitted with lances; my quiver and the bow case on my right shoulder, and my battle axe on the left, and hanging from the baldric on my left side, a Nibah sword. Then he hands me two katara knives that I slip into the top of each boot.

This ritual of donning combat apparatus has always been my favourite part of going to war; every tug of metal and leather tightens my focus, every swish of chain mail quickens my blood, and every positioning of weapon heightens my anticipation. I can hardly wait to mount my horse and ride into the battlefield. For this battle, I will fight on horseback rather than on an elephant. Although Altunia and I have strategised a five-wing formation, we know that because

Dilli has a larger force, Muiz will try to resort to a melee as soon as possible, to overpower our smaller numbers. A horse in a melee puts me face-to-face with the enemy to cause maximum damage.

When I step outside my pavilion, I see Altunia, also in full battle gear, waiting for me, his horse impatiently prancing under him. After I mount Fawz, the Arabian I have selected from Altunia's stables, we ride together, towards the safe line of the battlefield, where our forces are assembling. He's very quiet, and I wonder if, like me, he too is concentrating on some ataractic mental activity to control the agitation; not faintheartedness—just the body's instinctive preparation for the blood rush of battle and the receiving of pain. My tactic is to tune out the world and sharpen my focus to such acuteness that by the time I enter the battle, the battlefield will cease to exist. My mind will know only the angle of my sword, the tension of my bowstring, and the velocity of my lance. Even the enemy will only exist as a single point target to execute the perfection of a weapon.

Riding beside Altunia, I start to tune him out as well, so that I can begin to attenuate each of my senses.

'Do you remember your first battle, Razi?' Altunia's voice interrupts my focus.

I don't want to answer him, but then I think that perhaps this inconsequential chit chat is his way of calming his mind. There's still a little distance to the battlefield, so I have a few moments to spare.

'Yes,' I reply.

'How old were you?'

'Eighteen.'

'Which battle was it?'

'Tabarhind,' I say and turn to smile at him. 'Remember, it used to be one of Qubacha's territories before Baba annexed it?'

'I was sixteen when I went into my first battle. It was in this very battlefield of Torwan. Against Chand Rai. Yakut and me. For both of us; it was our first battle. I was in such a state, I unsheathed my sword even before we began the march. But Yakut was calm—not a breath out of pace. I envied him.'

'I envied him, too. Nothing ever fazed him. That's one reason why...' I become quiet.

'Why you loved him,' Altunia completes my sentence. 'I know. Maybe, it was one of my reasons for loving him, as well. Just being with him was calming. Like standing on the bank of a peaceful river. I should have been satisfied with that love. Instead, I let jealousy take over. I'm sorry.' The eyes he turns to me are deep with some emotion—sadness, remorse, an appeal for forgiveness ... I can't tell.

I shake my head. 'Let's not talk about that now.'

'Let me just say this, please, Razi. In case ... in case, I don't get a chance later.'

'I don't want to think about all that, Altunia. Not now.'

'I used to hide behind the trees and watch you two meet in Qasr-e-Shamsi.'

I look at him sharply. Yakut and I used to take so many precautions not to be seen. We would come and go separately. We always waited till after sundown, and we left before sunrise. I would use a different horse every time and wear a plain cotton burqa. I would also hide till Hindu Saras secured the area. It was so difficult for us to meet, but for those seven months that we were lovers, every obstacle made the meeting with Yakut that much sweeter. 'How did you know?' I ask Altunia.

'I met him once when he was on his way to meet you and asked him where he was going. He told me. You know he couldn't lie. He didn't have it in him. So, he told me, and I followed him, and then I stood and watched him disappear inside the qasr. Sometimes, I would wait all night for you to come out. I was so insanely jealous of him, I even told your father. If I could have, I would have broken down the door of the qasr. But Hindu Saras was always there, like an iron wall.'

'What ...' The world suddenly stops; the sun on my face, the air around me, the shimmering of dew on leaves, the soil crunching under my horse's hooves—everything grinds to a halt. A chasm of silence. 'What did you say?' My voice is the other side of silence.

'I wanted to break down the doors of the qasr.'

'Before that ... about my father. What did you say about my father?'

'I think I may have told him about the two of you. I'm sorry.'

A roar begins to fill my ears and something terrible shifts in me, like a deluge. 'What did you say to him?'

'Oh, nothing very direct, really. Just that you and Yakut had become very close. And that I thought I was worthier than he was. And then I made a proposal of marriage.'

'What ... what did he say?'

'Nothing. He was too sick. I don't think he heard half the things I said.'

'When did you tell him?'

'I don't remember. One of those days ... I used to visit him quite often when he was sick.'

'On the morning of his death, I saw you leaving his room. Is that when you told him?'

'Perhaps,' he says, but his face betrays him. He remembers the day exactly. 'Sorry, Razi. I was so angry at you. And so jealous of Yakut. After I left his room, I felt terrible. So ashamed of myself. I thought I would go back the next day and tell him I had been mistaken. But I never got a chance. He ... he ... you know. Allah rest his soul.'

The chasm is inside me, and I am sinking. I see Baba's eyes—pained, disappointed. I had wondered why. The one thing he had asked of me—'Promise me, you won't marry, Razi. A Sultan must never be subservient.' I remember when I asked him why he never promoted Yakut. 'He's a Habshi,' he had said. 'I can't place him above the other Turki nobles; they'll never accept him. It'll create dissension and hurt the unity of the Sultanate.' So, that's why Baba changed his decree. He named Rukn his successor because he thought I might marry Yakut. It wasn't Husni or the Ulema or his nobles who persuaded him. It was Altunia who changed his mind. And all these years I blamed Baba. I carried his betrayal like a taint in my blood. All these years that I couldn't forgive him. It was he who didn't forgive me in his dying hour. And Yakut—caught in the crossfire of Altunia's heedless words and the tragedy of Baba's broken trust. Ah, Yakut! I close my eyes and let myself sink.

I enter the battlefield with the sight of Yakut's head flying in the air and the sound of its thud at my feet. And wherever I look, Baba's disappointed, fading eyes are looking at me. When the air erupts with the battle cry: 'Al-naṣr aw al-shahāda,'—victory or martyrdom—I try to shake myself free of the images. Trying to regain my focus, I purposefully plant myself in the midst of the layered four-wing formation I designed and rally our troops to make the first strike. Our archers let loose an arrow shower so dense that for long moments the front lines of the enemy are shrouded, and when the dust settles, hundreds lie prone on the ground.

Exultant shouts of this early triumph from our ranks embolden my heart, but my vision is too wide; it's all over the battlefield. I notice the immense numbers on the other side and worry that our soldiers will lose heart. I see the same wing formation of Muiz's forces but with war elephants concentrated on the sides, and I fear that they will begin an early melee combat and encircle us. Even my weapons have lost their acuity. My lance throws are a little too short and my arrows' velocity, not enough. I'm so out of sorts with myself that I also become apprehensive about the stiffening muscles in my thigh.

Even before the sun can climb to the middle of the sky, most of our foot soldiers and light cavalry are demolished, and the melee fight we had hoped to delay, is upon us. Suddenly, I am face to face with Muiz. I strike, he counters, I thrust, he blocks. What a swordsman he has become, I think, and for a moment I even feel pride at the choreography of his striking and parrying, his concert with the horse that responds to the smallest pressure of his thighs, clench of muscle, and shift of weight. But then I give myself a mental jolt to halt my wandering mind. Executing a quick manoeuvre, I get behind Muiz and thrust a short-handled lance into his upper back. He shouts and circles around, his sword flashing, but before he can strike, Altunia is by my side, blocking the strike.

Somehow, Altunia and I manage to cut our way out of the melee, but, in the process, I lose my sword and shield. And then there is Muiz again, shouting, advancing, along with half a dozen more men. 'Retreat,' Altunia yells at me. Instead, I reach over my shoulder for the battleaxe and prepare to face the enemy. 'Come on,' Altunia grabs Fawz's bridle and pulls. 'They're too many, and you have no weapons.'

'No,' I shout at him. 'Let go.' He tightens his grip and spurs his own horse. In a daze I see Fawz's head turn, and we're fleeing, Altunia's hand still on my horse's bridle.

As though of its own volition, my hand swings in an arc and I pitch the battleaxe. It lands on the ground in front of Altunia's galloping horse, along with his head. For many moments his headless body remains seated in the saddle, spurting blood, and then it suddenly topples to the side.

31

I RIDE FOR AN ETERNITY. MAYBE IT'S JUST FOR ONE GHADI. MAYBE even less than that. I have no sense of how much time has passed, or where I'm going. My mind has emptied of all thought. I just keep going and going—away from the battlefield of Torwan.

Coming to the end of a line of trees, I am suddenly at the edge of what looks like a dry field. In the distance, I see a farmer ploughing a small tract of land. On one side of the field is a clump of bushes and, near it, I see a low parapet of what appears to be a well. I realise then that my throat is parched.

Circling the field, I ride to the other side and hail the farmer. He stops ploughing and comes to me.

'Can you give me some water?' I say.

'Who are you?' he asks, looking at me curiously.

'I'm ... I'm ... ' I don't know how to answer him. Who am I? I, who used to be Sultan Iltutmish's daughter; who used to be Dilli's Sultan Razziat; who used to be Malik Altunia's Malika. Who am I now? I shake my head.

'Are you a soldier of Dilli?' the farmer asks.

I nod, grateful to him for giving me this nameless identity.

'The water level is low,' he says, pointing in the direction of a well. 'But help yourself.'

'Thank you. Do you mind if I sit and rest there for a while?'

He nods and returns to his ploughing.

I walk Fawz up to the well and leave him to graze on whatever he can find in the bushes. Then, taking off my turban and removing the helmet, I draw water from the well. After I've had some myself and washed my face, I bring some of it to Fauz. Then, I sit down. I'm so tired, my bones ache. And I'm burning up in my kazaghand. Releasing the top two bindings of the padded coat, I lie down, letting the breeze cool my neck. Within moments, my eyes are heavy, and I drift into sleep.

I come awake suddenly. Somebody is pulling at the front of my tunic. I open my eyes to see it's the farmer. He has opened my kazaghand and is cutting out the ruby and gold clasps on my tunic with a hunting knife and stuffing them down the front of his shirt. Knocking his hand away, I pull myself up, but he suddenly turns the knife and drives it into my stomach. I'm engulfed in a breath that I can't seem to release.

As the afternoon heat bears down, an eerie calm begins to spread. A dust storm is coming. Tinkling sounds at the other end, like a child's ankle bells, as sand rubs against sand. Then a cloud wall arises from the ground up and begins to roll in. I lie, watching it approach—waiting. And, suddenly, I'm in it and it's all around me. The roaring wind, the swirling grit, the orange darkness, all the way up to the sky; the sun a shadowplay, a fiery copper outline. Within moments, it's all over the field. Everywhere a glitter of mica dust raining down in the orange light. This moment in time is separated from all the rest. And when it has passed, people will say, a storm came this way.

Acknowledgements

A couple of serendipitous encounters, an exchange concretising into an idea, research materials sent by a generous soul, and a quick character profile drafted over the phone. This is how Razia came to be, and I owe utmost gratitude to the people who helped me discover her. Instead of simply writing a note of thanks, I would like to give context to the role that each one played in my eight-year relationship with Razia's story.

I am grateful to the little boy who followed us to Razia's grave and became the inspiration for this book.

I went to see Razia's grave in Old Delhi about eight years ago. As my friend and I trudged up Pahari Bhojla Hill in Mohalla Bulbuli, a little boy, about seven or eight, followed us up the hill and into the courtyard, where the grave is located. The site is quite underwhelming—a watery, white-washed qibla wall with an unassuming mihrab on one side and, on the other sides, hodgepodge rears of grimy apartments, some with buzzing air-conditioners protruding out of windows. And in the middle of all this, two unmarked eroding graves of rough-hewn stone. As we stood wondering which one could be Razia's, the boy pointed in the general direction of the graves and declared, 'Razia Sultana!' 'Do you know which one is Razia Sultana's?' I asked him. He nodded, and touching the one nearest to him, said, 'Razia,' and then pointing to the other, he said, 'Sultana.' Smiling at his simple logic, I asked, 'Do you know who Razia Sultan was?' He shrugged his shoulders. 'Two girls who died,' he said.

Karthika, my friend, encourager and writing advisor, I want to thank you for planting Razia's idea in my head and for giving me Kiran Nagarkar's *Cuckold*.

While visiting Karthika in her office to talk about another book, I mentioned to her my encounter with the little boy at Razia's grave. 'Don't you think it's sad and shameful?' I said to her. 'The first Muslim woman emperor of India and no one really knows where she is buried. Let alone make her a tomb, they didn't even mark her grave, if indeed that is her grave.' (There are other contenders—in Kaithal, Haryana, and Tonk, Rajasthan) 'Why don't you tell her story?' Karthika said to me. 'You mean, like a historical novel?' I responded. 'I'm not sure I can. I've never attempted one.' Karthika got up and, reaching into her bookshelves, pulled out a copy of Kiran Nagarkar's *Cuckold*. 'Read this,' she said.

Sunil Kumar, renowned historian and brilliant scholar of the Delhi Sultanate—I owe him a deep debt of gratitude. I wish I had had a chance to thank him.

After a few months of research, I was in despair. I was drowning in material about the Delhi Sultanate; but I could hardly find any information about Razia. She is no more than a footnote in the chronicles. So, I contacted Sunil and asked him for help. He immediately sent me links to his own class lectures and articles on Razia and also helped me narrow my reading list. In fact, throughout my research, his advice not only anchored me but also gave me direction. Sadly, Sunil passed away earlier this year, around the same time that I finished the final chapter.

My daughter, Asawari, advocate of women's rights, unapologetic feminist, psychiatrist—thank you for illuminating Razia for me and for making sure my medical facts are accurate.

One day, sitting in a café, after numerous attempts at trying to create a profile for Razia, I finally called my daughter. 'I can't figure out who she is,' I said to her. 'I need to know her, but I only have a few disjointed facts.' 'Tell me what you know,' she responded, and when I rattled off the key events in Razia's life, she laughed. 'She sounds a little bit like me,' she said. 'But here's who I think she is ...' Somewhere in my notes there is a Corner Café napkin on which Razia's character was shaped.

I am deeply grateful to Hari Singh ji for becoming my impromptu tour guide for Lal Kot, Razia's home.

I met Hari Singh ji by chance in Adham Khan's tomb, near the Qutb Complex. Trying to locate the excavation site where archaeologists had dug for the Sultanate's royal palaces, I asked him if he knew where that was. 'Come with me,' he said. 'I can show you. I was part of that archaeological team.' He quickly climbed down the stairs of the tomb and began walking north, away from the Qutb, and then veered off up a forested hillock. After some minutes of arduous climbing, he suddenly stopped and, pointing to one side, said, 'Look. Remains of one of the bastions of the qila.' I looked but couldn't see anything except for foliage. Hari ji then picked up a sturdy stick and began to beat away the thick overgrowth. And there it was—a jutting, rounded structure of packed stone. What a sight! From that point on, Lal Kot—whatever remained of it—was all around me. The oblong stone-packed boundary walls, the dozen gates, the horse tracks, the wide paths along which elephants were led—I could visualise it all. Some distance further up, Hari ji started descending, till we came to a few huts with a small, marshy patch behind them. 'This used to be Anangtal, the water tank that the Tomar king constructed,' he informed me, and, going into the nearby shrubs, pointed out the area where the test pits had been dug to excavate the palaces. I stepped into what may have been the foundation of Kushk-e-Ferozi, the zenana in which Razia grew up. When I looked south, I could see the top of the Qutb, just as Razia must have seen from her veranda, as each new storey of the minar was built.

Finally, a very special thank you to my editor, Sanghamitra—my comrade in arms.

A few days away from a looming deadline, I realised that the manuscript we had been working on, for days, was the wrong draft. I panicked. 'I'll manage it. Don't worry,' Sangha said to me and sent me a photograph of her handsome little guy, smiling widely at the camera. Recently, a little guy has come into my life, as well—my grandson—and sharing his almost-a-smile photo with Sangha in camaraderie was just the thing I needed.